FROM **FEAR** TO **FREEDOM**

FROM **FEAR** TO FREEDOM

Based on True Events from WWII

GARY JAMES SUMNER

Gary James Sumner

Eagles Peak Publishing LLC

Eagles Peak Publishing, LLC

ISBN: 978-0-9864439-1-6
The photos in this book can be found on line and through:
http://www.archives.gov/publications/av-records.html
Drawings in this book are from Carol Tabacco
Book cover design by Peter Holm, Sterling Hill Productions,
G. Leigh Cropper, Gary J. Sumner.

"I believe there are two kinds of fear. One is good, it keeps us safe, and the other keeps us from being great."

— Gary James Sumner

DEDICATION

To my father, Ray, who fought in the Korean War, and to all those who served and are now serving in the U.S. Armed Forces. My father, like so many others, had to leave behind his young bride and their newborn baby girl. He put his trust in God that he would one day hold the two of them again. It would be a long time before he could do that. He was lucky. Many soldiers never returned home.

I'm reminded of the saying "All gave some, some gave all." Theirs is a debt we cannot repay; perhaps if we as a people let our voices be heard by those we send to Washington, and remind them of their promises and responsibilities to those who serve this great Nation, that will be a start.

To the first responders and to all those who go to work each and every day, who push fear aside to put their lives on the line to protect us.

Thank you to all.

My mom and dad with my sister Renie.
Photo from the private collection of Gary J. Sumner

AUTHOR'S THOUGHTS

As we travel down the road we call life, we come across challenges that appear as walls trying to stop us. Those walls are there to help us grow. Some walls are easily stepped over, while others appear to be the Great Wall of China. Whatever the challenge is before you, don't be discouraged, be excited. Look at every wall as an opportunity. Remember, what a small wall is to you, could be that Great Wall to another and vice-versa, there's nothing wrong in asking or giving help. Start taking that wall down one brick at a time with knowledge and understanding. For example, if your wall is reading and you're having difficulty between "their, there and they're;" once you understand the differences, congratulate yourself, you just removed a layer from your wall. When you get discouraged and want to quit — stop and look up to see how far that wall has come down; then celebrate your successes.

Appreciation For The Reader

Thousands of hours of research, including personal interviews, have been condensed into this heartfelt historical novel. It's my hope to create a spark in the reader to want to learn more.

Every author knows that the reader is not only going to spend a few hard-earned dollars, but something even more valuable: the time to read it. It's my hope and prayer that when you close the book, you will have gained something from the experience.

Here is a short list:

• To feel an inspired gratitude for and love of country.

• Have an understanding and knowledge of true events, where integrity sets good examples for us to live by.

• Appreciate freedom from those who helped us keep it.

• Inspire others to share their stories—to preserve the accounts of history and to learn from them.

• Knowing that facing our fears is an opportunity for growth, and that fear is a part of life. What we do with that fear is a choice.

UNFORGETTABLE EXPERIENCE

We all have experiences in our lives we never forget. For me, I was thirteen and though it was many decades ago, it seems like yesterday. I learned of a WWII commandant who ran his prison camp with an iron fist. Every infraction of his rules had its own punishment — escape attempts carried the death penalty. There were those who tried and the ones who failed were given a choice, the known, which was the firing squad, or an unknown that the commandant kept secret deep in the woods. Whatever was out there had to be worse than the firing squad, because all were led into the woods, and all but one returned to be shot. When I learned what the other choice was, I found it so profound I have used that event my entire life to give me the encouragement I needed in facing my fears. It's my hope it will do the same for you.

I wrote this novel much like eating a buffet. Let me explain. At the age of seventeen, I worked at a buffet restaurant: "Take your tray and get in line. Pick and choose what looks good to you and enjoy." This book is written as a historical novel, based on true stories and events that can be confirmed through research. I created Nikki as a means to tell history the way I like to learn. I suggest you "go through the line," so to speak, and get a taste of everything. Even though you may be tempted to stop and look something up, I suggest you first read through for pleasure. Then go back, and when you come across something you want to know more about, be my guest and dig in.

Enjoy your journey with Nikki.

BUFFET ANYONE

I wrote this novel much like eating a buffet. Let me explain. At the age of seventeen, I worked at a buffet restaurant: "Take your tray and get in line. Pick and choose what looks good to you and enjoy." This book is written as a historical novel, based on true stories and events that can be confirmed through research. I created Nikki as a means to tell history the way I like to learn. I suggest you "go through the line," so to speak, and get a taste of everything. Even though you may be tempted to stop and look something up, I suggest you first read through for pleasure. Then go back, and when you come across something you want to know more about, be my guest and dig in. Enjoy your journey with Nikki.

CONTENTS

PART TWO: THE HUNT FOR COMMANDANT SCHMIDT

THE **EDUCATION** OF **NIKKI BROWN**

Introduction

Ray and I were sitting on a hand-carved bench, overlooking the Pacific Ocean at his grandfather's estate in San Diego, California. Hundreds of feet below us, we could hear the waves coming to the shore. It's late fall, and we were waiting for the sun to set. Ray could see my light sweater wasn't enough to keep me warm, so, like the gentleman he is, he took off his jacket to keep me warm. As he was doing so he made his move to put his arm around me. I don't know if he was nervous or cold, but I could feel him shaking a little. I like to think he was a little nervous. I leaned into him and rested my head on his shoulder. After all, it was the least I could do to keep him warm.

Not being from the West Coast, I had never seen a more beautiful sunset as it sank into the water. . . The day had started by Ray's grandfather telling me the most amazing story I think I had ever heard. What I refer to as "Part 1" of the family secret; and tomorrow morning we start on Part 2. It's a little after seven-thirty, and though the night is still young, I'm calling it for the evening. I told Ray how much I had enjoyed the day with him, but there was something I needed to do before I met with this grandfather. It was something that had been weighing heavily on my mind all day. He understood. Putting his arms around me, he paused and gave me our first kiss. Now I was the one shaking, and it wasn't because I was cold. If I had to rate that kiss from one to ten . . . with that sunset, it was definitely a ten.

What has been weighing so heavily on my mind that won't leave me is this: I'm an investigative reporter and have many stories of the people I've interviewed, each one as different as the individ-uals themselves, yet in many ways the same. So many of the veterans I interview to get their story seem to all start off by asking, "Why do you want to interview me? I haven't done anything special." Or, "I'm no hero." I have their stories, but not one of my own, and I hear myself saying, "Why do I want to take the time to tell my story? I haven't done anything special, and I'm certainly no hero." Maybe not, but it's an itch that won't go away and I feel compelled to at least try, but where and how to start? Perhaps I should start by introducing myself.

ONE
How the Seed Was Planted

My name is Nikki Brown. I was one of the few girls at my college to become an investigative reporter. Over a month ago I returned home to the States from Germany. I had been on a quest to find out what had happened to a POW from World War II, whom my grandfather told me about. Any prisoner who tried to escape Commandant Schmidt's prison camp was sentenced to death. To each of those who were to die, Commandant Schmidt gave a choice: Face the firing squad in front of everyone, or face the unknown of whatever was out in the woods.

My grandfather saw many who tried to escape, only to fail. Each would be led out into the woods, his hands tied behind his back, only to return and then be shot. Whatever was out in the woods was more terrifying than a bullet, because each escapee picked the firing squad. My grandfather did, however, witness one who never came back; one had chosen the unknown. Who was he? My grandfather didn't know, nor did he ever know what was in the woods. The commandant kept that a secret. I just had to find out what the other choice was, and that's what took me to Germany. What I found there led me back to the States with a mission—to find out the rest of the story.

There are two parts to this story, which are referred to as a family secret. The first part I heard just today, and it's remarkable. Earlier today, I sent it off to the newspaper that paid for my trip to Germany. My assignment was to find out what was in the woods and if at all possible the name of the one who never returned to face the firing squad.

Tomorrow I start to learn about part two. I'm told it's going to take several months. Anticipating what I will learn, I find many thoughts running through my head. Like the one my grandfather told me about that I just couldn't get off my mind, which drove me to Germany. While I was there I realized just how much I love and appreciate America. Whenever I see the American flag flapping in the wind, I can't help but feel a great pride for my country. When I see someone in a military uniform, if at all possible I'll go up to that person, a total stranger, and thank him or her for their service. I'm so grateful for those who paid with the ultimate sacrifice.

I'm going to do this journal in a story form, the way I remember it, and fill in the blanks with some creative writing. Most of the day, I spent wondering what to write about, when I realized how much my grandfather had influenced my life. If someone were to read this, I would want them to know my grandfather the way that I know him, a kind and loving man.

As I was growing up, Grandpa would tell a story, and sometimes he would get off track, one thought leading to another, and the next thing he knew he was what he called "off in the toolies." But I learned his idiosyncrasies to get him back on track. When he would stare off into the distance, I knew he was reflecting back. When he took in a deep breath, and by the way he let it out, would depend on how much he thought I was ready to learn. I'm thinking about putting in some of the photos I've collected, mostly from my grandfather. He was an artist and taught me how to draw. I might even put in some of my own drawings. I don't think my life has been all that eventful, so this journal shouldn't take too long. I will say this: I've researched the stories my grandfather told me, and they are true.

I grew up living practically next door to my grandparents. From the time I was a child, my grandfather taught me history. All that training makes me wonder about the civilizations who lost their freedoms. Could something like that ever happen to our great country? Glenn Ford said it best. "Let's never forget that to remain free we must always be strong. That's an important lesson I learned in my Navy career in World War II. National defense must be the top priority for our country. If you are not strong, you are safe. Now is the time for every American to be proud. This is the land of the free and the home of the brave. If we are not brave, we will not be free." (2004)

One of my earliest memories is of my Grandfather Vince, reading the newspaper. I must have been five, because I remember I was in kindergarten when I came running into his living room all excited.

"Grandpa, Grandpa, look what I found!" Grandpa Vince put down his paper. He chuckled as he sat looking at me. I was smothered in his old flight jacket, his dog-tags and goggles draped around my neck and a leather helmet balancing on my head, held there by my two tiny hands.

He reached over to the end table, opened the drawer, took out his Kodak camera and took my picture. He then stood, went to attention, and gave me a salute. Leaning over, he lifted me up and put me on his lap.

Look What I Found
Photo by Bryan McClure Photography

My First Salute
Photo by Bryan McClure Photography

"Well, it looks like somebody has found my treasure chest, but I wish you had asked first."

"Sorry, I didn't know it was your treasure,"

"So you discovered my old flight jacket that I wore when I was a pilot in World War II, did you?"

"Uh-huh," I nodded, grinning from ear to ear.

"These glasses you have around your neck are called goggles and these two metal plates are called dog tags." He laughed as he tilted the helmet back, "This was my father's leather skull-cap." He took the helmet off my head, rubbing his hands over the worn leather. I'm sure memories of his father ran through his mind. "He was a pilot in World War I. They were called 'Knights of the Air.' He was a wonderful man, full of passion for life; he would have loved you." He choked back the tears. "I sure miss him. He gave this helmet to me when I turned eigh-teen. "Pun'kin, would you like to see the rest of the treasure?"

I nodded, he lifted me off his lap, took my small hand in his, and together we went to the bedroom as I eagerly pulled him forward. Grandpa could see the mess I had made. A quilt that my grandmother made hung out of the chest, the lid closed on top of it. Kneeling down to be eye level with me, he put his hand on the latch, looked at me, and said, "Are you ready?" All I could do was nod my head. Together as we slowly opened the lid, Grandpa made a creaking sound. I looked at him, my eyes wide open and legs crossed. The excitement was more than I could stand.

"Wait! I have to go potty!" I took off the jacket, dropped it on the floor, and raced out the door and down the hall. "Don't open it yet!" I yelled all the way down the hall. "Almost finished!" echoed off the bathroom tile. While I was gone Grandpa quickly folded the quilt and straightened up the things I had disturbed while rifling through the chest. Running back down the hall, I picked up the jacket and put it back on. "Okay, now!"

Once again we slowly opened the lid, as Grandpa again made his creaking sound. Inside we found the quilt on top. As he picked it up he said, "This is your grandmother's first quilt. She made it when we were married; we put it in the treasure chest for safe keeping." Under the quilt was an ivory-white wool blanket, with a navy blue strip. Inside the strip was, "U.S. Navy."

"My brother Ellis, who served in the Navy, gave this to me. Our son, Kent, had outgrown his baby blanket, so Ellis cut in half the blanket he brought back with him and gave it to us for our son. Your grandmother put this stitch on the side so it wouldn't fray. Ellis kept the other half for when he would have a child. Doing things like that was quite common back then. We didn't have a lot money, so we found ways to make it stretch."

The next thing he pulled out was a beautiful white dress. "This is your grandmother's wedding dress; I'll bet it still fits her.

"Looking at this dress reminds me about another wedding dress. There's an old term called 'hit the silk.'"

"Mommy says I shouldn't hit anyone." Grandpa smiled.

"It means jump out of your airplane and open your parachute. You see, back then parachutes were made out of silk. An old friend of mine by the name of Lt. Ken Parkhurst was the co-pilot of a B-24. He and his crew were on a mission to take out an oil refinery in Linz. Oil refineries were heavily protected and they had to fly twenty minutes through flak to get to their target. That's when engines three and four were hit and they had to be shut down. I've never flown a multiengine plane before, but I've been told that with two engines out on the same side of the plane and the other two giving you trouble, it's next to impossible to fly. They knew they would never be able to make it back to their home base, so looking at the map they decided to head for the Russian lines. They were losing altitude fast, and I'm sure they all prayed they would make it. They just passed over Lake Balaton when the pilot called for everyone to bail out."

"Hit the silk!" I was so proud to add.

"That's right, Pun'kin, hit the silk. Now, I've never jumped out of a plane, mind you, but I'm told by those who have, that nothing feels better than to feel the jerk when that parachute opens. When Ken hit the ground, he gathered up his parachute and stuffed it back into the pack as best he could. He told me the whole population of a small nearby town came out to greet him, and he shook the hands of all of them. He didn't have any cigarettes to barter with, but he found that the fabric from his parachute worked just as well. He was left with a big piece of it, which he brought back home with him for a souvenir after he was discharged in 1945.

"Nikki, I don't know how he did it, but a beautiful girl by the name of Elaine said yes to his proposal. She and her mother decided to make the wedding dress and though there were many fabrics to choose from, she decided she wanted to make the dress out of silk. Nikki, where do you think she got the silk?"

"From the parachute!" I said excitedly. Grandpa smiled and nodded.

The Parachute of Love
Photo from Elaine Parkhurst's personal collection
Thank you Elaine

"After the wedding, the dress was cleaned, and Elaine rolled it up and put it in her cedar chest, much like this one. They had a daughter they named Janet, and I'll just bet when she was your age she found the wedding dress and fell in love with it and the story, because many years later she asked her mother if she could be married in that very dress, and of course her mother said yes.

"Now the dress that Elaine and her mother made had what's called a sweetheart neckline. Don't ask me what that is. I'm a guy and have no idea. What I do know was how beautiful she looked. Her daughter, Janet, wanted to update the dress to make it her own, and she incorporated a mandarin neckline with lace. Permission was granted, and she and the dress were stunning."

When I was much older, I met Elaine, who told me her granddaughter, Julia, also wanted to wear the dress for her wedding. Like before, she asked to update the dress to fit her style, and of course Elaine said yes. I've seen the photo that has all three of the brides, mounted proudly on the wall at Elaine's home. Each of the brides in her wedding dress is, as my grandfather would say, stunning. Julia chose March 2 for her wedding day, a very special day not only for Julia, but for her grandmother, Elaine, as well. You see, March 2 was the day my grandfather's friend, Lt. Ken Parkhurst, 15th Air Force, 465 Bomb Group, 781 Squadron, had to hit the silk to save his life. That's when this love story of the parachute all began. Elaine's first great-grandchild, Madeline, also wants walk down the aisle in the parachute of love; until then, her aunt Julia will hold on to it for safe keeping. With seven more great granddaughters in line, I doubt this love story will ever end.★

Elaine *Janet* *Julia*

Photo from Elaine Parkhurst's personal collection

There we were, Grandpa and I, looking at my grandmother's wedding dress as he lovingly placed it on the bed. Next he pulled out his dress uniform and smiled.

★ Interview at the residence of Elaine Parkhurst, 2016. Thank you for letting me share your love story.

"Nikki, believe it or not, I used to fit into this. That was a hundred years and a hundred pounds ago."

One by one we went through the items. At the bottom was what looked like a pencil and a booklet next to a knife, fork, and a big spoon, along with a small, beautiful wooden box with an envelope on top. Grandpa picked up the pencil and booklet. "This brings back memories. Your Grandmother put these in here to remind us just how scarce things were back then and the sacrifices Americans went through. This booklet is a Ration Book; back then, everything was rationed, and I mean everything." Grandpa realized I had no clue as to the word ration.

"Let's say the next time you went shopping with your mother and she needed butter and sugar, if she didn't have this Ration Book, she wouldn't be able to buy them, and even with the book she could only get a small amount. Americans gave up a lot back then; everything was needed for the war effort. Because we had metal drives, people who collect old cars today have a hard time finding them; they were melted down to be made into planes or tanks. People who had cars that ran would take off their bumpers to help with the cause. I remember the local theater would have tin can days for the kids. Every Saturday matinee, the admission fee was a tin can. Speaking of tin cans reminds me of the grease we collected from cooking, mostly from bacon. About once a week a neighborhood Girl Scout would come by to collect all the cans of grease from the neighbors and put them in her little red wagon. The glycerin in the fat was used to make explosives."

Rita Hayworth 1942

Photo provided by the National Archives (NARA)

Grandpa looked at the pencil and started to laugh. "This pencil is an eye-liner. If a woman saw a line of ladies outside a department story, not knowing why, she would get in line in hopes it was a line to get silk stockings. If a woman didn't have silk stockings, she would make her own by using this eye-liner. Silk stockings were sewn together with the seam going up the back of the woman's leg. The women who didn't have stockings to put on, they would take this eye-liner and draw a black line up the back of their leg."

Grandpa looked at me and shook his head. "It's a woman thing. I don't understand it, but I suppose one day you will."

I reached in and took out the spoon. On the handled was stamped "U.S.N."

Grandpa picked up the knife and fork. "This brings back memories. After the war, there were army and navy surplus stores on every corner and we could pick up whatever we needed for a song. We didn't care if it wasn't real silverware, we pretended it was and we were happy. The reason that spoon is so big is because, on a Navy ship, there are a lot of men to feed and you never knew when you were going to be attacked, so you had to eat quickly."

Only two items left, the envelope and the wooden box. First the envelope. Grandpa carefully opened it, and inside was a yellowed paper, dated September, 1945, congratulating his brother Joe for a job well done at the flag-raising ceremony with General MacArthur in Tokyo, Japan. Joe was one of fifty for that Honor Guard. Last was the wooden box. He held it in his left hand as his right hand lovingly stroked the wood grain on the lid.

"What's inside, Grandpa?"

He turned to me: "Silver and gold. Do you want to see?" I shook with anticipation. He opened it slowly. There before my eyes were the medals he had received while he was in the service, including his Purple Heart. "Not many people know this, but medals and ribbons are not owned by the person they were given to. They're owned by the government and should only be worn by those who earned them. They can be handed down to family, but should never be sold."

To this day, whenever I smell cedar, I reflect on that experience and the sacrifices people made for their family and country.

I call this one, "Daddy don't go."
Every time I see this photo I think of my uncle Kent.
Photo provided by the National Archives (NARA)

TWO

Let's go fly

When I came to visit, my mother knew I would make a beeline for the treasure chest and then come running to my grandfather, the flight jacket, helmet, and goggles in tow. Holding them up, I would say, "Let's go flying, Grandpa." He would put on the jacket and reach into the pocket for the clothespin to take up the slack from the leather helmet on my head. On went the goggles, which had the strap stitched, so they would stay on my head. Around my neck I wore a blue scarf that my grandmother had made for me to match my blue eyes. I would take my grandfather's hand, and we would walk to the airport, which was the living room. Together we cleared the runway by moving the coffee table over to the bookcase. Underneath the table, we had hid our makeshift yokes, two sticks that Grandpa had cut from old broom handles, which we'd put between our knees as we sat on the floor, the couch to our backs.

"What kind of plane are we going to fly today, Grandpa? Can we fly the 'Jug'?"

Sorry, honey, the T-Bolt is getting fixed from our last mission."

That was the plane my grandfather flew. He loved the P-47 Thunderbolt. It went by several names, but I liked "Jug." Grandpa called it a seven-ton tank that could fly. He would say, "It could take quite a beating and keep right on going.

Couldn't climb worth a darn, but could that bird dive. It was great at protecting our boys on the ground; it was one hard-hitting ground-attack aircraft, I'll give it that."

Grandpa on Patrol
When Grandpa showed this one to me he smiled and said, "That's me in the front. Can you see me waving to you?" For years, whenever I looked at this picture, I really could see him waving at me.
Photo provided by the National Museum of the U.S. Air Force.

I found out years later that the P-47 was what he was shot down in and became a prisoner of war. He was like a superhero to me. I remembered telling him that, but he said, "I'm no hero. I was just doing my job. The true heroes are the ones who never came back."

You name it, the two of us flew it, from fighter planes to bombers. He taught me all about each one of the planes: what made them different: their strengths, their weaknesses, and what they were used for.

As we flew into enemy territory, I would call out, "Incoming bandits at ten o'clock, Captain. Bank left!" That was the signal for Grandpa to lean into me, and together we would make the engine sound. Then he would say, "Look out! Focke-Wulf 190s at two o'clock. Bank right!" Now it was my turn to lean into him. Banking left and then right, climbing up and diving down as we flew into danger head on, keeping the enemy at bay by protecting the fleet and the men on the ground.

The first time we flew a bomber, it was a B-17, known as the "Flying Fortress." We had to make plenty of room in the middle of the living room so I could run to all the guns. Suddenly Grandpa would point and shout, "Triple A straight ahead!" I looked at him. "What's triple A?"

"Triple A is anti-aircraft artillery shot way up into the sky by large guns. They would be placed in areas the Germans needed to protect, like oil refineries and factories. These large guns in groups are called a 'flak battery.' When the Nazis would shoot the large artillery shells into the sky, they would explode at different altitudes with a puff of black smoke into many pieces of shell fragments called flak. The black smoke would help the Nazis put a fix on our altitude. Usually by the third round they knew how high we were. There's a saying, 'You only take on flak when you're getting close to the target,' so in a way it's a good thing—you're getting closer to completing your mission. There is of course the bad thing: if you fly into the flak it could rip through your plane and you could go down."

Grandpa shook and rocked back and forth, while making dramatic sound effects of the downward crash; we would pull up in the nick of time. Sometimes we would bail out and parachute to the ground behind enemy lines and make our way back to safety.

Whenever we flew the bombers, Grandpa sure knew how to give me some exercise. He would be the pilot, and I would be the co-pilot, along with the left and right waist gunners, tail gunner, top and lower ball turret gunner, as well as the navigator, who fired the cheek guns. Grandpa would call out, "Here they come, twelve o'clock high." I would run to the top turret and let them have it. Then he would call out, "They're coming in on our six." I would run to the tail gun as they came from behind. From gun to gun I would run, protecting the squadron as we made our way to the drop zone. Once again Grandpa would call out, "Pilot to bombardier . . . approaching target." I would run to my station, and with me as navigator, the plane was now in my control. "Bombs away, let's get out of here." Banking left, we headed for home. Again Grandpa had me running from one gun position to the other as the enemy aircraft swarmed all around us as we headed for safety. You name it, we shot it down, from the Me 109, to the Germans' secret weapon, the 262, the first jet fighter.

One day when we were headed for the living room, my Grandmother Clea stopped us. "Not so fast, you two." When we turned around I saw her holding up a jacket she had made for me. I couldn't believe it—my very own flight jacket! It may not have been made out of real leather like my grandfather's, but that didn't matter, it was real to me. Grandmother helped me put it on. It fit like a glove, and I felt like a true pilot. I gave a salute and my grandmother snapped to attention. As she returned the salute she urged, "Go get 'em."

As we walked to the airport I asked, "What are we going to fly today, Grandpa?"

"Today we're going to fly the P-40 Kitty Hawk. Did I ever tell you that's the plane The Flying Tigers flew?"

I giggled, "Grandpa, tigers can't fly."

He couldn't help but laugh. After all, I was right. He told me, "The Flying Tigers" were the 1st American Volunteer Group of the Chinese Air Force before America got involved in the war. The pilots were from the U.S. Army, Navy and Marine Corps.

Flying Tigers
Hell's Angels, the 3rd Squadron of the 1st American Volunteer Group "Flying Tigers," Over China in 1942.
Pilot Robert T. Smith

Their planes were painted to look like sharks. John Wayne made a movie about the Flying Tigers, and later on I must have watched it with my grandfather half a dozen times. I really enjoyed watching old movies with him. He showed me a picture of one of the planes the Tigers flew. I loved looking at the art work that went on the planes of World

War II. Grandpa had a collection of books he would show me as a child, but because they showed a lot of scantily dressed women, he had to cover a lot of them up.

Whenever we would fly, there was a routine procedure we would do. Grandpa would say, "Are you ready for the preflight inspection?"

"Ready, Captain!" I'd say as I snapped to attention and gave him the customary salute.

"All right, then, let's give this baby a once over to make sure she'll fly. How's everything over there look?"

"Looks good, Captain, just a few bullet holes, but she'll fly."

As we walked around in a circle, he would call out the checkpoints, "Ailerons? Flaps? Elevator? Vertical rudder? Guns? Ammo? Fuel?" With each item, I would call out, "Check!" Together, we would step onto the wing and climb into the cockpit, with me on his left. Once inside, we'd pick up our sticks and hold them in place with our knees, while Grandpa would take me through the check list for the preflight inside. While working the foot pedals and the yoke, together we watched the flaps on the wings go up and down as we flipped on the switches. He'd call out, "Check the wind sock!"

"Wind coming in from the west, Captain!"

"Start the engine!"

I remember jumping up, dropping the stick and putting one hand on my hip, and with the other hand pointed my finger in a scolding manner. "Grandpa, we didn't call clear."

He just put his hand on his forehead. "You're right, Pun'kin, how could I have forgotten?" He didn't forget. He was just testing me. I sat back down all excited; we were getting to my favorite part. "Don't forget to strap in," he would tell me, and together we called out, "Clear!"

I reached over and started the engine. Together we made a low rumbling sound, and started to bounce up and down. Faster and louder we would bounce as I reached over and increased the RPMs. As we went down the runway, I would call out the speed. Grandpa would get louder and louder, so when we reached air speed I would have to yell, "Now!" And together we would pull back on the yoke, leaning back as we gained altitude. I would call out "one thousand, two thousand," until we reached ten thousand feet.

Grandpa's Little Co-Pilot
Photo by Bryan McClure Photography

Pushing back on the yoke, we'd sit up and I would call out, "Leveling off at ten thousand feet, Captain. What's our mission today, Grandpa? I mean Captain?" I had no way of knowing then, but learned later, that every imaginary mission was a real mission that had happened in World War

II. Oh how I loved this time with my grandfather!

After each mission, my grandmother would always have lunch ready for us. I was always captivated by the stories my grandfather would tell me about world history as we ate.

One time after lunch Grandpa looked at his watch. "Your mother won't be back for about another hour or so. What would you like to do?"

"Let's go fly!"

Grandpa smiled. "Aren't you tired of flying?" I shook my head no, took him by the hand, and led him back to the airport. Once again we would bounce down the runway.

We were flying patrol looking for men who were pinned down by the Germans. Grandpa pointing down, 'There's the G.I.'s were looking for,' and we dove down to give them cover. After our mission I asked, "What's a G.I.?" He smiled.

"General Infantry, but among the fighting men it stands for Government Issue. Like everything else that was given to us, we were disposable."

THREE

Fighting the Odds

By the time I was ten, I felt I was too old to be sitting on the floor bouncing up and down. Grandpa told me he knew this day would come sooner or later, and that he would miss it. But I still loved to hear the stories. We had flown every plane known to my grandfather. We had shot down enemy aircraft, captured generals, rescued starving prisoners, and bombed targets designated by headquarters. Some missions were what we called milk runs, low priority, which meant "little triple A." Others were valued targets, like ball bearing factories or oil fields and refineries, always the most dangerous. The Nazis protected them with heavy antiaircraft guns.

On the day I told Grandpa I was too old, he put his arm around me. "If you feel you are too old to play pilot with me, I understand. Maybe there are other things we could do."

"Like what?" I asked.

"I don't know, like visit aviation museums and maybe sit in real World War II planes. I'm sure there are lots of things we can do; we just have to use our imagination. What do girls your age like to do? This old dog can still learn some new tricks. I know, how about the mall? I know girls love to go shopping, or perhaps we could go to the movies."

I knew he was fishing for interesting diversions, and

some of them did sound fun. He was true to his word; we found all kinds of things to do. I tucked away my childhood jacket and scarf in my newly made treasure chest, and a whole new world opened up to me, especially in aviation museums.

There was an air show about two hours away, and we made a day of it. I think I was fifteen, I remember because I wanted to help my grandfather drive, but he wouldn't let me. When we got there, I couldn't believe it . . . so many World War II airplanes that I thought I'd died and gone to plane heaven. There were bombers, including the Flying Fortress, B-17; the B-24, Liberator; the B-25 Mitchell. Along with the bombers were a myriad of fighters. My grandfather went right to the P-47 Thunderbolt and talked to the pilot, who also was the owner. Those two could have talked shop all day. And what kind of an air show would it be if there wasn't a P-51 Mustang. We were introduced to the pilot of the B-17, and he showed us around.

B-17 Flying Fortress

Photo from the private collection of Gary J. Sumner

B-24 Liberator
Photo from the private collection of Gary J. Sumner

B-25 Mitchell
Photo from the private collection of Bryan McClure

P-47 Thunderbolt
Photo provided by the National Museum of the U.S. Air Force.

P-51 Mustang
Photo from the private collection of Gary J. Sumner

Grandpa and I aren't that tall so we didn't have too much trouble standing; the catwalk, however, was a different matter. I laughed when Grandpa turned sideways and sucked in his gut. When he got to the end he stood up and poked his head into the top turret, and I got a great shot of him looking at me.

Grandpa in his Summer Shorts
Catwalk of the B-17
Photo from the private collection of Gary J. Sumner

Grandpa looking at me from the top turret of the B-17
Photo from the private collection of Gary J. Sumner

The bombers weren't made for tall men, and that's for sure. The guy behind me told me he was six-foot five and I just had to take his picture. He didn't mind, and he gave me a nice smile.

Inside a B-17

Photo from the private collection of Gary J. Sumner

The next thing I knew my grandfather and I were strapped in the seats going through our pre-flight checklist. I may have been too old to be sitting on the floor bouncing up and down, but not when you're sitting in the real thing. We finished all our "checks," called clear, and started to make the engine sound, bouncing up and down in our seats. I called out the airspeed and the altitude, "Leveling off at ten thousand feet, Captain. Here comes the triple A." I pointed, but Grandpa didn't move. He sat, staring off. I noticed a tear rolling down his cheek. "Grandpa, are you all right?" He gave a slight jerk, then wiped his face with his hand. "I'm fine, Pun'kin. I was thinking of my four brothers.

"I always get a kick out of people's faces when I tell them I have four brothers, and when I tell them I also have five sisters, they almost faint. Yup, ten kids all together. Back then, that wasn't all that uncommon, especially if you lived on a farm, that's just what you did. Nikki, your Great-grandmother Caroline was a saint if there ever was one. I'll lay you ten to one odds, angels looked down on my mother in total awe and amazement."

Grandpa reached into his wallet and pulled out a picture of the five of them standing together in their uniforms. They looked so young, like little kids playing army and navy. Pointing to the photo he said. "That's me, that's your Great Uncle Ellis, Evan, Joe and George. George was the baby of the family until Louise was born. George was so happy, 'I'm not the baby anymore,' he would state matter-of-factly. Joe and I were one year apart, and we did everything together, which was mostly getting into mischief. George would follow us around like a puppy dog from the time he could walk. Mom told us that he looked up to us so we better behave ourselves. I'm sure Mom told Ellis and Evan the same thing to them about me, because I looked up to the both of them. We wanted to serve together, but after the "Fighting Sullivan Brothers," we didn't even ask."

"Who are the fighting Sullivan brothers?"

"They were five brothers who wanted to be together, and they were given permission to do so. But on June 1st in 42, their ship, the U.S.S. Juneau, was torpedoed by the Japanese. After that, the government made sure that would never happen again. You should look up their story. It's quite amazing. A movie was even made about them.

I loved my brothers, and we did about everything together, which was mostly getting into mischief, right up until Ellis and Evan left home. Then it was just the three of us, Joe, George and me.

Fighting Sullivan Brothers
Photo provided by U.S. Naval Historical Center #NH52362

"I was just finishing my second year in college when the Japanese bombed Pearl Harbor. I was married to your grandmother, and we had our first son, Kent. I sure as heck didn't want to leave them, but I knew I was going to be drafted, so I volunteered. I knew I had to do everything I could to keep them and others safe.

"Ellis went into the Navy and was trained to be a mechanic. He loved working on the airplanes. Evan was a flight engineer on B-32s."

I interrupted, trying to sound like Arnold Schwarzenegger, and said, "The Dominator." Grandpa shook his head.

"That's right, Pun'kin, the Consolidated B-32 Dominator. Evan wrote telling me about his first flight. The B-32 barely made it off the ground when one of the engines caught fire. The pilot radioed in, declaring an emergency. Before they could touch down, Evan had the fire out, props turned so they wouldn't cause a drag on the plane, and they safely touched down. Joe went to the Pacific Theater; he drove trucks, along with many other duties.

"Joe was one of the first to set foot on Japan and was one of fifty for the flag-raising ceremony with General MacArthur in Tokyo."

"I remember that from when we went through the treasure chest for the first time."

"That's a day I'll never forget. I went into the Army Air Corps and learned to fly fighters. When my group landed in Italy, we were assigned P-47s . . . I loved that plane."

"What about George? Where did he go?"

"George, being the youngest of the boys, we were all hoping and praying the war would be over before George turned eighteen, but he wanted to be like his older brothers and volunteered two months before his birthday. I tried to convince him to go to college first, but he'd hear none of it. George was the right height to be trained as a gunner for the ball turret in a B-17, just like the one we're sitting in. George wrote me a letter telling how he and his crew were going up at 0500, and how the only thing they were afraid of was that the war would be over before they could do their part. They were excited to be finally getting into the war after the many months of training. When you're young, you think you're invincible . . .

"When I didn't get a letter from George, telling me all about his first mission, I knew something was wrong. I kept hoping it was just the slow mail service, so prevalent at that time. When I received the word that his plane had gone down, with no survivors, I was so angry with God, I remember saying it should have been me and not my baby brother. Then my thoughts turned to my mom and dad and my brothers. I knew what they were going through, because I was going through it myself. I asked God, 'If one more of us had to die, let it be me.'"

There was a long pause, and then Grandpa told me, "When I entered the war, if you flew a bomber and made it through your twenty-fifth mission, you were able to return stateside. But the odds of you making it through twenty-five were not in your favor. You had a one-in-eight chance of being shot down each time you went up. If you think those were good odds, think about playing Russian roulette with one bullet in an eight-cylinder gun. Spin and close it each time, put the gun to your head, and pull the trigger. You have a one in eight chance that nothing will happen. Try doing it twenty-five times, and you'll start to get a feel for what those men went through.

The air corps was losing so many planes and men that it couldn't let crews go after twenty-five missions, so they upped the number from twenty-five to thirty-five, then fifty, missions. The air corps needed experienced men to carry out the missions. Many a plane went down on its forty-ninth or fiftieth mission. Sometimes our planes were shot down by accident by our own plane—friendly fire. Accident or friendly fire, the results are the same—men died for their country.

"Those who filled their quota could rotate out, or could stay on if they wanted to. But who in the heck would want to?"

FOUR

Philip McClure

"What about your friend who went 59 missions? You know, the one in the photo who was sitting on a bomb with his crew."

Smoke'em if you got'em
Photo from the private collection of Bryan McClure

A warm smile came to Grandpa's face. "I forgot I told you about Lieutenant Philip Leonard McClure."

"I remember because of the way you laughed when you told me how he and a buddy of his made themselves sick of milkshakes." That made Grandpa chuckle.

"I can't remember how much weight Phil and Stan had to gain, but it was enough that they had to put down milk-shake after milkshake, day after day, to make the weight. Phil must have made weight first, because Stan joined three months later.

"Phil ended up in Italy flying B-25s, and Stan, though he could have been assigned anywhere, he, too, was sent to Italy. It was quite a surprise when their paths crossed."

"Tell me about Mount Vesuvius."

There She Blows
Photo from the private collection of Bryan McClure

Grandpa smiled. "When that volcano went off, debris flew everywhere. Rocks ripped through the canvas tents like they were made out of paper. Men dove under the wings and body of the planes for cover. When it was over, not one of the planes was air worthy. If I remember, Phil told me there were close to thirty new planes that had just arrived."

"Tell me again about the Battle for Rome."

"That was one of the names. Officially, it was the Battle of Monte Cassino, and yes, Phil's 340th Bomber Group was part of that offensive. The Germans had no regard for that historic landmark, and I guess we didn't either, because we bombed the hell out of it. It was founded in A.D. 529. At least after the war our tax dollars rebuilt and restored it to its original state, from the cornerstone to the top stone.

Monte Cassino

Photo from the private collection of Bryan McClure

"It took four assaults by the Allies to take that high ground and drive the Germans off, but we did it. That piece of real estate came with a high cost, fifty-five thousand Allied soldiers, and all good men who would never be reunited with their families again. Among the dead was a high number form the 442nd Infantry. On the German side, the cost was twenty thousand, all because of that madman Hitler, their families paid a price, too."

442nd Infantry
Photo Courtesy of UC Berkeley, Bancroft Library

"Who was the 442nd Infantry Grandpa?"

"Something not too many people know, they were Japanese American volunteers from the internment camps. Even after President Roosevelt interned the Japanese, they sent their sons out to help protect America. Let me tell you, they were valiant and they fought with great honor, perhaps to prove a point on how wrong Roosevelt was for what was done to their parents.

Grandpa paused, "How did I get started talking about The Battle of Monte Cassino?"

"You were talking about after flying fifty missions you could rotate out, and I remembered your friend Phil who flew fifty-nine."

"That's right; he and his flight leader shared the same tent and became the best of friends. When they reached the fifty mark they thought, 'What the heck? Let's go for sixty.' They were flying in formation, with the flight leader just off Phil's wing. It was then that the plane exploded right before his eyes. When Phil finished the mission he went to the flight sergeant and told him he had just flown his last mission. The flight sergeant, knowing Phil had gone the extra mile, granted him his wish.

"There may have been others, but Lieutenant Philip McClure was the only one I knew." Grandpa stared off into the distance, and then continued.

"I don't think I would have flown past my quota. Fighter pilots were lucky to make it past fifteen missions. I tell you this so you'll know the sacrifices your family, like so many other families, made. And also when I'm gone and no longer able to tell my story, my song can still be sung. No one knows the sacrifices that were made, not only by those who served but by the family members left behind." Grandpa paused, and I could see the hesitation in his face. I'd seen that look many times.

"Nikki, I think you're old enough to hear about some of the unsung heroes. Ask people today to name the heroes of WWII, and you'll get blank stares. If you're lucky you'll hear names like Clark Gable, Ronald Reagan, Jimmy Stewart and Audie Murphy, to name just a few. There's no doubt, every one of them and others, are all heroes. But what about all the ones who quietly went about their jobs, who made it possible for the well- known heroes? Everyone, from the cooks, to the doctors and everyone in between who worked endlessly doing their jobs.

"What about the mechanics and ambulance drivers. Ever stop to think about what they went through? Can you imagine what they had to do to clean things up so others wouldn't have to look at it? They all had a job to do, and they did it. Not to be called a hero, but to serve. I wonder how many of those men later wake up in the middle of the night in a cold sweat, reflecting back on their experience. I just remembered, Queen Elizabeth, when she was the Crown Princess of England during World War Two, was a mechanic and an ambulance driver. Let me tell you, not only did she pull her own weight, she was definitely easy on the eyes."

Crown Princess Elizabeth
Artist Rendition

My grandpa sure thought he was the ladies' man.

FIVE

Hank Tussy

"Nikki, do you remember my good friend Hank Tussy?"

"Isn't he the one who, as you put it, 'Was a lucky bum to have married such a beautiful girl'?"

Hank and his lovely bride Judy

Photo from the private collection of Gary J. Sumner

Grandpa chuckled, "That's him. Hank's wife, Judy, never ages. She just gets better looking as time goes by, and if you tell your grandmother I said that, I'll deny it."

"Your secret is safe with me, Grandpa, but if I told her, you could deny it all you want. Grandma knows you too well." Grandpa smiled and agreed.

"Hank is definitely one of those unsung heroes." Grandpa chuckled. "Boot camp for most of us took two months, but Hank took three. Poor guy, he came down with the mumps. He went from boot camp in Idaho to the University of Illinois to be trained on engines. From there he went from the frying pan, Operation Tiger, into the fire, D-Day on June 6, 1944."

"I've never heard of Operation Tiger. What was that?" I'd seen my grandfather with many different expressions, but fear has never been one of them, until that day.

"I can't tell you."

"You know I'll just look it up."

"You can't, it's classified, I shouldn't even know." It took some doing . . . but my grandfather finally opened up.

"D-Day had been planned, and Eisenhower felt the rookies needed some toughing up with a joint mock invasion. A beach called Slapton Sands in southern England was selected. It was so top secret, the entire village was relocated until the exercise was over.

"The plan was to make it as real as possible; the Brits would shell the beach on the left and right side of the beach from their ships as the G.I.s stormed out of the landing crafts. From there, the men would crawl under barbed wire, all the while machine guns would be firing live ammo just over their heads, close enough they could hear the bullets as they whisked by. Just one problem: for some reason the timing was off, and the shells went right down the middle. The men didn't stand a chance. It should have been called off right then and there, but it wasn't.

"The next day was when the LST's were to land with all

the heavy equipment."

"What are LST's?"

"They were massive ships that could haul anything from tanks to jeeps and everything in between. The LST stands for, 'Landing Ship Tanks,' but the men called them 'Large Standing Targets.' The U.S. built so many of them, instead of giving each a name, only numbers were painted on the side. Eight of them headed for Slapton Sands, and Hank Tussy was on one of them. Normally radio silence would be in order, but for some reason it wasn't, and to make things worse, we and the Brit's weren't on the same radio frequency. The German's picked up on the miscommunication and sent out nine German S boats to investigate. Those babies were a hundred feet long and made of wood. Let me tell you, they were the fastest boats on water at the time, and they were deadly with their torpedoes.

"It was around 0130 hour when the S boats opened up, and we didn't stand a chance. When it was all over, two Allied ships went down, and a third was badly damaged, with over six hundred men dead. Some died due to poor instruction on how to abandon ship. At the time there were two types of life preservers: one, the most popular issued to the Navy, was called a Mae West. I'll let you research the reason why they were called Mae West. The other one issued to the G.I.'s was life belts. Imagine taking an inner-tube and strapping it around you, and you had to blow up. It should go under your arms, but there were those who put them around their waist. Those who had them around their waists, drowned, because the belt forced their heads down. There was another problem: when the men jumped from the ship with their helmets strapped under their chin, if they jumped from a high point, the force of the water going into the helmet would snap their neck."

"Grandpa, that's terrible."

"That's war. Sometimes it's a learn as you go. It was such a disaster and black eye that Eisenhower ordered a wall of silence for security reasons, and any man who talked about it would be court-martialed, regardless of rank. That's all I can tell you. I shouldn't have even told you that. Maybe someday it'll be declassified, and we'll know what really happened."

"I knew not to press for any more information, so I turned my attention back to Hank Tussy. "I remember you showing me a photo of Hank in his boat on D-Day."

Hank Tussy #72 (Center)
Photograph from the U.S. Coast Guard Collection in the U.S. National Archives.

"That's right, number 72. I'm not surprised you remember; that's why I never showed you a photo of his LST. If I did, knowing you, you wouldn't give up until I told you what I just did. Anyway, the engines he was trained on went in that very boat. It had a four man crew and was called an LCVP. Those babies transported the men who stormed the beaches on that day."

"I know what LCVPs stands for, Landing Craft Vehicle Personnel. They were also known as Higgins." Grandpa was so proud I knew that.

"I've trained you well, Pun'kin." Grandpa took in a long, deep breath and let it out slowly. In order to get to Berlin, we had to go through France. Our point of entry? Normandy. The Americans were to hit Utah and Omaha Beaches, while the English were to hit Gold, Juno, and Sword. Hank's beach, Omaha. Early that morning, the first wave hit the beach. It was their job to secure the beachhead, making it safe for all the men behind them. Nothing went as planned that day. A German general by the name of Erwin Rommel had fortified Normandy so well, it was a miracle any of the men survived.

"The plan was to drive the men in on the landing craft at high tide, and bring them closer to the cliffs for cover. Just one problem: Rommel must have been a chess player, because when he first arrived at Normandy, he took one look at the board and saw what he had to do to protect it. I don't know which of the many measures he took first, but the first obstacles we had to face were the land mines he placed on long stakes that the LCVPs would have hit at high tide. Lucky for us, recon planes had photos of these stakes at low tide, so we knew they were there. The only problem now was that the men had a long march on the beach out in the open. The men were told not to worry—the Germans would have been obliterated with massive shelling.

"Just before O600 hours, eighteen ships cut loose with close to 440 tons of shells. Next in line came the B-17s, numbering 446. They dropped 1,200 tons of bombs. After that, ten minutes before the men were to hit the beach, nine rocket ships sent 9,000 rockets flying into the air.

"When we hit the beaches of Normandy, we thought it was going to be checkmate. Company A unloaded and walked twenty yards onto a quietly eerie beach. Could it be true? Had all the Germans been annihilated? Sadly no. Even with all the heavy bombardment, not one German had even a scratch. They were waiting patiently for our men to enter the trap, like a spider waits for its prey to enter its web. Then, at the precise moment, all hell broke loose, with as few as 120 guns, each with a man in its sights. It was like shooting fish in a barrel. The weapon we feared the most was a machine gun that had a very distinctive sound. It could spit out 1,500 rounds a minute, twice as fast as any other gun at that time. It was the MG42, better known as Hitler's buzz-saw. When it was used in a heavily wooded area, if a soldier hid behind a tree for protection, the tree would be literally cut down, along with the man behind it. Company A didn't stand a chance. In ten minutes they had a ninety-two percent loss.

"Even with all that, Rommel hedged his bet with even more coverage to protect the beach. He placed two 88mm guns on each end that you would think would be aimed out to sea to take out the ships, but no, they were facing across the beach, able to fire as far as five miles each with pinpoint accuracy. Along with that, as far as six miles inland were artillery guns aimed at the beach. When the shells hit, the fragments were deadly for 60 feet.

"Rommel knew how determined the opposition would be. He needed the troops to stay on the beach as long as possible, so he strung out barbed wire to stop them in their tracks. But we were ready to clear the wire with Bangalore torpedoes. When the path was cleared, Rommel had another obstacle to keep us from advancing. He placed 40,000 landmines like seeds of grass. Most landmines were designed to take out the man who stepped on them. But these mines were different; when a man set them off, they would shoot upwards, exploding in the air, with fragments flying everywhere. The G.I.'s called them the castrator.

"Just like Operation Tiger, foresight and hindsight came up a dollar short and a day late. The men had packs weighing up to 85 lb. If ever there was a time a man had to run as fast as he could, that was the time, and carrying that much weight was a death sentence. Some who had to leap out of the landing craft into the water sank to the bottom, drowning themselves.

"It took the rest of the day with massive loss of life, before we over took the Germans. So what went wrong? The Germans were hunkered down in bunkers of reinforced concrete, able to withstand a direct hit from the 440 tons of shells. It was said because of heavy cloud cover, the pilots in the bombers were ordered to delay the drop to avoid hitting the men below waiting in the landing crafts. Just one problem: with altitude and speed, for every half second in delay, the bombs landed off target by a hundred feet. Some missed their targets as far as three miles. The cloud cover story was just that, a story. The Navy didn't know the Army pilots and their crews were seasoned, battle tested, and hard as nails. By that time in the war, those boys could have put one down Hitler's chimney. But orders are orders, and the bombardier delayed. And as far as the rockets were concerned, they too missed their targets and fell into the sea.

"Hank was in the second wave, that dreadful day. Nikki, when you're nineteen you think you're invincible, but when you see the boat in front of you get hit and literally blown out of the water, that's when it really hits you: you're a sitting duck, and the odds of you getting out of this alive are not in your favor. I can't imagine what emotions the man steering the boat must have felt, knowing he couldn't stop to help the survivors and was forced to run over the ones who couldn't get out of the way. They were under strict orders not to stop; their mission was to get to the beach at all costs. With all that, the men who manned those boats kept coming, back and forth, wave after wave. Land, drop off the men, and then run to the beach, pick up the wounded, take them to the ship set up to care for them, and pick up another group of men and head back to the beach, only to be slaughtered. Hank, with the two of his crew, was on that detail, leaving the coxswain at the helm."

"Okay Grandpa, what's a coxswain?"

"I knew I'd get you on that one. He's the guy who's responsible for steering the boat."

"Grandpa, you never cease to amaze me."

"I try Pun'kin, I try. Now, where was I? Oh yes, Hank told me he couldn't remember a lot about that day. He thinks he was probably in shock most of the time. He said, 'I did what I was trained to do.' It was his job to assess who would get on the boat for the ride back and who had to be left behind to do the hard task of dying. Hank knew that taking a person who didn't stand a chance to survive would only take up a valuable space on the boat for someone who might be able to make it.

"Running to the men who were down, dodging bullets left and right to help those he could, he and his crew loaded up the boat, praying they wouldn't get hit. When Hank told me the story, he said, with a smile, 'We carried men back and forth, just like a taxi service, and wouldn't you know it, not one tip.' Enough time has passed where we can laugh about it now. We all carried two dog tags around our neck, so when someone was killed, one tag would go into the mouth to stay with the body and the other went back to start the paper work. That's what Hank and the others like him had to do as well.

"The cost was high on D-Day. A little fewer than ten thousand paid the price. Hank tried to describe the scene to me; but mostly he just shook his head. Nikki, Hollywood can try to recreate what happened but never will. Saving Private Ryan was as close as I think you can get, but the stench is something you can't capture on film and no words can describe it. Trying to describe all the different odors in the air mingled together, along with all the commotion around you, it can't be done. It's something you have to experience for yourself, and I pray to God, no one ever again has to experience what happened on D-Day.

"Late in the afternoon on that first day, the bulldozers came onto the beach. By the next day trenches were made to make temporary graves to cover the dead and to cover the foul odor in the air. Nor was it good for the morale of the men coming ashore to see all that carnage. Somebody had to carry the dead, and Hank was one of the many somebodies.

"Hank and his wife Judy went back to Normandy for the ceremony commemorating the fortieth anniversary of that dreadful day. President Reagan gave a stirring talk, telling how the men stormed the beaches and how the Rangers climbed the cliffs to take out the Germans, and set the path to free Europe from tyranny.

President Ronald Reagan
Artist Rendition

When Hank and Judy were socializing with the others, one of the Rangers told Judy, 'We may get most of the accolades, but let me tell you, your husband and the men like him were the heroes that day.' Neither Judy nor Hank could remember the name of the ranger, but they told me they saw his photo on the cover of Time magazine.

"Nikki, we have to plan a trip to San Francisco. The ship Hank was pulling alongside to take the men into the action was the S.S. Jeremiah O'Brien, and it's there at Pier 45. Hank tells me if we look on the starboard side of the bow, we'll see the dents that the LCVPs put there on that day. Hank told me he knows for sure a few of them are his."★

S.S. Jeremiah O'Brien

Photo from the private collection of Gary J. Sumner

I asked "How was it possible for you and all those servicemen to be able to go back, mission after mission, and battle not only the enemy, but the constant fear you faced?"

"The Nazis were trying to enslave us, so we put that fear aside and simply did our jobs. You had to put the risk out of mind. When you're in the heat of battle, you don't have

★ Interview at the residence of Hank and Judy Tussy's. 4-20-2016. Thank you for your time and for sharing your story so others can learn what you and so many went through.

time to even think about it; you're too busy trying to save your life and the lives of your buddies. Those of us who flew never saw the damage we did.

"It was the boots on the ground that saw the blood and carnage firsthand. Why did we do it? It was our duty. We were there protecting what we held most dear to us—our liberty and freedom, our God, family and country.

"I never flew in a bomber, but I can imagine how impossible it must have been to even hear yourself think, over the thundering of the engines in this tin can. The chill that would rip through the cabin at takeoff was nothing compared to the freezing temperatures at high altitudes—thirty to sixty degrees below zero. The military planes couldn't be pressurized because of the openings needed for the left and right waist gunners, not to mention the holes made by enemy anti-aircraft fire."

Grandpa looked at the photo and told me something I never knew. "George was the only one who never returned home. Evan may not have been the oldest, but he was definitely the strongest. We leaned on him heavily to help us get through some pretty rough patches. There have been a lot of names for it: soldier's heart, battle fatigue, shellshock, and PTSD. I'm sure there are other names, but for those who suffer from it, it's called HELL.

"Joe and Ellis had it the worst. Ellis fought his own demons, and we were helpless; we just didn't know what to do. Joe, like so many others who just wanted to forget, would self-medicate with alcohol to stop the flashbacks.

"Joe told me it helped him to better cope—at least it did for a little while." Grandpa stared off for a long time. "Nikki, I loved my brothers and I tried everything I could think of to help Joe, but it just wasn't enough. He drank himself to death."

Tears were rolling down his face when he looked one last time at the photo. He tucked his pain back inside his wallet. "I carry them with me always. I never want to forget." He took in a deep breath and let it out slowly. "War is hell, Nikki! Don't ever forget the soldiers who have stood up to fight for the rights you have. I lost two brothers because of that war, one a quick death and the other to a slow, agonizing death. Both were protecting the flag. Don't ever take your freedoms for granted."

I promised him I wouldn't, and after knowing what my family had sacrificed, this is a promise I'll easily keep.

I left the B-17 that day feeling more connected to my grandfather than I had ever felt before. He had lost much to the war; and I now could appreciate his pain and his passion. He didn't want his brothers to have died in vain. He honored their memory, along with all the Brave Knights of yesterday and today, who stood and stand strong on that "wall of protection."

SIX

They Flew with Crimson Tails

Whenever I visited my Grandfather, he would teach me about history, and we watched old movies about the war. I'm not sure who was my favorite actor, John Wayne or Jimmy Stewart. On my thirteenth birthday Grandpa gave me a card with a handwritten certificate, good for one round trip on an airline to the Smithsonian National Air and Space Museum, to be redeemed on my next summer vacation.

It was my first time ever to be on an airplane, and the thrill of going down the runway, being pushed against my seat, was nothing like our runway in the living room. The acceleration of the engines and the liftoff, along with the lunge forward on the landing—these are sensations I'll never forget.

It was amazing to see history before my eyes at the Smithsonian. When we came across a plaque memorializing the first all-black American military aviators, Grandpa stopped. "The Tuskegee Airmen. If I ever told you about them before, it's worth telling you about them again."

I nodded my head, "Good stories are worth repeating."

"They were the first black American military aviators in the U.S. Army Air Corps. They got their name from the base they were trained, Tuskegee Army Air Field, Tuskegee, Alabama. At first they flew what one would call hand-me-downs. After they proved themselves they flew P-51s, and they were in high demand over Europe.

"I remember at the Tuskegee base, the dining hall was divided in three parts. In the center was the kitchen and on one side is where the white officers ate and on the other is where the black officers ate. There wasn't anything special on one side or the other; after all it was only a dining hall. One day a few of the black officers thought segregation was—for the lack of a better word—stupid. So they came on the white side but the person in charge of the dining hall stopped them. One of the officers pulled out of his pocket a copy of the Army Regulations stating any of the facilities on army bases were to be open to officers. The man in charge looked at it, and let them sit wherever they liked. But a few white officers reported the incident to the base commander and complained. The commander looked at the Regs and he let it stand. The name of that commander was Noel Parrish and he treated the blacks as equals.

"One of the leaders of the 332nd was a man by the name of Benjamin O. Davis Jr. His father, Benjamin O. Davis, Sr., was America's first black general. Davis Jr. gave his Mustang the name By Request. I think he was a bird colonel."

I smiled, knowing that pilots called their planes birds, and said out loud, "A bird flying a bird, now there's a visual." I love it when I can make my grandfather smile. "Tell me again why they were in high demand?" I knew Grandpa loved to tell this story.

"Because it was told that they never lost a plane when they flew escort on bombing missions. They were called Red Tail Angels because they had painted the tail section of their planes red. Let me tell you, these pilots were the best of the best."

"By Request."
Photo from the Air Force Historical Research Agency

When I was older I did research on the Tuskegee Airmen. I was led to the Air Force Historical Research Agency where I was fortunate enough to meet, Dr. Daniel L Haulman PhD. . . . And I thought my grandfather was a walking encyclopedia. Dr. Haulman shared with me with what the Tuskegee Airmen went through.

I asked Dr. Haulman about the never lost a bomber story. He smiled and said, "It's a good story, but it's just that — a story." He showed me his research on just how the story got started.

On March 10, 1945, Liberty magazine, a highly respected, periodical, published an article by the influential black journalist Roi Ottley. Roi stated that the 332nd Fighter Group was in more than 100 combat missions, in which the Red

Tails hadn't lost a single bomber to enemy fighters. The fact was that they had. Was it a miscommunication on Mr. Ottley part? I'm a trained reporter, and it's not my job to speculate. My job is to gather the facts, and one fact that is true and will never be refuted is the valor and courage of the Tuskegee Airmen.

On March 24, 1945, the Chicago Defender published an article entitled "332nd Flies Its 200th Mission Without Loss." Was it a misinterpretation on the Ottley article? Again, that would be speculation. What was apparent is that the boulder was rolling down the hill, and once it's started, it's hard to stop. Much like the story of Columbus sailing around the world to prove it wasn't flat.

Dr. Haulman told me about a gentleman by the name of William Holton who served for the Tuskegee Airmen Inc. as the organization's national historian. When he was approached by a WWII veteran and told Mr. Holton he did not believe the "never lost a bomber" statement, what would any good historian do to prove a point? . . . research, of course. That's what started the ball rolling.

What Mr. Holton discovered was that among the daily mission reports of the 332nd, bombers might have been shot down by enemy aircraft after all. In 2004 Mr. Holton published a booklet which contained copies of selected mission reports.

Oblivious of Mr. Holton's research, Dr. Haulman, in 2006, had also been working on the "never lost a bomber" and wrote a research paper on the same subject, using much of the same daily mission reports. Later that year they exchanged some of their research. Mr. Holton sent a copy of his booklet he had published in 2004, and Dr. Haulman sent him a copy of his paper on the Tuskegee Airman aerial—victory credits.

The Tuskegee Airmen have a very impressive record: the average loss of bombers for fighter groups was 46. The Red Tails only lost 27. Dr. Haulman was so kind to give me his time, and wished he could give me more, but he had a meeting he had to go to. He gave me his card and the website where I could go to get all the information I could ever want or need. Thank you, Dr. Haulman. http://www.afhra.af.mil/

I remember my grandfather telling me, "To even be considered a pilot you had to have at least two years of college, and back then only about one percent of the black population was able to go to college. So out of that one percent, only a handful of young black men made it to be Tuskegee Airmen. The two—year requirement was later dropped during the war.

"It took a lot of work before they were given the opportunity to show what they were capable of doing. When they were finally given the chance, they flew with such honor and valor it didn't take long before other pilots gave them the respect they deserved, especially the pilots and the men who flew in the bombers those fighter pilots protected.

"It was believed by some that blacks would be cowards in the face of danger. Some even believed they lacked the intelligence to fly a plane or drive a tank. That's why the army called the Tuskegee group 'The Experiment.' There were those who made it hard on the black men, but not Noel Parrish.

General Davis Sr. Noel Parrish Colonel Davis Jr.
Photo from the Air Force Historical Research Agency

Those Tuskegee Airmen sure showed them just how wrong the skeptics were. Back then blacks weren't treated as equals; they really had to prove themselves. When I look back at the way blacks were treated, I'm thoroughly disgusted! Segregation should never have happened in this great country, but it did, thanks in part to Woodrow Wilson and his administration."

I knew what segregation meant, but at the age of thirteen I had never experienced it myself. The thought of a person not being able to go someplace just because of the color of his or her skin was to me incomprehensible.

Grandpa took a deep breath and let it out slowly. "The blacks were called Negroes or Coloreds back then, and they were treated like second-class citizens. Just when I was getting used to African-Americans, a black gentleman told me how he didn't like being called a 'hyphenated' American: 'I'm an American who is black,' he said. He also told me he was from Kenya, and proud of his heritage, and he made sure his children knew of their ancestry, but not to the point where it would have divided them from their new country. I got to thinking about it, and I wonder if we separate ourselves by saying where our ancestors came from? Whether we say I'm an African-American or Mexican-American or Chinese-American, we're all Americans. Except on Saint Patrick's Day. Then everyone is Irish."

Grandpa got such a kick out of his own joke, I couldn't help but smile along with him.

He continued, "Nikki, I've known a few white people that were born in Africa who are now citizens, and I certainly wouldn't call them African-Americans. I'm just an old white guy. What do I know? I sure as heck don't want to offend anyone. No, to me they're all Americans, and for those who serve or who have served, I call them my 'Brothers in Arms.'"

Grandpa paused. "It just hurts to think how they were treated. They couldn't go into a restaurant or a restroom unless it was marked 'For Colored Only.' Even the drinking fountains were marked. These men fought and died for this country, but when they came back to the States, segregation was right there welcoming them as they got off the ships. Whites were to use one gang plank and the blacks another. It took three years after the war before President Truman could reverse the segregation Woodrow Wilson had supported. Truman signed Executive Order #9981, ending segregation in the U.S. military."

President Wilson

President Truman

Artist Rendition

Grandpa continued. "As I look back, I think there were two events that started the ball rolling for President Truman to stop segregation in the U.S. military.

"One was the Port Chicago disaster in California back in 1944. If I remember right, over 300 were killed and about 400 injured, most of them blacks, due to segregation. They were loading munitions onto a cargo vessel headed for the Pacific Theater to fight the Japanese. There was an explosion that could be heard and felt miles away. That slowed things down for a while, but the war had to press on. About a month later things were back to the same-old, same-old, and the black servicemen refused to load the ships, for safety reasons. Fifty of those men, known as the 'Port Chicago 50,' were convicted of mutiny and sentenced to long prison terms. When that became known, the public outcry caused the Navy to change its practices and initiate the desegregation of its forces.

Damage at Port Chicago
Photos from Naval History and Heritage Command's

"The second event happened in 1945, known as 'The Freeman Field Mutiny.' I got this story from one of the Tuskegee Airmen by the name of Les Williams. Come to think of it, he and his daughter Penny wrote a book about Les and his life experiences. In the book, Les tells how he met his future wife, Elsie Miller. He saw her at a very nice nightclub in Detroit, and as soon as he laid eyes on her, it was love at first sight. Or as Les told me, 'That did it, boom, bam.' Elsie was working at the Office of Price Administration. She was in charge of the coupons—something, thank God, you've never had to experience. You had to have a coupon for just about everything, from tires and gas, to sugar and everything in between. And it didn't matter what color you were, that's just the way it was. In the book, Penny tells what her father and mother went through back in those days. If I remember right the name of the book is Victory, Tales of a Tuskegee Airman. Grandpa started to chuckle. "You'll probably have to go to the Amazons to get it."

Whenever he recommended a book I should get, he would always tell his Amazon.com joke. No one cracked up Grandpa more than Grandpa.

He was on a roll that day, and I love his sense of humor, but I had to get him back on track. "What about "The Freeman Field Mutiny?"

"It turns out there was a very nice 'whites only' officers club at Freeman Field, Indiana. Lieutenant Roger Terry and another officer got together and decided to do something about it.

Lieutenant Roger C. Terry
World War II (left), recently holding his photo (right).
Photos from the Terry family personal collection
Thank you. Anna Terry

"They all got dressed up; they wanted to look, as Les would say, 'spiffy,' and were told to behave like officers. They lined up in groups of three and started their way over the field. Wave after wave, they kept coming."

"Why three?" I asked.

"They knew they had to tread lightly and didn't want to be too provocative. The man in charge of Freeman Field was, Colonel Robert Selway, and he was well known for his segregation policies. In fact, Selway wanted all the black officers to sign orders stating they would observe the segregated facilities, such as the officer's clubs. Many of the officers refused to sign, and many who did wrote in "Under protest, or Under duress." Later in his career, Selway was fired as Commander of the 477th because of his policies, and Benjamin O. Davis Jr. took command.

Benjamin O. Davis Jr
Artist Rendition

"Les and two others were in the third wave. When they came up to the door, he was told he couldn't come in. 'Why not? Those guys in there are my friends, we fly every day, and we go up every day to get ready to shoot down the enemy just like they do.' With logic like that, I guess the officer didn't have a comeback, because Les and his two buddies walked around the officer and found themselves inside, sitting at the bar. Les said, 'Very posh, and it became clear very quickly, we were not welcomed. I was told by the enlisted man who was serving the others that he was under orders not to serve us, so we left.' When it was Lieutenant Terry's turn, he was told he couldn't come in. Terry went around him, and brushed the officer's uniform. Terry was arrested for striking an officer.

"Les told me, 'The black officers who were married didn't live in the barracks with the others; we lived in houses on base. When it came time for the officers of the 477th Bombardment Group to be arrested, the M.P.s went to every other house. Why every other house, I never knew. I had a fifty-fifty chance, and I got lucky.'*

"The word went out to all the black newspapers, from New York, to California, and they converged on Freeman Field. Just one problem: the reporters weren't allowed on base. That wasn't going to stop a good reporter, no way, no how. One of the reporters gave an enlisted man a camera that was hidden in a shoebox.

"When the photos hit the papers, it hit the fan, and the army had to back down. The army had to save face, or as I like to put it, they needed an escape goat, and Terry was going to be that man. When it was all over, three officers were court-martialed, but Lieutenant Terry was the only

* Interview at the residence of Les Williams, with his wife Elise and daughter Penny. 6-9-2013

one convicted, and that made him a 'felon.'

"It was hard enough to get a job to take care of your family when you're black—try being black and a felon. And to put salt on the wound, Terry was fined $150. Let me tell you, back then, that was a lot of money. I suppose he was court-martialed so the army could justify what they were going to do with all the others. In 1995, President Clinton pardoned Terry, restoring his lost rank. President Clinton offered to remove the reprimands for any who requested that the reprimands be removed. Many refused. The story is told that President Clinton took Roger Terry aside and offered to pay back the 150 bucks. Terry, in his own unique way, told the President, 'No thank you.' He, like the others considered his protest and the fine a badge of honor.* It may have taken over fifty years to correct a wrong, but let me tell you, Roger's family has a man they can look up to, and I know he's proud of them as well."

Long Overdue
Left to right, President Clinton, U.S. Secretary of Veterans Affairs Jesse Brown, U.S. Representatives Kweisi Mfume, Roger Terry, and Charles Rangel.
Photo from the Terry family personal collection.
Thank you, Anna Terry.

* Roger Terry told this story to Jay Richardson, Vice President of the William "Bill" Campbell Chapter of the Tuskegee Airmen. Interview with Jay at his residence 7-2013.

Two of my grandfather's good friends are David Cunningham and Jay Richardson. David is the president of the William "Bill" Campbell Chapter of the Tuskegee Airmen, in Hayward California. And if memory serves me right, Jay was the vice president. That's where my grandfather met four of the original Tuskegee Airmen.

Sergeant Clyde Grimes was in the intelligence operations end of it with the 477th Bomber Group Headquarters.

Clyde Grimes
World War II (left), recently (right).
Artist rendition

Lieutenant Le Roy Gillead flew in a B-25 and the Northrop P-61 Black Widow, as the navigator and bombardier. Grandpa said, "Let me tell you, you really had to know your stuff to hit your target."

Le Roy Gillead
World War II (left), recently (right).
Artist rendition

Burl Smith was a 2nd lieutenant who flew a P-47. Grandpa would say, "There's just something about us fly-boys who flew P-47s that drove women crazy."

Burl Smith
World War II (left), recently (right).
Artist rendition

Leslie "Les" Williams
World War II (left), recently (right).
Artist rendition

And Captain Leslie Williams was a bomber pilot of a B-25."

It was Captain Les Williams who told Grandpa the story about Roger Terry. Whenever he would talk about the Tuskegee Airmen he would be sure to tell me, "I'd be proud to be their wingman anytime." I just remembered Grandfather telling me about Le Roy, who wrote a book called The Tuskegee Aviation Experiment and Tuskegee Airmen.

I also remember Grandpa telling me, "Nikki, it took about 15,000 men to make the Tuskegee men who they were. From the guys who busted their knuckles with every turn of the wrench to keep their birds flying, to the men behind the desk, mapping out their course.

"It takes a lot of manpower to keep those planes in the air. Each one is just as important as the next; they worked as a team."

There was one Tuskegee Airmen my grandfather would have loved to meet who was part of that chapter: Leon "Woody" Spears.

Leon "Woody" Spears
Artist rendition

Woody flew many missions, and as luck would have it, his number came up when his plane hit some flak. He tried to make it to friendly territory but couldn't. He was taken prisoner by the German police and handed over to the Luftwaffe. They took his flight jacket, which was never returned. Woody loved that jacket, as well he should. When he was liberated by the Russians, he found they treated him worse than the Germans, with the exception of his flight jacket.

Jay Richardson also told this next story to my grandfather. Jay was there, so I know the story is true. I call it "Woody and the Navigator."

Angel from Above
Artist rendition

"Woody was flying a P-51 known as Kitten that was flown by Col. Charles McGee who named it. Woody was escorting a lone bomber back to safety that had been badly damaged. It was common back then for the other bombers to leave behind any stragglers; they had to, it was the only way the rest of the squadron was going to make it back alive. More times than not, the bomber left behind would be alone. Lucky for them that day, they had Woody. He was on the port side of the plane when he noticed four or five guy sticking their heads out of the plane. Waving back and forth, pointing over the top of the plane. There in the distance was something no one likes to see, especially in a crippled plane. Coming in for the kill with its unique silhouette was an Me-110. Woody pushed the throttle wide open and gave it all she had. Woody knew he had to take this guy out on the first pass. With the combined air speed of the two planes coming together, there wouldn't be time for a second pass. The bomber would be a sitting duck, and the lives of ten men would be on his hands. Woody stayed calm as he closed in. He had only a split second to hit his mark. A heartbeat later, as the 110 fell under the bomber, cheers of the crew rang out.

Not on My Watch
Artist rendition

Many years later, Jay was with Woody at Hiller Aviation Museum, where Woody was speaking before a large group of army men. As Woody was telling his story, a gentleman stood up and raised his hand. Woody, on seeing the man, wondered why on earth someone would stop him in the middle of his story. Woody, being the gentleman, looked at him and asked, "Yes?" The man who was standing continued with Woody's story. He was the navigator on that very plane Woody was talking about. The man's voice cracked as he told Woody, "Because of you, I was able to be a grandfather." Jay told my grandfather that he wasn't sure who teared up first, but there wasn't a dry eye in house. It was something Jay will never forget.

Grandpa sat with a smile on his face as he reminisced, then remembering he was talking about discrimination, his smile disappeared. "Nikki, you'd think after President Truman signed the executive order ending segregation in the U.S. military, it would end discrimination. If you thought that, you thought wrong.

"It took even longer before discrimination ended with the Civil Rights Act of 1964. Before President Kennedy was assassinated, he got the ball rolling, I believe, for the right reason. President Johnson may get the credit for having carried that ball over the finish line, but I question his motives. Up until then, LBJ never supported civil rights legislation, not even ones that would have protected blacks from lynching.

The Republican Party in 1957 and 1960 tried to get a Civil Rights Act through, but was stopped at every turn. The Civil Rights Act of 64 wasn't easy, I'll tell you that for sure. It looked like it would never see the light of day. Even Senator Berry Goldwater, along with five other Republican Senators, voted against it. On the Democrat side of the aisle, twenty-one opposed it. It passed, and over to the House it went, where ninety-six Democrats and thirty-four Republicans voted it down. But with both parties working together, the blacks were finally given equal rights." Grandpa looked me in the eye. "Promise me, Nikki, you'll always treat everyone equal."

I nodded my head. "I promise, Grandpa."

SEVEN

Who's Schooling Who?

There are so many things to tell about my high school days, most of which I would say were awkward and uneventful—the typical things everyone goes through. My first love who I thought was my one and only lasted three months until he met Marsha. Marsha, Marsha, Marsha. She was on the high school cheerleading team; no way could I compete with that. I might start another journal and put only my high school days in it, but I remember a few things that should fit quite nicely with this journal.

I remember that when I was a freshman, I thought I knew more about geography and World War I and World War II history than any of my teachers. Case in point: When my history teacher was telling us about the Battle of Britain, I was so uninterested in his reciting of names and dates, I unknowingly muttered under my breath how bored I was. Unfortunately, the teacher heard me and asked me to repeat what I said.

Embarrassed, I apologized, but he still wanted me to repeat it so the whole class could hear. I was sitting next to the teacher's pet, and since I wasn't going to repeat it, she did. The teacher thought he would teach me a lesson by having me come to the front and teach the class. Not wanting to embarrass myself further, I tried to apologize again, but he insisted. As I stood up and started to walk to the front of the room wondering what to say, a thought flashed through my head: tell the Battle of Britain as a story like my grandfather had told me. I decided I would tell it as though I were there, living every moment.

I cleared my throat and spoke in a soft voice. "The Battle of Britain is what the Americans know it as. The Brits however, know it by its German name, The Blitz, short for Blitzkrieg, it means 'lightning war.' It was the summer of 1940 when Prime Minister Winston Churchill delivered his famous speech." In my best impression of Churchill I boomed out: "The Battle of France is over. I expect the Battle of Britain is about to begin." It surprised everyone, and a lot of my classmates jumped in their seats and I could hear others laughing. I blushed for a moment, regained my composure and continued. "The French had lost; they were forced to line the street to pay homage to their new ruler."

The French had lost
Photo provided by the National Archives (NARA)

I continued talking, walking back and forth, keeping my eyes on the class. By now the students had settled down and I could tell I had gained their attention, even the teacher's. "Hitler's objective was quite obvious—gain control over the Royal Air Force. Bombing raids along the coastal shipping convoys were the main targets of the German Luftwaffe, along with airfields, aircraft factories, and other military targets. But the bloodthirsty Hitler wanted to reign terror among the people, and he soon targeted the infrastructure.

"One can only imagine the fear the people felt. Men on rooftops with binoculars in hand, peering at the horizon to sound the alarm.

Ever Vigilant

Photo provided by the National Archives (NARA)

Fighter planes overhead trying to defend their homeland. The sounds of engines roaring in the ears of the people as booming guns went off overhead. They could see the weavings in and out as the dogfights above them continued, the smoke from their planes trailing in their paths. As planes, both friend and foe, fell from the sky, hearts raced in terror, not knowing where they might crash to the earth.

Planes, Both Friend and Foe
Photo provided by the National Archives (NARA)

"Night after night as the bombing raids hit their targets and buildings burst into flames, the people huddled and even slept together in backyard bomb shelters called 'Thompson huts,' or in wine cellars. Most people went into large neighborhood bomb shelters or the tube, what we call subways. At night, families pulled blackout curtains over windows, so as not to give their positions away to the enemy planes up above. Brave men and women fought back with courage. Many wondered if the bombings would ever end, but at last they did. Adolf Hitler's 'Operation Sea Lion' had failed, but it was a long way from the war being over, and much damage had been done. Where a building once stood, there was now rubble. Children were homeless, many now orphaned. But the strong will of the people proved out."

Will the Battle of Britain
Photo provided by the National Archives (NARA)

As I went to sit down I was halfway to my desk when the whole class started to applaud, including the teacher. I have to tell you it felt pretty good.

I'll never forget what happened in my senior year of high school. My economics teacher was a firm believer that when governments print more money it stimulates the economy, which is a good thing. I couldn't help myself and raised my hand. "Can't that lead to hyperinflation, like it did during the Revolutionary War, and the Civil War? I remember reading where the soldiers were being paid with money that was worthless because there was nothing behind it, and that almost started an uprising with the army."

He looked at me with contempt. "I assure you, Miss Brown, that that could never happen, because governments would never let it happen again."

That made no sense to me, so I raised my hand again. "Forgive me, but the government is already doing it. My grandfather gave me a two dollar bill for my tenth birthday.

He could tell I wasn't impressed, and that's when he explained that my two dollar bill was a silver certificate, which means it could be redeemed for silver. Take a look at any printed money today, it's a note. My grandfather is what you would call an entrepreneur. Back in the 1960's he had all kinds of different vending machines. My grandfather knows history, and he knows history has a way of repeating itself. He saw the government take us off the gold standard then the silver; he even saw the government make silver dimes out of steel. It didn't take long before they stopped that practice but my grandfather could read the writing on the wall, so when he had his vending business he took all the silver coins and put them aside, he even collected pennies. People thought he was crazy and they laughed at him, but in 1964, that was the last year the government made coins out of silver. My grandfather got the last laugh. And as far as pennies go, if you have a penny prior to 1982, he'll trade you one of today's pennies for that one all day long."

I looked at the teacher. I could tell he didn't have an answer, so I asked, "And what about the Weimar Republic? In the 1920s Germany stimulated the economy by printing so much paper money without anything like gold or silver to back it up, prices of goods doubled every forty-nine hours. It was cheaper to burn the money to keep warm than to buy firewood with it. My grandfather served in World War II, and he told me a story about how it took a wheelbarrow of money just to buy a loaf of bread. Money was also used as wall paper and building blocks for the children to play with. It had become worthless, and the street sweepers found it annoying. With what the government had done to the money, the people didn't stand a chance."

Going to the Store for a Loaf of Bread
Photo provided by the National Archives (NARA)

I Wish People Wouldn't Litter
Photo provided by the National Archives (NARA)

I'm so Rich, I have Money to Burn
Photo provided by the National Archives (NARA)

Since the teacher hadn't stopped me, I went on. "Austria in the early 1920s did the same thing and suffered hyperinflation at a peak of 134 percent. Hungary went through two hyperinflationary periods in the '20s and '40s.

With This Much Money we can Build a House
Photo provided by the National Archives (NARA)

"Things were bad enough when we were in a recession in 1930 due to the stock market crash in 1929. But when F.D.R. took us off the gold standard in 1933, we went from a recession into a depression that lasted far longer than it should have. If it weren't for the war, there's no telling how long it would have lasted. I realize there is more to the story than taking us off the gold standard, but I contend it didn't help matters."

I could see my teacher wasn't, let's say, looking very happy with what I had to say, so I thought that maybe if I explained my position, I could gain his respect.

"I know I've taken a lot of your time and the class's, but this is a topic, as you can see, I'm very passionate about. Whether from the founding of our country or today, whenever money is not stable there will always be unrest with the people. Even ancient Rome had to learn that lesson the hard way. The Emperor Diocletian, in AD 270 started his own stimulus package, by lowering the metal content of the Roman coins and issuing large amounts of inferior copper coins into the population. The people weren't stupid; they knew they had to increase the price of their goods in order to compensate for the devaluing of the money.

"Of course Diocletian, when things started to get out of control, he blamed the merchants of greed, and thirty years later he issued his own version of 'Price Control.' Anyone selling above what he declared to be fair would be put to death. So the merchants stopped selling altogether; they had too. If it cost more to produce something than you could sell it for, then why bother? The Emperor had a solution to this problem as well: any merchant who stopped selling could be accused of hoarding and be put to death. So the merchants simply left their trade. Diocletian countered that with laws saying that every man had to pursue the occupation of his father. If they didn't, the penalty was— you guessed it, death. Don't you love it when the government gets involved in your life?" That comment came out of my mouth before I could stop it.

I concluded, "President Nixon tried price controls, and it didn't work for him either. At least he didn't have people put to death for finding ways around it. But like I said, history has shown us that whenever the currency is unstable, fear and panic set in, and chaos takes over. I believe that's how rulers like Hitler can take over. They will make promises they can't keep, but it sounds so good in the ears of the masses that they are willing to give up some of their freedom for security, a little bit at a time. Wasn't it Benjamin Franklin who said something like 'Those who are willing to give up a little freedom for security deserve neither?' I truly think that's how civilizations can be slowly led into captivity."

I took some pictures to class the next day. I thought that they were photos that everyone had seen before, but I guess none of them had grandfathers like mine. I was sure I had earned my teacher's respect after my dissertation, but for some reason I could only pull a C+ out of his class. There went my 4.0. I contested, but it was no use.

EIGHT

A Burning Desire

As a little girl, I always thought I wanted to fly. But when I took my first airplane ride to Washington DC, that's when I knew I wanted to become a pilot. When I asked my grandfather what I needed to do, you should have seen the look on his face.

"Are you sure that's what you want? It's a lot of work. You'll have to save all your money, and you won't have much time to play with your friends."

I looked at him and said, "That's what I want."

"All right, then," he said, rubbing his hands together. "Just knowing what you want puts you halfway there. Next, you have to have a burning desire, and not let anything stand in your way. Then you need to write it down. A goal not written down is just a wish." Then he added, "If wishes were fishes, we'd never go hungry."

I laughed, shaking my head. "That's a new one."

"Just trying to keep you on your toes." Grandpa taught me a little trick about goal setting. We went to the bookstore and found a magazine with a lot of pictures of airplanes. Instead of the typical posters that you'd see in any other teenage girl's room, mine was filled with airplanes. I ate, drank, and slept with my mind on becoming a pilot.

From that day on, every nickel I earned was put aside so I could one day fly. Any odd job I could do for my age, I would do it. As I grew, the jobs got bigger, and so did my stash of nickels.

I took to flying like a duck takes to water. I was scared and excited all at the same time when I took my first solo flight. I must admit, however, I did have a challenge when it came to navigation, because I had always had a hard time with math. With tutoring help from my grandfather, I was able to get a good grasp of the basic principles of navigation.

It was on my eighteenth birthday, one month before graduation, that I was able to cross off one of the biggest goals from my long list: I earned my pilot's license! I didn't think anything could top this event on my big day, but leave it to my grandfather to do just that. He handed me a box, nicely wrapped, with a big bow on top. It was heavier than I expected. "What's inside?"

"You'll have to open it to find out."

I don't know who was more excited, me or my grandfather. I tore off the paper and lifted the lid. I couldn't have stopped the tears had I tried to. Inside was his old flight jacket, with his goggles and dog tags on top, along with my great-grandfather's leather helmet. With my arms around his neck, all I could say was "Thank you, Grandpa. I'll always treasure these."

When I showed them to my flight instructor, he said, "You never told me your grandfather was an Ace."

"What do you mean?" I asked. He pointed to the lining in the flight jacket.

"It's red. Only pilots who shot down five or more enemy planes were given the title of ace, and it was at that point they could change the lining in their jackets to red. Didn't he tell you that?"

"No, that was something he neglected to tell me."

"I can also tell he was an Army Air Corps pilot."

"How can you tell that by the jacket?"

"Simple, the pockets are different from the Navy's. But the easiest way to tell is on the back of the jacket; the Navy had a leather piece going across the back, the army didn't. Didn't you tell me your grandfather flew P-47s?"

"He did."

"Let me tell you, your grandfather had to have been one heck of a pilot to be an Ace. Not many were, and to do it in a P-47? Those babies weren't known for their maneuverability."

At eighteen, I thought I knew everything about my grandfather, but I couldn't have been more wrong. Over the years he would let me into his world a little at a time. I found that for most vets, they would keep their stories to themselves. Grandpa Vince didn't like to talk about being an Ace. He felt he would come across as a braggart, and that was so not him. It also meant that it represented the lives he took. He would say, "It was me or them, and I preferred it to be them." The only way he could live with himself was to focus on the lives he saved by taking theirs.

I may have been taught many things by my grandfather, but it was my mother who taught me not only how to read, but how to love reading. As a small child, I would climb up on her lap, and she would read to me all kinds of books. My favorites, because of Grandpa, were history; and because my mother loved mysteries, I also fell in love with her old collection of Nancy Drew novels. As a little girl, if you had asked me what I wanted to be when I grew up, I would have said a detective who flew all around the world solving mysteries. As I became older, I would have said a mystery writer.

In my second year of college I had no doubt about what I wanted for a career. I had a burning desire to be an investigative reporter. I knew I had found the best of both worlds: a detective and a mystery writer.

To my disappointment, my journalism instructor was quite the male chauvinist. To put it politely, he should have been in a museum, not as the curator, but on display, next to the Neanderthal man. He had a face which a caricature artist would have loved to draw. Ichabod Crane comes to mind. He was harder on the girls than the boys, and he didn't even try to hide it; but he had tenure, and nothing could be done. His hostility created such an impossible environment that it didn't take long before some of the other girls dropped out, but my determined nature made me even more committed to prove his view of girls wrong.

After I graduated, I started working for a small local newspaper. I covered the typical things the new kid reporter gets assigned to. I covered exciting things, such as DUIs, visitors from out of town, mailbox vandals; and I was even given the glorious assignment to describe the delicious cakes Mrs. Johnson donated to the community cake sale. I can't complain; it was at that event where I received a tip that led me to a major scandal. The mayor, along with a few of the city council members, were siphoning off millions of public monies—from pension plans, payrolls and benefits they thought they were entitled to. They were brought up on charges, and luckily all served jail time. After I exposed them, it wasn't long after that that the small paper I was working for was bought by a large corporation, and doors started to open for me.

NINE

Hitler Knew

I had been trying to get my grandfather to tell his story since I was about sixteen, but I could never get him to open up. Later as I became a more seasoned reporter I found this quite common with many war veterans. They just didn't like to talk about the war; there were too many painful memories to relive. I knew, however, that their stories needed to be told so we could know of the countless sacrifices they had made for our freedom and we could learn from the mistakes of history, so as to never repeat them.

For my own personal interest I had been doing quite a bit of research about World War II that left me with several questions for my grandfather. The next time I visited him I asked, "Why didn't you tell me about Ilse Koch?"

Ilse Koch
Artist Rendition

He looked at me, surprise in his eyes. "I will always look at you and see my little co-pilot, bouncing up and down, picking up speed as we would go down the runway. There are some things I hoped you would never find out about; I was trying to protect you. Telling my little co-pilot about a woman who was called 'the Butcher of Buchenwald,' along with other names, was something I didn't think you needed to know.

"In the concentration camps millions were murdered, mostly Jews. They were starved and literally worked to death. Some were tortured, others were used as guinea pigs while the doctors experimented with different drugs. Bullets were too slow and costly, so showers were built, only instead of water coming out of the shower heads, it was Zyklon gas. Each camp had to dispose of the bodies. Most were buried in mass graves. Other camps had ovens. Before bodies were cremated, their heads were shaved and the gold picked from their teeth.

"Murdering so many was costly, but the Nazis found a way to off-set the expense. Bones were pulled from the ovens and ground up to be sold to the local farmers as fertilizer. Hair was sold to industries to be used to stuff furniture and quilts. All this was carried out by the hands of one man, Heinrich Himmler, Hitler's right-hand man.

"As the war was coming to an end, the Allied troops advanced and were able to liberate prisoners from hundreds of concentration camps. What they found— there are no words known to man that can describe it. Humans were being forced to live like animals. The Nazis, not wanting to be taken captive, abandoned the camps, taking prisoners that could still walk and murdering those who couldn't. This happened days, sometimes just hours, before they could be rescued. The Nazis left few witnesses behind to testify against their captors. The dead, however, spoke loud and clear of the Nazis' barbarism.

"Where the allies found survivors, aid was given immediately, but for over thirteen thousand, help came too late. Nothing could be done; their bodies simply gave out.

"People from the nearby towns were rounded up and walked to the concentration camps to see what had been going on in their own backyards. Allied guards made sure that none of these townspeople looked away from the gruesome sights.

"The concentration camp known as Buchenwald was probably one of the worst. Ilse Koch, the wife of the camp commandant, singled out the men with interesting tattoos to be killed so she could make lampshades out of their skin."

The look on my grandfather's face told me he wasn't going to say more. "I love you, Grandpa, but I'm not a little girl anymore. I need you to tell me what you know. I want to hear your story." After years of persuading, Grandpa Vince was finally ready to talk. I think deep down he knew it was a story he needed to tell. It didn't take me long to learn why it was something that he would much rather have kept buried, never to be brought to the surface again — so many gruesome stories of the suffering of so many people; things no one should ever have to experience or endure would now forever haunt me.

"These are slave laborers in the Buchenwald concentration camp near Jena; many had died from malnutrition when U.S. troops of the 80th Division entered the camp." Pvt. H. Miller, Germany, April 16, 1945.
Photo provided by the Jewish Virtual Library Organization.

There are those who truly believe Hitler was oblivious to the holocaust because there are no known papers with his signature sanctioning it. Though Hitler was very careful to hide it from the people, there were those who saw the atrocities, but only one that I know of said anything about it.

Her name was Henriette Hoffmann; she was the eldest of Heinrich Hoffmann, Hitler's personal photographer for many years. Hitler met her when she was only nine years old. He became very fond of Henriette and called her "Henny."

Heinrich "Henny" Hoffmann
Artist Rendition

When Henriette was 17 she went to work for Hitler as his secretary. A year later they briefly dated. He was more than twice her age. A few years later she fell in love with Baldur von Schirach and was married. Both Hitler and Ernst Röhm acted as best man.

In 1943, Henriette was visiting in German-occupied Netherlands. It was late at night when she heard screaming outside the hotel that she was staying in. She decided to investigate. What she saw were Jewish women and children being deported by force. She walked up to the first German soldier she saw and asked what they were doing. The soldier must have been young and naïve, because Hitler would have had him shot for treason had he known. He told Henriette, "What Hitler is doing in Holland is wrong. We are making enemies of the Dutch people, which is a big mistake." He must have known that Henriette knew Hitler because he asked her to tell Hitler the next time she saw him.

What Henriette witnessed in Amsterdam troubled her deeply, and she vowed she would do all she could to stop it. She cut her visit short and called to make an appointment with Hitler. She was certain Adolf knew nothing of the treatment of the people, and he would put a stop to it immediately.

When Henriette first walked in, Hitler greeted her with warmth and kindness. After common pleasantries she told him what she had seen. She was quite taken back when Hitler told her she was too sentimental, that ten thousand of his best men die on the battlefield every day, the biological balance in Europe has to be balanced.

From there things got rather heated. Only Henriette could have spoken to Hitler that way and live, especially in front of the other leaders in the room. He stood up. That was her cue that this meeting was over.

Neither Henriette nor her husband was ever invited again.

TEN

Heroes who said No

There were those who said no at great peril to their lives. I'm reminded of so many Christians and good people who said no to Hitler, and did all they could to help the Jews during his horrifying reign, even to the peril of their own lives. There are the known who obviously get the recognition and thanks, as well they should, but to all the unknown, God knows you and thanks you, as do I.

Of all the known, Oskar Schindler comes first to mind. Yes, he was a member of the Nazi Party, but he was also a spy who saved over a thousand Jews during the Holocaust. He did this by employing them in his factories.

Oskar Schindler
Public Domain

Irena Sendler
Public Domain

Another whose name comes to mind is Irena Sendler, a social worker who, along with others, smuggled children outside the Warsaw Ghetto. They disguised themselves as nurses, who were allowed inside the ghetto. They had many different ways in getting the children out; one way for infants was in a false bottom of a tool box.

When Poland was occupied by the Germans, severe rules were put into place. Any infractions to those rules had only one punishment: Death.

Many cities in Poland had large sections fenced off where the Jews were relocated. With so many people stacked on top of each other with very little food and no means to up keep their surroundings, it wasn't long before they were turned into ghettos. With Poland's harsh winters, pipes would freeze and break. With no means of fresh water to drink or water to flush toilets, the waste was thrown out the windows into the court- yard. When the weather warmed and things began to thaw, it became a breeding ground for disease. With very little to eat to keep up one's strength, sickness and death were common. Bodies stripped of their clothing, rags though they may be, could be used to help save another from freezing to death. The bodies were placed by the sidewalk waiting to be picked up, as the people walked around them.

When the Germans started to clear out the Jews from the ghettos of Poland, everyone knew they were being led to their deaths.

I remember a story about a group of Jews who escaped the Germans by going down into the sewers. Men, women and children, doing all they could, just to survive. They hid there in the most putrid, disgusting conditions for over a year. Only with the help of non-Jews were they able to survive. There were many cities In Poland with similar stories. Perhaps the reason Warsaw stands out from among the other ghettos is because when it came time for the Germans to clear the ghettos out, they were met with a different kind of welcoming party. You see, there were those who fought back, and for once, German blood fell on the streets of Poland. The Germans were caught completely off guard; they thought they had removed all the guns. The resistance lasted for about a month until there was no more ammunition to fight back with, and the ghetto was soon set on fire to drive the Jews out or to burn them to death.

Jewish civilians: copy of a Berman photograph taken during the destruction of the Warsaw Ghetto.
Photo provided by the Jewish Virtual Library Organization.

I remember another group of Jews who went into the woods to survive, and they were armed. I believe the Germans left them alone because they knew they could put up a fight.

Before Germany invaded Poland on September 1, 1939, Warsaw, like so many other cities, was cultured and thriving. That is, until Hitler set out to exterminate any and all he found undesirable—Jews, Gypsies, homosexuals, the list was long.

When Hitler came to power, all Jews were forced to wear armbands displaying the Star of David. Some Jews considered it their badge of honor. Soon everything was stripped from them: the Germans blocked Jewish bank accounts, took away their homes and belongings, their work places and shops were closed. The sick who were in hospitals were also forced out. All schools for Jewish children were closed, along with synagogues. Even group prayers were forbidden.

The German occupiers by design created the Warsaw Ghetto in the heart of the beautiful city—a Jewish residential district. First fences went up with gates, and the people could still come and go as they pleased, as long as they had the proper papers. Soon came the walls, but the people could still come and go as they were being built. When the wall was built, coming and going was no longer possible, and the walls became higher and higher; over a hundred thousand Jews were "resettled," bringing the total to nearly half a million behind the walls of the Warsaw Ghetto.

Irena Sendler and others risked their lives to do all they could to get the children out of the grasp of the Germans. She kept a record of all the children, with their given names along with their new Christian name and where they went, in hopes that one day they could be reunited with their parents. Since I don't have any children, I can only imagine what it must have felt like to give up something so precious.

Irena Sendler was caught and tortured, but she never revealed her sources or the hiding place where she kept the names of all the children in jars and where they went. Irena was to be shot, but because a guard was bribed, she was spared. Irena, along with others, was able to save two thousand five hundred children. Sadly, when the war was over, many children were never able to be reunited with their parents due to the holocaust.

Then there are the lesser known, at least in America. I'm thinking of Count Folke Bernadotte.

Whenever I do research for a story, I try to use primary sources first. I also like secondary sources. But tertiary sources? I take that information, as my grandfather would say, "with a big grain of salt." But as my elementary English teacher taught me, there are exceptions to the rules.

It was my senior year and I was home for Christmas when I met one of my grandfather's closest friends. He is a great European source.

My grandfather's friend shared with me how Count Bernadotte was able to negotiate with Heinrich Himmler, who was Hitler's righthand man, in releasing well over 30,000 prisoners during World War II, including 450 Danish Jews.

On one account, Himmler, without Hitler's knowledge, gave the Count a surrender offer. Germany would surrender to the Western Allies as long as they could continue the war with the Soviet Union. The Count told Himmler he would pass it on through the proper channels, but it would most likely be turned down.

Not only was Count Bernadotte from the Royal Family of Sweden, he was a diplomat and a nobleman; he was also the vice-president of the Swedish Red Cross. It was with those connections that he was able to do the prisoner exchanges. Sadly, he was assassinated in 1948.

There is something not many people know: Hitler was an artist, some would say a rather good one at that. He tried to get into the Academy of Fine Arts in Vienna but was rejected twice, once in 1907 and again in 1908. I've seen his work, and when I look at it, I wonder how a man who could do such beautiful work could have so much hatred and evil coursing through his veins? I know I have already told my grandfather's story of the two animals that live inside us all, but I think this is a good time to repeat it. It made such an impact at a very young age, I never forgot it. He told me everyone has two animals that live inside each of us. One is good and the other is evil. They're always in competition with each other, and the one who will win is the one you feed the most. I wonder if Hitler had been accepted into the Academy of Fine Arts, where he could have fed the good, might history have been different? I guess we'll never know.

ELEVEN

Facing Ones Goliath

Those who said no to Hitler remind me when I said no to my grandfather. I must have been six when he asked me to clean up the mess I had made. I knew the rule and never had a problem with it, until that day. For some reason I folded my arms, stomped my feet and said, NO! The look on his face is hard to describe. Surprise? Hurt? Shock? Like I said, hard to describe, but my grandfather never let a good teaching opportunity slip by him.

"Nikki, clean up this mess you made and I'll tell you a story when it's good to say NO!"

Grandpa knew how much I loved his stories, and I quickly cleaned up.

As I climbed up on his lap he smiled, "Now, that wasn't so hard, was it?" I shook my head. "Is there something you'd like to say before I tell you the story when it's a good thing to say NO?"

I knew what he was talking about, and I felt embarrassed for what I had said. So I apologized.

"Thank you, apology accepted. Did you know everyone has two animals that live inside them? One is good and the other is evil. They are always in competition with each other; the one who will win is the one you feed the most. When you said no to me, you fed the evil animal. There are times when saying no is the right thing to do. For example, when someone wants you to do something you know is wrong, or when someone needs your help to say no to a bully. Even God had to say no to a bully."

I remember looking at my grandfather, confused. "Who would try and bully God?"

Grandpa always kept his Bible on the end table where he sat to read. Reaching over, he picked it up.

"Nikki, inside this book are many lessons and principles to help us have a happier life. God had men whom he called to be His prophets and to write down what He told them. God also told them to write down what was happening to the people at the time so we could learn from history. Unfortunately, we don't learn our lesson very well, and we keep repeating the same mistakes over and over." Grandpa looked at me. "So you would like to know who God had to say no to."

Grinning, I nodded my head. Opening the Bible, he turned to the book of Revelation, I think his favorite. Turning to chapter 12 he told me the story in the way I could understand it.

"Not only do we have wars here on earth, but there was a war in heaven as well."

"What?"

"That's right, in heaven there were good angels and bad angels. The Bible says the leader of the bad angels was a dragon. The dragon had many names, but I think the one he liked the most was devil, because it had the name evil in it. The dragon's army was a third of the host of heaven."

"Who won Grandpa?"

"Why the good angels, of course."

"But why did the dragon go against God?"

For that question Grandpa turned to Isaiah 14. "The dragon, being evil, had an evil heart. He wanted power to rule over all, even God himself. When the war was over, the dragon and his angels were cast out of heaven, never to return again. So you see, Pun'kin, even God had someone who wanted to control him, but God said NO! But that's not the story I want to tell you."

Grandpa turned to 1st Samuel 17. "The story I want to tell you is about a young man by the name of David, and his bully was Goliath.

"There is always someone wanting to have control over another, so there will always be war after war. I'm sure there must have been a time or two on this earth when there wasn't a war going on, but I'm not aware of it. You see, that dragon, from the time he was cast out of heaven to this day, loves war."

My grandfather may not have been a preacher, but as I got older I think he may have missed his calling; he brought the stories of the Bible to life like no one I ever knew.

In a soft voice he began the story the way I loved every story to begin with at that age.

"Once upon a time, in a land far far away, lived a boy by the name of David, who had seven older brothers. The three oldest brothers were off doing battle against the Philistines. David was told by his father to take supplies to his brothers, but when David got there, there wasn't a battle but what looked like a standoff, and it had been going on for forty days.

"The Philistines were on one side of a mountain and the Israelites on an opposite mountain, a valley between. When David arrived he wanted to know what was going on. He was told there was a giant of a man by the name of Goliath who was challenging any one man to come up against him, and whoever should lose the fight would become slaves to the others. Every day the giant would come down off the mountain in the morning and evening and give the same speech. David probably asked, 'So why hasn't anyone challenged him?' to which the reply came back. 'Have you seen this man?' He was close to ten feet tall and had on heavy armor from head to toe.

"David told King Saul, 'Thy servant slew both a lion and a bear: and this uncircumcised Philistine shall be as one of them, seeing he hath defied the armies of the living God.' David knew the Lord had delivered him out of the paw of the lion, and claw of the bear, and he would deliver him out of the hands of this giant. And Saul said unto David, 'Go, and the Lord be with thee.'

"Saul armed David with his armor from head to toe and finished it off by putting his sword around David's waist. Poor David had never worn armor before and could hardly move in it, so he told the King, 'Thanks, but no thanks.' What the King didn't realize was that David already had on the armor of God.

"David went to a brook, picked out five smooth stones, put them in his shepherd's bag, and with his sling went before the giant. When Goliath saw David, he was angry to be challenged by a young boy.

"In his anger, Goliath said, 'today I'm going to feed you to the fowls of the air, and to the beasts of the field.' David just looked at him and said, 'You come to me with a sword, and a spear and a shield: but I come to you in the name of the Lord of hosts, the God of the armies of Israel, whom you have defied. Today the Lord will deliver you into my hand and I will feed you to the fowls of the air and to the beasts of the field so everyone will know there is a God in Israel.'

"That made Goliath angry, and he started toward David. The giant probably thought that David would run away. David ran all right, but not away, he ran toward the giant, and as he did he reached into his bag and took out one of the stones. Putting it into his sling he whirled it over his head and let it go. Even though the giant had armor from head to toe, there was a small opening in his helmet; that's where David aimed, and it was lights out for the giant."

David and Goliath
Artist Rendition

As I got older, Grandpa would go into more detail as to what happened next.

Grandpa closed his Bible and put it back on the end table. Looking me in the eyes he said, "Nikki, we all have Goliaths in our lives that we face and we need to know in advance how to say no. When someone we don't know wants us to do what we know is wrong, it's easy to say no. But what do you say when it's someone you look up to and all your friends are going along with it? Then is not the time to come up with an answer. You need to know what to say beforehand."

"Like what, Grandpa?"

"Like, what if a boy wants to kiss you?"

I wrinkled up my nose with a face as though I had just bitten into something sour and said, "No way. I'll get cooties."

"You see, you already have an answer. By the way, you'll change your mind on that one. But what if someone wants you to take something that's not yours, or to try smoking or do drugs?"

Grandpa always said, 'Show me your friends and I'll show you your future.' He was right about picking my friends, and I did change my mind about boys. When someone wanted me to do something I knew was wrong, I had a quiver full of ready answer "no" arrows. One of my favorites was to look at them with a rather incredulous look and ask, "Why on earth would I want to do something that is going to mess up my future."

Growing up, whenever I had a problem that I would share with my grandfather he would say, "Looks like you have a Goliath to slay."

TWELVE

Patty O'Kelly

I would stop by from time to time and share a morning cup of coffee with my Grandfather. He would relate to me his experiences during the war, which I recorded. I was the first person he ever told his story to; not even my grandmother knew it. She went to her grave not knowing much about his story, and it was just as well. Grandpa told stories of men starving, in threadbare clothing, freezing in the winter with little means of heat. One blanket to be shared by two, sometimes three men. Barracks that had so many gaps between the siding that it was impossible to plug them all. The floor, always a few feet off the ground so the Germans could look under the barracks, making sure no tunnels were being built. That was convenient for the Germans but not for the prisoners. The cold air ripped through their quarters day and night.

The POWs had roll call every morning, and it didn't matter if you were on your death bed or not. Sometimes if a prisoner couldn't get up due to illness, others would cover for him by calling out his name and moving down the line. Sometimes it would work, but for the most part it didn't. The guards would take their dogs and drag the prisoner out, punishing him, along with all those who tried to help. The punishment was usually less food, as if that were even possible, or no time out of the barracks.

It was almost more than I could bear at times to hear those stories, but I knew I had to be strong for Grandpa. I could see that getting this heavy load off his chest was painful, but at the same time therapeutic. I couldn't help but notice that after only a few times of our meeting together, his countenance was becoming much brighter. We had developed a very special bond, the type of bond one would have with another after fighting in the trenches side-by-side in battle. I remember telling him how terrible it had to have been. To which he replied, "At least we had the Pat O'Kelly show."

Grandpa chuckled. "In camp there are many personalities. There were those who were withdrawn and reclusive, while others went out of their way to help lighten the load on others' hearts and everywhere in between." We were lucky to have Pat in our barracks.

Grandpa then did something he'd never done before, which I noticed he would do whenever he spoke about Patty. He would try to speak with an Irish brogue.

"Pat O'Kelly was from the Bronx. He had a raucous sense of humor, and he loved to ham it up. Many times the men would be so bored they would start fights over the smallest of things. Pat would step in and defuse things with a joke. He even had a way of looking at you as if to say, 'Are you kidding? You're going to fight over that?' Sometimes when we were locked inside the barracks, Pat would wet down his red hair to look like Hitler, take the soot from the stove with his finger, and give himself a Hitler-like mustache. Then he would parade around, goose stepping, all the while doing the 'Heil Hitler' salute and speaking in a thick Irish-brogue, German accent. He had us rolling with laughter. We always had lookouts to keep close tabs on the guards; if they had caught him, I shudder to think what they would have done."

"Pat loved history, and he could see trouble on the horizon when Hitler was coming into power. So when Hitler invaded Poland on September 1, 1939, it was no surprise to him.

"One time Pat put on a twenty-minute show for us with his Hitler routine. 'So you would like to know how I came to control zee people, ja? I vill tell you, zee formula, is quite simple. First, tell the people their problems are not their fault, and blame it on someone else. Use the press to sympathize with you. Tell whoever you are talking to, you will give to them whatever they want. For the farmer, who breaks his back to feed us, higher prices in the market. For those who buy the food, lower prices. To the tenants, lower rent, putting more money in their pockets. To the landlords, promise them higher rent. And of course, to the workers, higher wages, making the wealthy pay. While all the time telling the owners not to worry, their little slaves will be paid less.

Once in control, guide the people to follow you unconditionally. Designate yourself as God and have the children sing songs of how you are their savior and hero, and that they live and die for you. Take control of what they read, hear and see. Anyone speaking ill of you—severe punishment, including death. Enforce your laws with judges you put in power. And by all means, control their capability to defend themselves.' When Pat said it at the time it was both funny and sad. Funny because of the way Pat did it, and sad because it was true."

To all the men who did their best to make life easier in all of the POW camps, Thank you.

THIRTEEN

Charlie

On one visit Grandpa said, "Nikki, I know I told you about Pat, but did I ever tell you about my good friend Charlie?"

That name wasn't familiar. "No, Grandpa, I don't believe you have."

"Pat, Charlie and I became great friends. You couldn't have gotten more different kinds of personalities together in that camp if you had tried. Pat was the entertainer and Charlie . . .

Grandpa smiled. "Charlie, now there was an American hero if there ever was one." A warm smile came to his face.

Charlie
Artist Rendition

"I never met a man who had more love for both America and his Chinese heritage. If they ever make a movie about his life and what happened to him in World War II, people won't believe it. They'll say, 'That's Hollywood making up a good story to sell tickets.' He came from a farming family and was tall with a solid build. He was what you call down-to-earth and approachable. I loved his great sense of humor. The best way I think I could describe him would be to say he was a dignified farmer. Once we got to know him and his personality, we quickly became good friends, he had such a good heart. I found out he was drafted, eleven months before Pearl Harbor.

"Because he could read, write and type, he was offered a desk job as an orderly in the war. He just said, 'I didn't come over here to ride a desk, I came over here to fight a war!' Charlie had a background in heavy equipment, and with high test scores in machinery, he was assigned to be part of the 1st armored division. It was almost a year to the day when Charlie was drafted that he found himself in his first battle. American troops were going up against Rommel's troops in North Africa."

Rommel
Artist Rendition

"Rommel! The "Desert Fox"? Didn't you tell me he was a brilliant tactician?"

"I did. I'm just glad we had Patton on our side. It's too bad Patton wasn't in charge of the Battle of Kasserine Pass. If he had been, maybe Charlie wouldn't have spent over three years as a POW with six more months as an escapee.

As Charlie got closer and closer to the front, it was learned that the Third Battalion had already been destroyed. It was in the afternoon on February the 15th of' 43 when the battle commenced, and in a little over an hour, it was over. The battalion was surrounded by German tanks, which were hiding behind big mounds. The Germans couldn't believe the tactic being used; they were sitting ducks, just waiting to be plucked. The Americans were taking on heavy fire when Charlie's tank was hit with such force that he was thrown up against the inside the tank and his leg shattered. No, the force pulverized his leg, and he was on fire. The tank commander was too scared to open the hatch, so they couldn't escape the burning tank. They all thought for sure that as soon as they popped their heads out, they would be cut down.

"Charlie yelled at the commander, telling him they had to get out of there. He came to his senses, and the crew jumped from the tank. Charlie hit the ground and rolled, trying to put out the fire. Once the fire was out, he thought for sure he would be shot, but he wasn't. They were taken prisoner."

"Grandpa, how on earth did Charlie, on fire, with a shattered leg, do all that?"

"When endorphins kick in, you'd be amazed what a person can do. You've heard of mothers picking up cars to save their babies, haven't you?" I nodded my head. "That was endorphins kicking in.

"Charlie had shrapnel wounds in his left hand, but what was really painful was his leg and the burns on his face. He was first taken to a German field hospital, where doctors wanted to amputate his leg, Charlie refused. All the wounded were transported to an Italian hospital, if that's what you want to call it. No beds, no doctors, and no medicine. There wasn't even a bathroom. You had to go outside. Charlie said it wasn't so bad in the daylight, but at night, you couldn't see where you were stepping."

Grandpa chuckled. "It's easy to laugh about it now, especially since it didn't happen to me. Charlie did tell me the only thing that came close to resembling a hospital was the lousy food.

"From there, Charlie was put on an Italian hospital ship. If you were a Catholic, you were treated well. If not, back of the line you went. Not only were you last for food, but for the doctors as well.

"It was on that ship where Charlie met a soldier with both of his legs shot off. He noticed Charlie carried an army-issued pocket Bible and thought he was a minister. Charlie wasn't a minister; he wasn't even a Christian. You don't have to be a Christian to be a good person. This soldier told Charlie he wanted to die along with his friends and didn't know why he was spared. Charlie looked at him and told him, 'You're not needed yet. When they need you, they'll call for you up there.' The soldier thanked him. It seemed as though that was what he needed to hear to make peace with his plight.

"I think I remember Charlie telling me he had escaped six times. Unfortunately, he kept getting caught. When he was brought to our camp the commandant assigned him to our barracks."

"Six times?" I asked.

Grandpa nodded, and then continued, "I think Charlie's first prison was in Italy, in camp 59. It was also the first camp he and a native Italian soldier escaped from. They were able to get past the fence and into the countryside."

"Grandpa, what was an Italian soldier doing inside an Italian POW camp?"

"He was there because he was an anti-fascist who was headed for the American side to help free Italy. Charlie's new friend may have blended in with the people, but Charlie, not so much. They were on the lam for six months. They thought they were being helped by an old farmer, but it turned out the farmer was a fascist. The Germans interrogated them and put them in a small cell with forty other prisoners. Half would have to stand so the other half could lie down and get some rest. There was no bathroom, only a wooden barrel that leaked."

"That's terrible."

"That's war. The enemy has little regard for captives. Charlie's adventures were, to say the least, incredible. When the prisoners were transferred, they were put on busses with armed guards, with their fingers on the trigger the whole way to their next destination. Where Charlie was sitting, a guard was behind him, and he could feel the gun on his back. He thought for sure that with every bump in the road, the gun would go off and his ride would be over.

"With all the times Charlie escaped and was caught, he spent a lot of time being transported to different camps. Buses, trains, trucks, sometimes walking on a leg that never really healed, but Charlie never gave up. One time he was loaded in a truck that stopped in Florence for a rest. A lady came over to the truck. Because Charlie had spent so much time on the run with the Italian from Camp 59, he was able to speak a little Italian. He told the woman he was a POW and very hungry. She ran home and brought him a big bowl of spaghetti. The guy next to him grabbed it, and four or five of his buddies ate it, without giving any to Charlie."

"I can't believe it! None?"

Grandpa shook his head. "Starvation will turn a civil man into an animal. I know starvation, and I don't know but I would have done the same. I hope I wouldn't, but I just don't know." Grandpa paused for a while, staring off to another time in his life.

Coming back to the present, he said, "Pun'kin, I'd like to tell you more, but so much may still be classified. There is one story, though, I'd like to tell you. Charlie's last escape was with the help of a Russian officer and two Germans."

FOURTEEN
Off to the Salt-Mines

"Charlie was put in camp 7A. It was there he was reunited with many from the 1st Armored Division.

"Then smiling, Grandpa added, "This is one of the parts where if Hollywood made a movie, it would be hard to believe, even though it's true. When Camp 7A was taken over by the Russians, American trucks came to take the prisoners out. The Russians however, wouldn't let the prisoners go, and the trucks had to go back empty; they became prisoners of the Russians."

"I don't understand. The Russians?" I asked. "Weren't they our allies?"

"We were more their allies than they were allies of ours. Do you remember one of the things you need to do when playing chess?" I looked at him with a look as if to ask which one? "Always be looking beyond your next move. The Russians are well known for their chess players. They knew that after the war with Germany, we would no longer be on their side but would be going up against them.

"Charlie learned that the Russians were going to send them off to the salt mines to work as slaves, and he knew he had to do whatever he could to escape. Inside that prison camp were about five thousand POWs. Charlie made two escape attempts, each time getting caught. He drove the Russians crazy, so they put him in another area with about eight hundred POWs, where they could keep a better eye on him.

"Pun'kin, what I'm about to tell you, some people may pooh-pooh this, but I believe it to be true."

My grandfather used many different expressions for "not believe." There's "hooey, bull feathers," and "hogwash," just to name a few. But the one I remember giggling at, at the age of five, was "pooh-pooh."

Grandpa continued, "It was while Charlie was at camp 7a, that his father came to him in a dream. He told Charlie he was going to be okay, and he would get back home. When he did get back, he found his father had passed away the very night he was told he'd make it back."

When Grandpa told me this, I found tears rolling down my face. "I believe it, Grandpa."

"So do I, Pun'kin, so do I."

"What happened? How did Charlie escape?"

"It was the darndest thing. It was Charlie's second escape attempt when he was being marched back to see the day officer for discipline, which most likely meant execution. A high-ranking Russian officer happened to be driving by in his staff car when he saw Charlie. Because Charlie was Chinese, the officer thought he was a part of the Mongolian Russian troops; he stopped and wanted to know where he was going. Charlie had no idea what he was being asked. Nikki, I don't know why this officer, after trying to talk to Charlie and realizing he wasn't part of the Russian Asian troops, even bothered to want to know more, but he did. He went and found two American Yugoslavs from Wisconsin who could interpret for him. They told the officer Charlie was an American soldier, and all he wanted to do was to get back to the front line.

"Nikki, you can't tell me his father wasn't looking out for him. Do you know what that officer did? He took Charlie and the two interpreters aside and told them they had to escape that night, because tomorrow they were going to be shipped out to the salt mines. Charlie told him he had already tried escaping twice, with no success. That Russian officer could have been court-martialed for what he did. He made arrangements for them to escape.

That night, he drove them to the crossing at the Elbe River. The guard at the bridge told them he couldn't let them cross through until ten o'clock that night, when the other guard would be gone. They were told to go to a nearby building to hide and wait for his signal. Charlie's new friend said in broken English, "Good luck, until we meet again." At ten o'clock they heard a whistle and went to the guard post, where the guard wanted to be paid."

"I'll bet the guard waited to be alone just so he wouldn't have to split it with the other."

"I hadn't thought about that, but I'll bet your right. The price was a gold cigarette case and a gold ring. I don't know why there was a guard at the bridge. It had been bombed. The middle part sat in the water. From there they would have to swim to an island down river. For Charlie, that was one of his worst nightmares. You see, Charlie didn't know how to swim. He left what little he had behind, knowing that if he tried to take it with him, it would only drag him down to a watery grave.

"When they made it to the island, a German came out of the bush and scared them half to death. They didn't know the Russian officer had made arrangements for their escape.

The German spoke English. He said he owned the island and that he was willing to take them to the other side. The two Yugoslavs from Minnesota didn't trust him. Charlie was told the two would distract him long enough for Charlie to get a club. If anything went wrong, Charlie was to kill him. When they got to the other side of the island, the German blinked his flashlight. Back came the reply, two short, one long. A few minutes later a rowboat came into sight, and a man in a German uniform was at the helm. Charlie was ready to club the man before his accomplice could make it to shore. The Yugoslavians said something to the man in the boat, and with his reply, Charlie was told they were safe."

"Grandpa, you have me sitting on the edge of my seat. What happened next?"

"They climbed in and went down river. Around each bend of the river, Charlie thought for sure there would be enemy soldiers just waiting to pick them off. They went about ten miles when their guide beached the boat. A quick blink from the flashlight, and another man came from the thicket of trees. The guide told them it would be safer if they split up. The new guide spoke English, so Charlie went with him and the others went with the man from the boat. Charlie didn't even know their names. He told me, 'Somewhere in Minnesota are two guardian angels.'

"Twice, Charlie and his guide came within feet of German troops. Had they been seen, both would have been shot, Charlie for being the enemy, and his guide for treason. When a German soldier was accused of treason, his entire family would be executed. The third time, they weren't so lucky. Charlie was in front when they walked right into a

German patrol that had stopped to take a break. It was too late to duck back into the woods. Charlie quickly raised his hands as though he was being held captive. That move saved his and the guide's life. The German patrol congratulated the guide for capturing one of their enemies. From there, Charlie was put into Commandant Schmidt's Camp, where Charlie told me his story.

"There's so much more to his story. Perhaps one day his family will write a book about his adventure; it will make for a fascinating read, for sure. After the war he went back home to his small town in Bakersfield, California, where he was well known and loved."

FIFTEEN

The Phone Call

"I remember getting a call from Charlie that scared me to death; I thought something bad may have happened. You see, back then, to make a long-distance phone call, you had to go through several operators, and it was very expensive. It turns out Charlie was fine. He was calling to invite me to a parade the town was putting on in his honor, right down Main Street. Of course your grandmother and I put on our Sunday best and flew out; we wouldn't have missed it for the world."

I just had to ask about something my grandfather said. "You put on your Sunday best to fly?"

He looked at me. "Back then, everyone did." With a smile he took his hand up to his collar and pretended to straighten a tie that wasn't there. "We old-timers had class. Today, getting on airplanes is as common as getting on a bus."

Grandpa's smile faded, and I knew something was troubling him. "What is it, Grandpa?"

"Thinking about Charlie and meeting his family brings back such warm memories and sadness at the same time."

"I don't understand, why sadness?"

"Your grandmother and I got to know Charlie's family, and let me tell you, harder working people you'll never find. Let's just say I'm glad I'm not a farmer. The sadness comes from some of the information Charlie shared with me over the years."

"What kind of information?" Grandpa paused, took in a deep breath and let it out slowly.

"You know I don't like it when someone doesn't like you just because of the pigment of your skin or if your heritage is a certain place." I nodded my head. "I remember Charlie's family telling me about the Chinese Exclusion Act of 1882."

"I've never heard of it."

"Don't feel bad, Pun'kin. I was a lot older than you when Charlie's family told me. For some reason our schools don't teach a lot of history. America is beautiful, and I'd climb back into the cockpit to protect her if that's what it took to keep her free. But with all her beauty, she does have some warts. I suppose that's why some things are not talked about. It's not polite to talk about someone's imperfections. Still, if you don't know your history, warts and all, how will you see how far you've come?

"From the beginning of time, it seems men can't get along with each other, what with all the wars and rumors of wars, one group of people putting another group into slavery. Just read the Bible and you'll see what I mean.

"Take America, starting at the beginning in the early 1600s. True, America was a colony of England, and slavery was a tradition brought over, but still . . . " Grandpa shook his head. "At least America got its act together with the Constitution, which was the beginning of the end of slavery." I saw his eyes water. "All that blood being shed on the ground to put an end to that ugly practice of slavery—over fifty thousand in the Battle of Gettysburg alone. I just wish it had put an end to hatred.

"As America grew, different groups of people came, and

it seems like every group that came were never welcomed. When the Irish came to New York, all you could see were 'Irish need not apply' signs everywhere."

I could see Grandpa going down one of his rabbit holes. "Grandpa, what about the Chinese Exclusion Act?"

"What? Oh yeah, sorry about that. I know where I got lost. You know that the Civil War ended slavery for the blacks, but it didn't include the Chinese."

"Wait. What?"

"You didn't know about that, did you? I'll also bet you didn't know you could buy a Chinese slave in San Francisco up until the year 1929."

"How can that be? Slavery ended after the Civil War."

"It did for the blacks but not for the Chinese." Grandpa took a long pause. Shaking his head, he continued. "When I think of the government prohost or when it turns a blind eye to what is wrong, I stop and think the founding fathers must be turning over in their graves."

"Prohost? Okay grandpa, that's a new one, what does it mean?"

"In short, it means government-sanctioned bigotry. Charlie's family told me farmers couldn't own chattel."

"Why would a farmer want to own cattle? After all, their farmers, not ranchers, a few milk cows maybe along with some chickens."

Grandpa laughed out loud. "Not cattle, chattel. It means property, and not just land, everything and anything, including chickens and cows."

"Then how were they able to farm?"

"They would find someone they thought they could trust and give them the money to buy the land and whatever they would need. It would then be put in that person's name so they could work the land, sometimes for generations. Sadly, many times after raw land was cleared and producing, the legal owner would charge rent, sometimes at a very high price. He could even legally take the land, leaving the Chinese family with nothing.

"The Chinese weren't the only ones who had trouble with the government. After Pearl Harbor, the Japanese were put into internment camps, and their property was taken as well. The Italians also had a bad time, and it didn't matter if you were famous or not. You're way too young to remember Joe DiMaggio, but his family lost everything they had because they were Italians. Joe's family were fishermen, and when the war broke out, the government confiscated their boat, because they didn't want anyone who was Italian to have the means of transporting the enemy. . .

"At least the Italians could interracially marry. The Chinese, on the other hand, couldn't. Not until 1967.

Charlie has a niece who married a Caucasian, and had they married before '67, they could have been prosecuted for a felony."

Charlie, like Pat, taught my grandfather a lot of things he never knew. One story Grandpa told me was when Charlie was captured by the Nazis the first time. The Nazis lined up all the new prisoners and demanded to know who among them were Jewish. Charlie and the others knew who were Jewish, but they weren't about to tell the Germans.

Dog tags had a place for a stamp telling what religion they were—P for Protestant, C for Catholic, J for Jewish, and so on. Not all the Jews had the J stamped on their tags, for obvious reasons. The Nazis brought in German Shepherds, and those dogs were able to sniff out those who were of Jewish heritage. They were all removed from the line and were never heard from again. Charlie told my grandfather that for the rest of his life, he would be the voice for those who no longer could be heard, his Jewish brothers in arms, and for the prisoners who were led to their deaths in the salt mines.

When Grandpa told me about the dogs, I had never heard of such a thing, so I asked how that was possible.

Grandpa explained, "I myself wondered about that for years. I told a good physiologist friend of mine the story and asked him about it. He told me the explanation was quite simple. The human body can have a hundred or more chemicals on the surface of the skin. Each person has his or her own unique formula that dogs can detect. That's why when someone is lost, a dog can smell something the person wore and separate it from all the other scents. Even though all of us have our own unique combination, there are common scent groups within each race. Dogs are trained to do all kinds of things that need detecting; it stands to reason the Germans simply trained them to detect the common scent of the Jewish race. Mosquitoes have a similar ability; they are more attracted to certain chemicals over others. That explains why whenever your grandmother and I would go for a walk, if there was a mosquito within five miles, it would find me and leave her alone. There's something about me they just love—lucky me."

SIXTEEN

The Resistors and the Punishment

Grandpa and I would share stories back and forth; I learned from the research I gathered that there were Germans in Hitler's military who tried to assassinate him. They put their lives on the line for their country. They knew that what was happening was wrong, but they faced their fears to try and stop it. Many were discovered and executed. Some stories my grandfather had heard, others were new to him. Some of the stories came from my interviews with other vets. For example, when I asked Grandpa if he had ever heard of "The White Rose," he thought I said something else.

"Yes. They were judges; at least that's what they called themselves. They were called 'The Red Robes' because that was the color of their robes. They were also known as 'The Blood Robes.' Hitler set up a 'People's Court' against Germany's constitutional authority. Anyone who appeared in that kangaroo court was as good as dead. That's how they got the name 'The Blood Robes,' because of all the blood on their hands. Look up the name Roland Freisler. That, that . . . " He paused, I never heard my grandfather swear, but I almost did that day when he talked about this so-called judge. Once he composed himself, he continued. "Let's just say when he was killed in his own court by a bombing raid, and when his body was brought to the hospital, someone said, 'It is God's verdict.' There was no love lost there; even his grave is unmarked."

Roland Freisler
Artist Rendition

I didn't want to embarrass my grandfather, because that wasn't the question I had asked. So I told him, "I never knew that." I knew about the "People's Court," but not about Roland Freisler. I asked, "How about the 'White Rose'? Have you ever heard of the 'White Rose'?"

"The 'White Rose,'" he repeated. "I don't think I've ever heard that one."

I told him, "The White Rose was a group of students from the University of Munich who resisted Hitler's regime. They started a leaflet campaign, knowing it would result in certain death if they were caught, but they didn't let their fear stop them and did it anyway. Six of the core group were arrested by the Gestapo and beheaded. Even after they were executed, there was another member who helped distribute 'Leaflet 6' in Hamburg. I can only imagine what must have been going through his mind as he distributed that last leaflet. He was caught and executed for his participation as well."

I told my grandfather, "I understand the members of the 'White Rose' are considered to be among Germany's greatest heroes and are honored at the University of Munich, where they attended.

Hans Scholl, His sister Sophie and good friend Christoph Probst.
Photo provided by the National Archives (NARA)

"I learned all of this from a gentleman I interviewed last week. He also informed me that when he went back to Germany a few years ago, there were streets and schools named after the heroes who had participated in the Resistance. He made it a point to tell me that he wasn't able to find anything named after Hitler or his henchmen.

"Another hero was a fifteen-year-old boy named Helmuth Hübener.

Helmuth Hübener's "mug shot."
Gestapo would place the same hat on all men to show what they would look like on the streets if wearing a disguise

"Helmuth had access to a shortwave radio, and although it was strictly forbidden, he secretly listened to the news of the war on the BBC, the British Broadcasting Corporation; the penalty for doing so could be death, but he did it anyway. Hitler wanted the people to listen to only what he wanted them to hear, and he appointed Joseph Goebbels to be his propaganda minister. You would think with a title like that, no one would trust him. Goebbels had all power over what Germany would hear on the radio, read in the press, or watch in the cinema and theater. It was Goebbels who said, 'If you repeat a lie often enough, it becomes truth.' Hitler knew he could control the people if he could control what they knew.

Joseph Goebbels
Artist rendition

"I'm sure Helmuth knew Hitler was a liar and a murderer from what he learned outside his media, and he said as much in the pamphlets he had printed. He and two friends would secretly post the flyers where people could read them. When they were caught, they were tried in 'The People's Court.' Helmuth was sentenced to death; his friends were sentenced to time in prison. Hitler himself signed the death warrant.

The Nazis would give the prisoners who were to be executed a drink that would keep them calm, and then take them to a room where the charges were to be read. Helmuth Hübener didn't believe in strong drink; it was against his religion. He knew his fate and was ready to accept it. Even though he didn't want to take the drink, he knew he had no choice; the Nazis would have broken his teeth to get it down him.

"The room was divided by a black curtain that was pulled back as soon as the charges were read, to reveal the guillotine. The Nazis had it down to a science: eighteen seconds from the time the charges were read to the execution. Helmuth Hübener was only seventeen when he was beheaded. His mother found out about his execution on her birthday by reading about it on a bulletin board.

"The bodies of those who were executed, like Helmuth Hübener, were put in metal containers with their heads and then sent to medical facilities for study. They were never returned to the families for proper burial. The Nazis executed hundreds, if not thousands, this way. I wonder how many of those were ones who got involved and took a stand against what they knew to be wrong, or were they in the wrong place at the wrong time.

"Grandpa, I've been thinking about the tremendous fear the resisters must have all felt, knowing that what they were doing could lead to their own deaths. Yet there were a few who found the courage to act and took the risk to follow their hearts."

SEVENTEEN
Joseph Banks

Grandpa slowly shook his head, "Hitler had no regard for human life; his hatred had no bounds. He believed the aged or mentally ill needed to be disposed of. Even though Hitler himself had an aunt who was mentally ill, he thought these 'defective' people were a burden and a drain on society. He was able to convince his followers that there was nothing wrong with killing them, including his aunt. To Hitler, the blacks were also an inferior race that deserved death. Of the eleven million killed, about five million were non-Jews: Polish leaders, Gypsies, homosexuals, priests and Christian leaders. There's a poem by Pastor Martin Niemoller that goes something like this.

> 'First they came for the Communists, but I was not a Communist so I did not speak out. Then they came for the Socialists and the Trade Unionists, but I was neither, so I did not speak out. Then they came for the Jews, but I was not a Jew so I did not speak out. And when they came for me, there was no one left to speak out for me.*'"

* Jewish Virtual Library Organization

Grandpa sighed with disgust, "I doubt if it will ever change. People wanting to rule over others seems to be part of man's history." He sat silent for a while, tears in his eyes, and then spoke. "I don't know why, Nikki, but that story of Helmuth Hübener reminds me of a book I read some time ago about the Death March."

"The Bataan Death March in the Philippines?" I asked. Grandpa nodded.

"The Bataan Death March was in the Philippines, and it was about seventy miles long.

"The death marches I'm referring to took place in Germany, and they were hundreds of miles long. Toward the end of the war, Hitler ordered the prisoners who were being held in the camps in eastern Germany near the Russian border to be moved. The Russians had broken the front line and were moving in toward Germany. The Germans knew of the Russians' hatred toward them because of Hitler's betrayal.

Adolf Hitler
Artist rendition

Adolf Hitler had invaded Russia after he made an agreement not to with the premier of the Soviet Union, Joseph Stalin. If the German soldiers were caught, their punishment could be severe. I don't think Hitler gave two hoots and a holler for his men. I think he didn't want the Russians to have the satisfaction of liberating the prisoners, so he marched them from the eastern to the western end of Germany in the dead of winter. I use the word 'dead' with great meaning.

"The winter of 1944 was the worst winter ever recorded. With very little food, and less clothing, any prisoners who fell by the wayside were beaten, either with the butt of a rifle, or the heel of a boot, and left for dead." Grandpa sat in deep thought. "I can't remember the name of that book, but I can see its cover in my mind's eye. Help your old grandpa up, would you, Pun'kin?"

After I helped him up, he walked over to one of his bookcases. "The book cover shows a B-17 flying through the clouds. The author was a POW who made one of those marches. He and his buddies had walked about five hundred miles when one of the friendlier guards told him that the next day the SS, Hitler's version of the Secret Service, would be taking over. They were no secret."

Having heard of the name "Brown Shirts," I thought it was just another name for the SS. When I told Grandpa that, he smiled and said, "Close, but no cigar. The SA were rivals." As he kept looking for the book, he straightened me out about the Brown Shirts. "Before Hitler's SS, there was the SA, and their uniform was a brown shirt. They were founded by the government in 1919 to deal with the threat of Communism. In the 1930s the SA's leader was a man by the name of Ernst Röhm.

Ernst Röhm
Artist rendition

The SS were the elite of the SA, and their uniforms were black. A man by the name of Heinrich Himmler was in charge of them, and he was one sadistic SOB if there were was one.

The SS were trained in their youth to serve as Hitler's attack dogs, putting down any insurrection by the people. They were fanatics and, to say the least, they were inhumane.

Heinrich Himmler
Artist rendition

"Another name you should know is Hermann Göring. He founded the Gestapo in 33."

Hermann Göring
Artist rendition

"I thought the Gestapo was just another name for the SS."

"No, the Gestapo was Secret State Police. They did have many things in common, one of which was that they both hated Ernst Röhm."

Grandpa continued to talk while he searched for the book. "As I recall, this POW, when he learned the SS would soon be taking over command, he and three of his buddies knew that if they didn't make a break for it before that happened, they would probably never see their families again.

"Devising an escape plan was the most frightening thing they had ever done. The POWs didn't know where they were or which way they needed to go. They were easy targets with a big PW painted in white letters all over their clothing to show they were prisoners of war. If they got caught, they would be forced to walk barefooted, just as the others who had tried to escape had been forced to do, a death sentence for sure. In spite of all that, they knew it was worth the risk. They did escape, and when they were rescued it was learned that the SS had locked the remaining prisoners in an old barn and set it on fire. Some of the desperate men managed to break the door down and run from the inferno, only to be cut down by machine-gun fire."

I stood in unbelief next to Grandpa as he ran his fingers back and forth over each shelf as he told me that story.

"I wonder where that book is. I wish I could remember the name of it. I've got to find it before it drives me crazy."

Smiling inside, I knew that once my grandfather had something on his mind he couldn't let it go. He checked all the bookshelves, and wouldn't you know it, in the garage is where he found it. As he came down the hall I could hear him yell, "I found it! It's titled A Distant Prayer, and there are two authors, Joseph Banks and Jerry Borrowman. I was right! It has a B-17 on the cover. Do I know my planes or do I know my planes? I just remembered, Joseph Banks was on his forty-ninth mission when his plane was bombed by the plane above him. One more mission and he and his crew were headed home, I think you'll enjoy this one."

Grandpa was right, what an amazing story.

I was going to stop writing and get ready for bed, but first I went to get something to eat. I carved off a slice of ham and made myself a sandwich. The only knife I could find was a long bread knife. With the thought of the SA on my mind I remembered something else. The SA were gaining power when Himmler and Göring convinced Hitler that Ernst Röhm was planning a coup. Hitler, outraged, used the SS and the Gestapo to murder the leadership and imprison their leader, Ernst Röhm. Röhm was given a Browning automatic. Clearly, he was to shoot himself. Röhm said, "If I am to be killed, let Adolf do it himself." He was then shot twice in the chest. As Röhm lay on the floor moaning, it is said his last words were, "Mein Führer, mein Führer" A final round to the head and he was dead.

It was called "Operation Humming Bird" but is best known as "The Night of the Long Knives." That was in 1934 from June 30th to July 2nd, and when it was over, the SA and SS were one under Himmler's control. Hitler made the military take an oath, swearing them to pledge loyalty and allegiance to him and not to Germany. In 1936, Himmler was given control of the Gestapo and Göring was Commander-in-chief of the Luftwaffe (air force).

Hitler controlled the people through indoctrination in the schools and media. He knew if the people felt it was their patriotic duty to turn in their neighbors for doing anything anti-Nazi or against the regime, they would do it. The fear was too great—if they didn't turn someone in, they could be charged with treason and also be executed. The SA were also known as "Storm Troopers."

My mind went back to my going to the movie Star Wars with my girlfriends. We were at Pizza Hut, waiting for my dad to pick us up. I made a comment about how George Lucas had named the evil army of Darth Vader after Hitler's "Storm Troopers." My friends didn't have a clue to the connection.

EIGHTEEN

Yalta and the Candy Bomber

As I was eating my sandwich, my mind wandered in thought about Berlin and all that had happened there, before, during, and after the war.

I remember one of my grandfather's favorite stories, and I just have to put it down on paper before I go to sleep. It's a story about Gail Halvorsen, better known as the Candy Bomber of Berlin.

Gail Halvorsen

Photo from his personal collection

Thank you Gail, It was an honor to meet you.

It was in 1948 when the Berlin air drop began. . . . Sorry, I'm getting ahead of myself, and I can hear both my professor and grandfather telling me, "Nikki, lay the ground work."

Hitler fought in WWI, and he knew he didn't want to have a two-front war, so in August of 1939, he made a nonaggression pact with Stalin.

August 23, 1939 the signing of the nonaggression act
Photo provided by the National Archives (NARA)

But a few years later, Hitler invaded Russia with Operation Barbarossa, and he now has a two-front war—big mistake.

"Operation Barbarossa"
Germany invades Russia June 22, 1941
Photo provided by the National Archives (NARA)

It was February 1945; the war would be over soon, and President Roosevelt, Prime Minister Churchill and Premier Joseph Stalin met in Yalta, Crimea, southern Ukraine. This meeting is known as the Yalta Conference.

Yalta Conference
Left to right Joseph Stalin President Roosevelt, Prime Minister Churchill
Artist rendition

They were united that Germany would have to surrender unconditionally. Unlike the Armistice at the end of WWI, this time Germany would have to dismantle its military, including the Luftwaffe (air force). They also decided to divide Germany into four sections. The Soviets would control East Germany, while West Germany would be controlled by the US, UK and France. They also divided Berlin, the capital of Germany, into four parts among the superpowers, the Soviets controlling the east and the others controlling the west.

The Yalta Conference has been much debated; many think it was the worst thing President Roosevelt could have done just months before he died. But in all fairness, I'm sure he thought it was the best deal he thought he could get under the circumstances. He really thought he could control Stalin. There is a saying that has been around forever: The enemy of my enemy is my friend.

I can see my grandfather shaking his head and saying, "Why do we have to have enemies?" He hated war; he saw so many good people die, and for what? So someone could have more power over others. He lost so many close friends, some right before his eyes. People you don't like for what they do to you . . . that he could understand, but going to war, that he couldn't. There goes his voice in my head again: "Pun'kin, get back on track with the candy bomber."

After the war, Germany was divided up into four zones. Berlin itself was divided in half with East and West. Russia controlled the eastern half, while the western half was divided up between France, Britain and the U.S.A. There were millions of people homeless and starving in western Berlin.

To get food to the people in western Berlin,, trucks by the hundreds would carry the supplies needed. The trucks were allowed to travel through Soviet-controlled roads, but the alliance we had with the Soviets broke apart in the summer of 1948. The Soviets would no longer let the trucks get through, leaving over two million people to starve to death. Stalin could not care less about the people in West Berlin, and the food in all those trucks rotted on the side of the road. President Truman went against his advisors. They thought flying food to that many people couldn't be done and we would look foolish. Truman knew we had to try, so he set the wheels in motion. "Operation Vittles" began. Now, I don't know how exact this story is, but it's the way my Grandfather Vince told it to me.

C-54 transport planes loaded down with food and supplies came into Berlin, landing one after another, at times every two minutes. As soon as the planes were unloaded they took off to get another load. Three times a day they would do this, pulling sixteen hours shifts. Gail Halverson was a 1st lieutenant then, and he was one of those pilots. He could see Berlin from the air, but he wanted to see it from the ground and get some pictures. He made arrangements to have a jeep take him around, but it would take about an hour before it would show up. Gail had an 8mm movie camera, and he wanted to get a shot of the planes coming over the apartments.

Gail found himself up against the barbed wire getting the shot he wanted when he noticed a dozen or so kids, ranging in age from what looked to be 8 to 14. Children were taught English in school, and several were quite proficient. He talked to them for a little while but soon had to leave and says his goodbyes. As he was walking away, he wished there was something more that he could do for the kids. He knew the food he was bringing in was a godsend, but still he wished he could do more.

Gail put his hands into his pocket and felt two pieces of gum. He knew there wasn't enough to go around, even by breaking it into the smallest of pieces. Not only that, he knew for sure there would be bloody noses fighting over the gum. Gail felt he had to go back, and so he did. Breaking the gum in half, he handed out the four pieces. To his surprise, there was no fighting, and those who didn't get the gum took turns smelling the wrapper. One by one the delight on the kids' faces from smelling the wrapper told him he had to do more. A thought came to Gail Halverson's mind, and he told the kids that if they didn't tell anyone, he would fly over the next day and drop enough for everyone and to share it.

They all agreed.

Gail knew that to do something like that took special permission; you see, in Uncle Sam's Army, as my grandfather would put it, "You have to get permission to go to the bathroom." Gail also knew it would never be granted. He knew he could get into big trouble, even court-martialed, but he rationalized it to be the right thing to do. Besides, he would do it only a few times so nobody would be the wiser. What could it hurt? As he turned to walk away, one of the kids asked how they would know which plane to look for, there were so many. Gail thought for a moment, "Look for the plane that wiggles its wings." The kids looked puzzled, so Gail held out his arms and wiggled them back and forth. All of them giggled from the wiggle.

The next day Gail flew over, wiggled the wings and dropped to the kids below the gum that was tied to three handkerchief parachutes.

Gifts From Above
Artist Rendition

When he got ready to take off he looked over to the fence line and saw three handkerchiefs waving through the fence, with all the kids chewing the gum. Three times he and his crew did this. One day Gail needed to know the weather so he would know where to land in West Germany. He went to the base operations and found a big pile of mail addressed to Uncle Wiggly Wings. Gail knew he was in trouble. He and his crew decided they had to stop with the candy drops.

Each time they flew over, the crowd grew larger and larger, and they could feel the disappointment from the kids below. They looked at each other and decided, "One more and that's it." On their next trip, Gail wiggled the wings, and the jubilation was reward enough for their last drop. Six more parachutes found their targets. The next day Gail was told to see Colonel James Haun immediately. Into his office he went. Gail knocked on the door. "Enter" came from the other side. Gail walked in. "You wanted to see me, Sir?" There was a pause,

"Halvorsen, what in the world have you been doing?"

"Flying, Sir."

"What else are you doing?"

"Nothing, Sir."

"Halvorsen, I'm not stupid. What else have you been doing?"

Gail knew the jig was up; he knew he was about to get his wings clipped. "I've been going over your file. Didn't they teach you in ROTC to keep your boss informed?" Colonel Haun took out a newspaper and placed it on his desk. Pointing at the paper, he said. "You almost hit a reporter in the head with one of your candy bars in Berlin yesterday. The story of Uncle Wiggly Wings is all over Europe. I received a call from General Tunner congratulating me on a great PR move, and I didn't know anything about it. So why was I left in the dark?"

Gail knew he wasn't in the clear yet, so he figured the truth was the best answer. "I didn't think you would approve it before the airlift was over, Sir."

"You mean to tell me that after we dropped thousands of bombs on that city you didn't think I would approve dropping a few sticks of gum? The general wants to see you first thing tomorrow morning. It seems there is an International Press conference set for you in Frankfurt. Fit them into your schedule."

Gail thought he was about to be dismissed, but Colonel Haun wasn't through. With sternness in his voice he added. "Lieutenant, keep flying, keep dropping, and keep me informed." It was only then the colonel smiled and shook his hand.

The press called the project "Operation Little Vittles." Little Vittles was unofficial and had to be voluntary. Grandpa would say, "Some things just work better without government getting involved."

In May of 1949, the Soviets lifted the blockade and by the end of September the airlift came to a close. In fifteen months, over two million tons of supplies were flown in from over two hundred thousand flights, along with twenty tons of candy.

During that time, Grandpa Vince had a good Catholic friend who went to Elms College in Chicopee, Massachusetts. He told Grandpa how they took an old abandoned firehouse, cleaned it up and turned it into a national clearinghouse for donations to the "Little Vittles." Candy came in from all over the country. From firehouse to Candy house, I can't think of a better use for an abandoned building. Over twenty schools helped. They wrapped, packed, and shipped over eighteen tons of candy attached to parachutes.

It was many years later when I actually got to meet the "Candy Bomber" himself.

Me and the Candy Bomber
Photo from the private collection of Gary J. Sumner

NINETEEN

Jessie and Louie

I remember Grandpa rubbing his leg and then smiling. "I'll bet you didn't know your old grandpa was quite the track and field star in high school." I got the hint; he wanted to change the subject. "It's true. I'm proud to say I set quite a few records in my day. Mind you, I was no Jesse Owens or Louie Zamperini, but I sure loved to run."

"Who are Jesse Owens and Louie Zamperini?"

Grandpa look shocked. "Who are Jesse and Louie?" He shook his head. I thought he was going to disown me. "I can't believe you don't know who they are. What I can't believe is that I haven't told you about two of my heroes.

"Jesse Owens put on one heck of a show in the 1936 Olympics in Berlin, Germany. He won four track and field gold medals. One in the 100 meters, 200 meters, the long jump and the 4 x 100 meter relay. When I ran the relay, I loved being the anchor. If memory serves me right, I think Jesse was having trouble qualifying in the long jump. One of the German athletes noticed what Jesse was doing wrong and suggested he try something that worked for him. Talk about good sportsmanship, because of that tip Jesse took gold in that event, making him the most successful athlete in that Olympics. I'm sure watching a black man win that many gold medals put a burr under Hitler's saddle after he had told his people how inferior the black race was."

Jesse Owens
Artist Rendition

Grandpa grinned from ear to ear. "The race I remember most would have to be the 5,000-meter." Grandpa's eyes sparkled, and a grin came to his face. "It was the first time I heard the name Louie Zamperini.

Louie Zamperini
Courtesy of the Louis Zamperini Trust

"I thought for sure he would be from the Italian team, but he wasn't. He was on our team. I remember sitting around the radio and hearing the announcer describe the race. The Finns were well known for the sport and were a shoo-in for the medals, but they sure played some dirty pool that day.

The lead runner was Don Lash, and he was on our team, with the Finns right behind him. As the race wore on the Finns got around him and started to rough him up a bit. On the eighth lap, one of them planted an elbow right into Lash's chest, causing him to fold.

"It was in the last lap when we started to hear the crowd roar and the announcer described the speed of Louie Zamperini as he passed runner after runner. He came in eighth place, just a breath away from seventh. Let me tell you I was on pins and needles that day. He ran his last lap so fast there was no doubt in my mind: he was going to be the first man to break the four-minute mile. He would have done it too, I'm sure of it, if it hadn't been for the war, which started soon thereafter. I met Mr. Zamperini once, and I'll never forget it. I was home reading the newspaper when I saw an ad for a cruise ship. What caught my eye in bold print was 'Come Meet Louie Zamperini.' So I took your grandmother to meet one of my heros . . . it was like a second honeymoon.

"At one of the dinners, Louie and his wife, Cynthia, sat two tables away. He and his wife are the two warmest people I ever met. It was a week–long cruise, and we had a chance to get to know each other. When I told Louie I flew a P-47, he smiled and told me he preferred being a bombardier. He didn't care too much for the ups and downs we fighter pilots go through. Being a POW myself, we had a lot in common. I thought my captor was bad, but he was an angel compared to Louie's. What Louie told me, someone should make a movie of his life."

"What happened, Grandpa? Was he shot down?"

"No, he wasn't shot down, but down he went. Nikki,

we lost a lot of good men without the enemy ever firing a single shot. Sometimes the bombers had mechanical problems, taking the crew down with them. Sometimes human error and sometimes a little of both. That's what happened to Louie over the Pacific. He and only two others survived, and for days they floated closer and closer into enemy waters. With only the rain to quench their thirst and whatever they could catch for food, it was a miracle two survived. If I remember right, I think they were on the raft for forty-six days when they spotted land."

"Forty-six days? That's impossible!"

"Definitely a record breaker, that's for sure."

"Then they made it!"

"Not quite. As they were paddling, a patrol boat saw them and picked them up, and believe it or not, it was all downhill from there. Louie ended up in the hands of a man by the name of Mutsuhiro Watanabe. The POWs called him 'The Bird.' That man was certifiable. What he did to Louie and the other prisoners was unspeakable, and for some reason, the Bird made it his mission to make Louie Zamperini's life a living hell.* How Louie ever survived, God only knows. Louie told me he had forgiven him. Louie Zamperini is a far better man than I ever could be. I hope there's a special place in hell for both the Bird and my captor, Schmidt."

* The Mutsuhiro, AKA, "The Bird" story came from Laura Hillenbrand's book Unbroken.

TWENTY
Crash Landing

My Grandfather had always walked with a limp because of a broken leg that happened in the war, but I never knew how he broke it.

"Tell me how you broke your leg, Grandpa."

He hesitated, and then spoke. "My squadron was hanging around the base playing cards, and Graig was manning the radio when the call came in. Two platoons were pinned down and needed our help. Graig sure loved working that radio whenever he could. He had been a ham operator before the war. He could pound out a CW (Morse-code) message on his Vibroplex Bug (telegraph key) so fast it would make your head spin. When you were off to college I got to thinking about him after I read an article about keeping your mind sharp and started to look into becoming a ham radio operator myself. Did you know you can send a message from earth, bounce it off the moon and back to earth? Some of those guys can even bounce microwaves off rain drops."

Grandpa was, as he puts it, "Going off into the toolies," and I had to bring him back. "What about the men who were pinned down?"

"Sorry, I guess I got sidetracked. The call came in and we took off. Our squadron leader spotted them first, five miles ahead at two o'clock. We dove down, picking up speed. We could see our guys in a wide-open space behind a small ridge that was keeping them safe, with the Germans about two, maybe three hundred yards ahead of them. Whoever led them out in the open like that should have been court-martialed. Behind the men about a hundred feet were enough trees for cover; if they could make it to them they would be safe. But if they so much as lifted a head, they would be an easy target for a sniper. We could see quite a few of the dead as we flew over them. We leveled off at about twenty feet. One of the guys said something about if we were any lower we would be giving them a haircut. The squadron leader told him to pipe down and stay focused.

"We came in so fast the Germans never saw us coming. We kept them busy long enough on our first pass for about a quarter of the men to make it to the tree line. The next pass we weren't as lucky. We no longer had the speed we had after coming out of a high dive or the element of surprise. That's when they broke out the 'double A' guns. They had three anti-aircraft guns, and they were all aimed right at us. We kept crisscrossing, laying down fire power, banking left and right, trying to avoid the double A. It looked like one more pass would do the trick and the rest of the men would be safe.

"My good buddy Graig was out of ammo, so the squadron leader ordered him to head back. But if you knew Graig you knew he would do whatever it took to get those men out. I heard him over the headphones: 'Sorry, Sir, you're breaking up. I can't hear you.' He started to make one more pass. I tried to get in front of him to give Graig cover, but before I could he was hit and his plane went down. He became, as the ham radio operators would say, a 'silent key.' I was so angry I gave it all I had. I took out one of the guns, but that left them with two more, and one of them took down my plane.

"They say any landing is a good landing if you're able to walk away. I guess my landing wasn't so good. I worked my way out of the cockpit and managed to crawl about fifty feet before I passed out from the pain in my leg. When I came to, I was being dragged into the back of a troop transporter. I had to hop on one leg into a building to be interrogated. After a few days they dragged my keister into a prison camp. I thought they'd never take me to a doctor, and when they finally did, he shoved my belt into my mouth, told me to bite down, and then set my leg with one big yank. The next time I woke up I was in my assigned barracks with two wooden slats strapped to my leg. It never did heal right."

My heart went out to my grandfather, and tears ran down my face. Leave it to my grandfather to try to cheer me up.

"If you keep crying, you'll have to put on some new makeup. Besides, it could have been worse; I could have been fighting in the Pacific Theater. I heard of a B-24 pilot by the name of Fred Garrett who broke his ankle when he was shot down by the Japanese. They took care of it by strapping him down, giving him a spinal anesthetic, and made him watch as they sawed off his leg."*

The look on my face must have been one of horror and disbelief. "How could anyone be so cruel?" I asked.

Shaking his head, he mused, "I have often wondered that myself until I learned that the rulers of Japan had planned for decades to rule over all the Far East.

* The Fred Garrett story came from Laura Hillenbrand's book Unbroken.

They knew that if you want to control the masses, control what they know and believe; and they did that for decades. They started by controlling the curriculum in schools as to what students learn and believe, drilling violently into them their superiority and their right to rule over others. The rulers built up a very sophisticated army and navy to do just that. The military-run schools were ruthless in their indoctrination, including brutality to their own soldiers. It's of little wonder then why they were so inhumane to their enemies. Hitler also indoctrinated his people with the thought of grandeur and superiority. I guess sick minds think alike. At least Hitler didn't convince his people to commit suicide as a last resort, like the Japanese did."

I sat dumbfounded. "I guess it was lucky for you to have fought in the European Theater."

Grandpa nodded. "At least we didn't have the 'Rape of Nanking' in the back of our minds when we were shot down over Germany."

Having never heard of that, I asked him what the Rape of Nanking was. I knew the look on my grandfather's face—the "I wish I hadn't said that" look.

"You know I'll look it up, so you may as well tell me."

Grandpa, though reluctant, gave in. "It was in 1937 at the beginning of Japan's invasion of China. The Japanese took the city of Nanking with over a half a million civilians and close to a hundred thousand Chinese soldiers." Pausing and with a pained look on his face, he continued: "They executed them. They made a sport out of murder. Machine-gunned, bayoneted, burned alive, and I think their favorite was beheading. They found that if they wet the blade first it would cut easier.

Their thirst for blood couldn't be quenched. After they murdered the soldiers, they started on the civilians, raping tens of thousands of women. Taking babies from the arms of their mothers and putting them to death in the most inhumane way. The Japanese soldiers would take pictures of themselves with their trophies. In six weeks they murdered close to half a million people."

Grandpa looked at me, holding back tears. "There's more to that story, but that's all I can tell you."

I knew better than to press it, and I doubt I would have been able to hear much more. Grandpa stared off. "So many lives, and for what? Power . . . power to control? I just can't wrap my mind around it. I can't believe it took not one, but two—two atomic bombs, before the Japanese would surrender.

TWENTY ONE

Nearing The End

"I know there are those who believe we should never have dropped the bombs, and the taking of 120,000 Japanese lives was reprehensible. For those who think that, they have no clue as to the psyche of the Japanese people at that time. They had been trained from a very young age that they were superior, and to die for Japan was a great honor. Let me tell you, those two bombs saved countless Americans and Japanese lives.

"President Truman knew putting boots on the ground in Japan would come with a high price. Hideki Tõjõ who was a general of the Imperial Japanese Army, meant it when he said, 'The moment the first American soldier sets foot on the Japanese mainland, all prisoners of war will be execute.' Some Americans called it The Kill All Order.

"Japanese people were trained in the aspects of invasion to be personally involved in the defense of Japan.

"After the bombing of Pearl Harbor on December 7, 1941, the Japanese took control of most of the islands in the Pacific. It took a lot of work and a lot of blood, but we slowly gained a footing as we marched our way toward Japan. Early on Guadalcanal, 1942, that island was strategic for the Japanese. From there they could reach Australia and the States. After what the Japanese did to us at Pearl Harbor, we were anxious for payback.

"I don't think they took us seriously until we set our sights on taking control of the Marianas. From there it was just a hop skip and a jump to their front door.

"I can't remember much about all the battles, but I do remember Saipan, Guam, Iwo Jima, and Okinawa. I wish I could forget, but some things are so indelible you take them to your grave."

The only battle I really knew anything about was Iwo Jima because my grandfather and I must have watched John Wayne in the movie Sands of Iwo Jima at least a dozen times. My grandfather loved that man because he never took guff from anyone and stood for what was right.

"Tell me about Saipan. What do you remember?" He stared off thinking if he should tell me or not. "Please, Grandpa."

"I suppose you're old enough to know. The battle on Saipan started in mid June of 44 and went half way through into July. The Japanese had lost ground and were about to make their last stand. The commander of the Japanese knew they had lost and called for a gyokusai. (g-o-coup-sigh) We called it a 'bonsai attack.'"

"I thought bonsai was a small plant."

He smiled. "It is, but it's easier to say bonsai than gyokusai. It means an honorable suicide. What it really means is don't stop fighting until your dead. Early morning on the 23rd day, 3,000 troops came running into the front line. When it was all over, they lay dead on the ground, with 1000 of our own.

"What happened next was another example of the Japanese mind-set. The citizens on Saipan were told it would be better for them to commit suicide, rather than be taken by the Americans. They ran to the cliffs, mothers throwing their babies over to the rocks below and then leaping after them,

700 in one day. Loud speakers were brought in, trying to talk to those who were left to come out of their caves and they would be cared for. Many heeded the call and came out."

Grandfather was in deep thought when he gave a smile that I knew he was thinking of something humorous.

"What are you thinking of, Grandpa?"

"I was just thinking that some of those leathernecks walked on all fours. I don't think I've ever told you about the 3rd Dog Platoon known as the 'Devil Dogs.' Those dogs were inducted in the service with their own military service number." Grandpa smiled. "The only thing they didn't have were dog-tags around their necks. They were mostly Dobermans donated by the United Doberman Club. Not only were they trained for jungle warfare, they could detect land mines and booby traps. They made great watch dogs as well giving our boys a chance to get some sleep in their foxholes.

"Not all dogs came from the club; many dogs were family pets from neighbors down the street. I remember a story about a black lab that was lent by a 13-year-old girl from Butte, Montana, and she wanted to do her part. Her dog, Skipper was her cherished pride and joy which she loved with all her heart. With tears in her eyes, she gave Skipper one last hug and kiss as she sent him off to war. She knew Skipper was on loan and would be returning home after his service had been completed. I wonder at the age of 13, if she understood there was a chance he would never be coming home.

"The dog handler Skipper was assigned to quickly became close, and Skipper would do anything for his new master. Skipper's new handler would correspond with the 13-year-old telling her of his progress with the training. One night in a heavy fire fight, Skipper was by his side watching over him.

Skipper saw a Japanese soldier coming in from behind. Skipper leaped out of the fox-hole and placed himself between his master and the enemy. Skipper was shot, and died in the arms of the one he protected. With rage for what they did to Skipper, his master did something he should never have done; he jumped out of the safety of his fox-hole and started shooting. When daylight brook, the enemy lay dead all around the fox-hole. Skipper gave his life to save his masters. The handler wrote the young girl telling her about the bravery of her beloved pet. She never wrote back."

(After retelling this story I looked up "war dog memorial" along with, Always Faithful A Memoir of the Marine Dogs of WWII. There is a lot more to the story.)

I wanted to know more about the battle of Guam so I asked. "Tell me more about Guam. What happened?"

"Twenty-one days of intense fighting, is what happened. Guam was American territory before the Japanese took it over, and we wanted it back. After the first day, the Marines had only advanced 200 yards and were digging in for the night. All of a sudden 700 Japanese troops came running in on a bonsai attack. That failed, so next they brought in their tanks. Why they didn't start with the tank, who knows? Our tanks came in and took them out. Seven days in it was apparent we were going to take back our barracks that we hadn't set foot on for nearly three years. The Japanese who were left there to hold the ground, rather than surrender, committed suicide. On the eighth day the Marines finally took back their old barracks. A Japanese bugle was found, and as the American Flag was raised, 'To The Colors' was played while an honor guard presented arms. In 24 hours the airfield was repaired, but the fight was far from over.

"As the Marines pushed forward, the Japanese were running out of ammo and it was inevitable they were fighting a losing cause, but still they fought to the death."

On that island there were native citizens being held captive. Those American Nationals, some 20,000, had been living in hell for what must have felt like a lifetime. With tears running down their faces, they thanked the Marines for their freedom.

"Okinawa also had civilians who had been abused so badly they were willing to risk their lives in an escape attempt. It was late at night when they entered the vast area that is described as no man's land. It was pitch black when the Marines heard movement and opened up. At first light, battle-hardened Marines ventured out expecting to find dead Japanese soldiers. What they found horrified then. There were hundreds of emaciated civilians who were so gaunt one wondered how they were able to walk into no man's land in the first place.

"As soldiers, we're trained to kill an enemy who is trying to kill us, but not women and children. They quickly looked for any survivors. It was a miracle, but many survived. The civilians were so frighten they were shaking uncontrollably. The Marines did all they could to provide comfort with food and water, bowing before the elderly to show respect. One Marine came upon a young child next to its mother who was dead. He bent down, took out his canteen and helped the young child take a drink of water. Wetting down his handkerchief he cleaned the face of young mother, trying to give what comfort he could for the child.

"Nikki, I saw enough death to last me a lifetime, and I still have a hard time with it, mostly at night in my sleep. What I experienced was a fraction of what the men on the ground went through. I can't imagine what those Marines have had to live with after witnessing what they experienced."

Grandpa's eyes teared up as he took a deep breath and composed himself. "Truman had no choice but to drop the bomb. Japan would have fought to the bitter end, even if it meant the complete annihilation of the Japanese people. So you see, by doing what Truman allowed, he not only saved Americans, he also saved the Japanese as well.

"For Tõjõ and others like him, annihilation would have been more honorable than surrender. Surrender would bring great dishonor.

"Grandpa, I know the name Tõjõ. Wasn't he the prime minister of Japan?"

"He was. After the first atomic bomb in Hiroshima, the Japanese continued to fight, and we kept losing good men. Nagasaki was next. We wanted them to think we had an endless supply of the bombs and were ready to use them. Little did they know, two were all we had.

"After Nagasaki fell, the emperor of Japan was ready to surrender unconditionally. When Tõjõ learned of the surrender, he and a small group of very powerful men in the government took a vote to assassinate the emperor and destroy the recording of the emperor calling for the end of the war. I'm sure glad Tõjõ wasn't successful in the assassination attempt of the emperor, or the destroying of the recording, if he had been, there would never have been a surrender.

"When the recording was played before the people, it was the first time they had ever heard their emperor's voice. You have to remember, the people believed their emperor was a god."

TWENTY TWO

Grandpa and Life as a POW

I remember asking my Grandfather when I found out he was a POW what it was like.

Grandpa started by saying, "I'll never forget the stench of the prison camp. With so many men in such deplorable conditions, the smell was indescribable. We were deep behind the enemy line, as were most camps. Some were better than others, but this one was known to be among the worst. The man who ran the prison camp was a young commandant by the name of Schmidt. Apparently he had family connections to get the post. He was extremely strict, probably over-compensating for his age. Not only did he starve the prisoners, he also enforced his rules with an iron fist."

My grandfather took quite a long pause, longer than usual. I could see he was reliving the experience again. Then he continued, "We were starving, and I don't mean the kind of 'I'm hungry because I haven't eaten all day' kind of hunger. I'm talking about the kind of starvation you feel after your body has used up its excess fat and has gone into a survival-mode kind of hunger. Your body starts to shut down as it looks for anything to keep it going. It will literally eat itself from within. We were all young and had very little excess fat to begin with. We were fed just enough to keep us alive, if that's what you want to call it. If anyone was caught stealing food, it was solitary confinement for them with half rations."

"The reenactment movies you see about POWs aren't real. Remember, they're actors, and there is no way any of them would starve themselves enough to look the part. We were fed twice a day with black bread that had more sawdust in it than flour, and that was served with the soup of the day. I think the cooks went out, picked dandelions, or whatever else they could find, and put it in a pot of water. We were never given any clothing and lived in whatever we were wearing at the time of our capture. There was no water to shower or wash our clothes with, so you can imagine the stench.

"We all had straggly beards and matted hair because we didn't have anything to groom ourselves with. You could tell how long a prisoner had been there by how much of his ribs showed. Some of those guys looked like skeletons that someone had put paper maché on. Something I learned years later was that the prisoners in concentration camps who were forced to work, the camp officials would check for several things that could lead to their death, such as low body fat. Prisoners knew that this could be a reason to be selected for the gas chamber rather than continue as slave labor."

I watched my grandfather as he stared off, remembering.

"When we were allowed to go outside, one of our pastimes was to sit down, take off our shirts, and pick off the lice and whatever else was crawling on us." Grandpa rubbed his eyes. "I wonder if those who don't serve their country fully realize the sacrifice that is made for them. So many leaving behind loved ones they may never see again. That was the hardest part of prison life, not knowing if you were going to make it back home. Wondering what your family had been told, whether they even knew if you were dead or alive. We were given paper to write letters home on, but we had our doubts the Germans would ever send them. Just in case they did, I kept my comments short and to the point. Always saying how good we were being treated and not to worry, but most of all how much I loved your grandmother. Just the thought that maybe she would get it, the hope that a letter would slip through to her, letting her know I was still alive, lifted my spirits."

Grandpa leaned forward, looking me right in the eyes. "I would imagine your grandmother reading every word and holding each letter next to her heart, feeling how much I loved her."

He leaned back in his chair. "When I finally got home, I learned that my suspicions were justified. She had never received a single letter, just as I had never been given any of the daily letters your grandmother had written to me."

There was no way I could stop the tears that were rolling down my face after Grandpa told me that love story.

After I regained my composure, Grandpa continued his story. "We were also supposed to receive a package from the Red Cross once a month that contained food, candy and cigarettes. It was no surprise that the packages never made it into our hands. However, wrappers and cigarette butts were left on the grounds which the commandant would make us pick up to keep his camp clean. That really made us mad. Not only were they stealing our packages, we had to pick up after them, and that made our blood boil. But there was nothing we could do. Those Red Cross packages would have been a real treat.

"I'll bet you didn't know your grandpa used to smoke."

"You smoked?"

"Oh, yeah, young and dumb. But to be fair, back then nobody knew how bad it was for you, and everyone smoked. I think most of the fights we got into were from withdrawal symptoms, that along with boredom. When we were liberated, we were given food and cigarettes; I noticed most of us went for the smokes before the food. I had been controlled in every part of my life for well over a year while in that prison camp. I decided right then and there, I was not going to let anything have control over me again, and I never picked up another cigarette. Believe it or not, sometimes when I get stressed, I'll still get a craving for a smoke."

It was getting late, and I could see Grandpa was getting tired. He walked me to the door, gave me a kiss on my forehead, just as he had since I was a little girl, and said, "Have I ever told you I think you have the prettiest blond hair and blue eyes?" He didn't have dementia; that was his way of saying, "I love you." I would always say back, "Yes, Grandpa, but I never get tired of hearing it from you, and I love you too." He then wished me a good night and opened the door.

As I drove home that night, I started to reflect back on all the stories my grandfather had told me over the years and the ones I had just heard. All the sacrifices and trials so many had made excited young sons saying good-by to their parents at countless train stations across America as they head off to what they imagined to be an adventure, while moms and dads hold back tears knowing of the danger that lies ahead. Newlyweds and new parents embracing perhaps for the last time as they go off to war, just so others could be free, helped me to realize how trivial any problems and trials I was going through really were.

TWENTY THREE

An Unforgettable Story

It's late and I really should try to get some sleep, but sleep eludes me, so I'm going to keep writing. There is one story I have to put down; after all, this story sent me to Germany.

When my grandfather finally opened up about what it was like as a POW, he told me about his first encounter with Commandant Schmitt.

Commandant Schmitt
Artist Rendition

"I was lying on the floor bed because of my broken leg when the truck backed into the camp. Tailgate was opened and the canvas cover was thrown back. The light of day hurt our eyes and we were ordered out. Two G.I.'s helped as we got in line.

There must have been a few dozen or so new prisoners already standing in the middle of the courtyard when my group was dragged in. Guards with dogs surrounded us, and we watched as one lone prisoner, his hands tied behind his back, was rigorously led out of camp. The commandant himself, accompanied by a handful of guards with their dogs, escorted the terrified prisoner out of the compound. Those dogs must have been bred in hell. I think they enjoyed ripping a man apart."

It was then I understood why my grandfather had such a fear of dogs, especially German shepherds. He continued, "We were left standing in the middle of the compound until the commandant and the guards returned. The guards wanted us to stand at attention, but we were in no condition to do so. The guards finally let the prisoners on each side of me help support me in my struggle to remain standing on my one good leg. It was about an hour later when the commandant and the guards came walking back through the gate with the prisoner. We watched them blindfold him, lean him up against the wall, and then watched the commandant raise his hand and call out, 'Ready, aim,' and as he dropped his hand he called out 'fire.' We all flinched at the sound of the report as the guns went off.

"After the body was dragged off, the commandant turned to face us, and it was then he introduced himself to us and his rules. With each rule infraction there was a consequence.

One of the commandant's rules carried the death penalty if anyone was to get caught. But I guess when a man gets pushed to his breaking point, he figures he's got nothing to lose."

Again I could see my grandfather reliving it all over. Since I had been interviewing him, I learned several things that would get him back on track without losing his train of thought. I would touch him lovingly on his knee or hand, and ask a question that would bring him back to where he had left off.

"What was the one rule that warranted the death penalty, Grandpa?" He blinked his eyes as if coming out of a trance. "What was the one rule?" He looked at me, and then answered.

"Trying to escape." He seemed far off as he continued almost in a whisper, "I've often wondered if I would have had the courage to attempt an escape if my leg hadn't been all busted up. I was so beaten, in body as well as spirit, I guess I'll never know the answer to that question."

"Tell me about the POWs in your camp, Grandpa. Were there any who tried to escape?"

"There were. I didn't know it then, but what I witnessed on my first day in camp, was the results of a failed attempt."

Taking in another long pause, he continued. "I can still see the commandant walking around with such arrogance, in his polished black-leather boots and trench coat with gloves to match, and a high peaked hat. He carried a riding crop under his arm when he walked. As he was delivering his rules, walking up and down the line inspecting us, the commandant would tap the crop in his left hand; and when he wanted to make a point, he would hit it against his boot. It made such a crack we would all flinch.

When he came up to me he stopped. 'Why is not this man standing on his own?' One of the guards told him I had a broken leg. 'Why was I given this man? Do I look like a nurse?' If he had used a monocle, he would have looked more like Colonel Klink in the television series Hogan's Heroes, but we knew this was one man we didn't want to cross. Nikki, did you know that some of the actors in Hogan's Heroes were real victims of the Nazis?"

"No, Grandpa, I had no idea." Anxious to get him back to the story, I asked, "What happened next?"

"After he made is grand debut to us, I was carried to the infirmary, and my leg was finally looked at."

"Tell me about the prisoner. Why was he led into the woods and then brought back to the camp?"

"We learned that when a prisoner was condemned to death, he was given two choices as to how he would die."

I interrupted, "One choice was by the firing squad. What was the other choice?"

He raised his eyebrows. "I have wondered that very question all my life. No one knew. As soon as a prisoner came back from the woods, he was shot. Only one prisoner who was condemned to death didn't come back."

"Who was he, Grandpa?"

"I don't know. He was assigned to another barrack in the camp. It was forbidden for any of us to go into a barrack that wasn't ours, but I think I recall his name being Jim, or Joe, something like that. We were stacked in our barracks like cords of wood. Since we were confined there ninety percent of the time, there weren't many opportunities to get to know the men in the other buildings.

"It was a month or so before the war ended when Jim and the others were brought in. Of course we didn't know the end was so near. We had our hopes up so many times, only to be let down, that we got to the point where we stopped thinking about it. I still remember that day watching the trucks pull into the camp with their new loads of POWs, the tailgate open and a guard, with the butt of his gun, landing a blow to the midsection of this guy. He stood out because even with that heavy blow, he stood as if to say, 'Is that all you got?' I knew from his uniform that he was a fighter pilot. He was in rough shape; it looked like the Nazis had really worked him over. Sometimes, when you're shot down, you can hide from the enemy long enough to be rescued, but more times than not, the Nazis or the civilians would find you before help could arrive. This guy looked like he had been able to evade them for some time, but we could tell by the way he carried himself that in spite of his weakened body, his spirit was strong.

"Before I was taken captive, I was in the best shape I had ever been in my life; we all were. The service will do that to you. I was five-feet-eleven, and built like a rock. I always said I was six foot, and when I was around the ladies, I would stretch it a little more and become six one." He smiled and gave me a wink, then continued with his story.

"Shortly after Jim was brought into the prison camp, he saw an opening to make an escape. He chose a night when the moon was just a sliver, with a heavy cloud cover. If you could get past the searchlights, I'm sure you wouldn't be able to see your hand in front of your face. Jim saw an opportunity, and he took it. He timed the searchlights just right, got past the fence, and made it into the woods. More than a week passed before the guards brought him back into camp. Late that same afternoon he, too, was led into the woods. He was the only one I ever knew of who didn't come back. I'll never forget the look on the commandant's face when he returned. He looked as though he had done something terribly wrong. I kept thinking if only that pilot had waited a little longer he would have known freedom. I'm sure the fear of becoming skin and bones, like the rest of us, must have been a factor in deciding to take the deadly risk of trying to escape."

Of all the interviews I had gathered from other vets and POWs, this was the first time I had ever heard the story of prisoners being given a choice as to how they were to die. I couldn't get it off my mind, no matter how hard I tried. One night as I was lying in bed, it came over me like a warm blanket in winter. I realized I could use my position as an investigative reporter to help give my grandfather closure.

The next morning, I told my editor the story about the POW in the prison camp, adding, simply, "I wonder what the other choice could have been." Then I added, "After all these years, wouldn't the answer to that question make a great story?" And I left it at that.

After a few days, Mr. Baker, my editor, called me into his office to tell me about a great idea he had. He wanted to know, if I would be willing to go to Germany on an assignment to find out how that one prisoner who never came back died. To make things even harder, the paper would only pay for two weeks. I looked at him and said, excitedly, "I think that's a great idea! I would love to, and I am sure I can do it in two weeks' time." Even though I had no idea what I was in for. I could hardly wait to tell my grandfather the great news. After making the necessary arrangements, I found myself on a plane, passport in hand, headed behind old enemy lines in Berlin, Germany.

THE **HUNT** FOR **COMMANDANT SCHMIDT**

TWENTY FOUR

Behind Enemy Lines

It's just after midnight and I should be exhausted, but the very word exhausted reminds me of the first time I met the Professor. It was after four long layovers when the plane finally touched down in Berlin, a little after eight in the morning. By the time I got through customs, it was almost noon. When I went to the baggage claim, my luggage was nowhere to be found. While waiting in another line to see what could be done, I struck up a conversation with two other women with the same plight. One lady advised me not to hold my breath waiting for my belongings; this wasn't the first time it had happened to her, and it took weeks to get the luggage back. The other woman said she was lucky to have gotten it back at all.

When I finished reporting my missing luggage, I was starving and tired and couldn't wait to get checked into my hotel. I had changed my plans and decided to go to the U.S. Consulate in the morning after I was refreshed. I had trouble hailing a cab but finally succeeded. The cabby looked as if he had been working all night; still he was friendly and helpful. I couldn't help but notice the relief on his face when I explained that the myriad of packages and suitcases surrounding me belonged to the family standing next to me. I handed him my one small carry-on and the address of the hotel. With renewed energy, he popped the trunk, tossed in my one and only belonging, and ushered me into the back seat. I couldn't wait to get some much needed rest.

As we were making our way through the crowded streets to the hotel, up ahead I saw the USA flags flying outside of an impressive building. Two sharp looking Marines in full-dress uniform were standing at their posts on each side of the doors. I knew it had to be the U.S. Consulate building. Making a quick mental note of the location, I hoped it would be close enough to the hotel that I could walk and save the cab fare in the morning. Right now all I could think about was a hot shower and a bed. Just then, a car pulled out from the curb in front of the Consulate building and left an open parking space. I had a strong impression to take the spot. I had learned, sometimes the hard way, to follow those promptings whenever I had them. Without stopping to think, I asked the driver to pull over. In a matter of minutes, I had retrieved my one bag and tipped the cabby.

As I was walking up the steps toward the Marines, two men were leaving the building. I overheard them talking about where to go for a quick bite to eat. Looking up at them, I smiled and said, "Good morning."

They smiled and returned my friendly greeting, but then one of them, looking at his watch, replied, "Good afternoon!"

Not missing a beat, I tapped my head and said, "Sorry, blonde moment! I guess I lost track of time. I just got in from the States, and it took forever to get through customs."

The other gentleman smiled and pointed to my small carry-on. "It looks like you're running away from home."

I couldn't help but laugh. I'm sure that's what it looked like. Lifting it up, I told them, "I'm afraid this is all I'll have for a while; my luggage decided to take another route. Say, I'll bet you know a place close by where a girl might get a quick bite to eat."

"As a matter of fact, we were just on our way out for lunch."

Now it was my turn to have a little fun with them. I looked at my watch. "I set my watch by the clock in the airport, and unless it was wrong I see that it's two o'clock. They must really be working you hard in there." Then in a slightly flirtatious tone I added, "Or are you in charge of this operation and so busy making sure things are done right that lunch is an afterthought?"

Both smiled, and one of them said, "A little of both, I'm afraid." They introduced themselves. "I'm Scott, and this is Wayne."

"I'm Nikki – Nikki Brown."

Scott smiled, "Well Nikki, Nikki Brown, you're welcome to join us."

"I'd love to, thanks." And with a friendly smile I said, "But I must insist we go dutch-treat." They couldn't help but smile too.

"Would you like to leave your carry-on here?" Scott motioned to a young Marine. "All bags have to go through security, so if you don't mind security going through it without you, you can leave it here. I can have it left in my office until we get back."

"That would be nice, thank you."

Scott handed a Marine my carry-on and instructed him to give it to his assistant Jeanette when the inspection was completed. Over lunch, I asked my new acquaintances questions about themselves—where they were from, how long they had been working at the Consulate building—things I thought would interest them. In return they asked me about myself and what brought me to Germany. I told them about how my grandfather was a POW and how any prisoner who tried to escape was sentenced to death, but was given a choice as to how he was to die, but no one knew what the other choice was.

Scott said, "I think I know just the man you need to talk to. He is a liaison from the German government who works with us. When we get back I'll introduce him to you. Everyone calls him the Professor, which he loves, because of his knowledge of history. Every conversation I have ever had with him has left me in utter amazement. Some even call him Doctor History. He speaks very good English and can even pronounce th properly. Most Germans can't. It's not one of their sounds; it sounds a lot like a z, or a hard t. The word that will sound like zat, or tat.

Wayne added, "Sometimes it sounds like a d, dat, and don't forget their pronunciation of w."

"That's right, their w sounds more like our v: will becomes vill. But you'll get use to it rather quickly." With Scott and Wayne as my escorts, we quickly went through security. I was led into a large room lined with desks and crowded with people. It reminded me of some of the newsrooms I'd been in. We weaved our way through busy workers, and I soon found myself shaking hands with the man who would save me weeks, if not months, in my quest. I guessed him to be in his late fifties, early sixties. Scott briefly outlined my purpose for coming, explaining that I had just arrived.

The Professor graciously motioned for me to have a seat. In a beautiful German accent he said, "You must be exhausted."

"I am, thank you."

"So how may I be of service?"

I took my time telling the story of my grandfather, Commandant Schmidt, and the prisoner of war, in hopes that even the smallest details would be helpful. As I talked, I noticed that quite a crowd of people had gathered. My lunch companions had pulled up chairs, and they, too, were listening intently. I described how the camp had been laid out, everything from the buildings the prisoners were housed in, to the color of the dirt. I even recounted which way the sun rose and set over the guard towers. When I ended my story about Commandant Schmidt, the firing squad, and the prisoner who had not come back, the Professor's eyes were wide with excitement. He said, almost in a whisper, "So it is true."

My heart raced. "You know of this story?"

"Ja! Ja! I mean, yes," he replied eagerly. "It's one of those stories we hear as children about the war. I thought it was a made-up story, but if your grandfather saw it happen first-hand, then it must be true."

By this time, it seemed that everyone who worked on that floor was crowding around. I asked, "What was in the woods?" All eyes were now on the Professor.

"No one knew." I heard a few moans from the eavesdropping crowd. The Professor continued, "As children, we made up endings, always trying to outdo each other. But I think I might know someone who can help. He's an old friend in charge of a building that holds many of our records. I don't know if he can, or even will want to help. There is a lot of red tape, even for him, but I'll see what I can do."

The Professor stood up, my cue to stand as well. "I hope he is as curious as I to find answers. It will take some time going through all the channels and red tape. Perhaps two, three—" I quickly interrupted, "Days?" He shook his head. Then, with hesitation in my voice, "Weeks?" He shook his head again. That just left months or years, and I definitely didn't want to hear either one of those. So with a hopeful smile I put my hand to my chest, and with a sigh of relief said, "Two or three minutes! Great! I'll wait." I could hear several people laughing at my comment, knowing that government never moves that quickly. I raised my eyebrows as if to say, "Please." He couldn't help but smile as he gave me his card.

"Give me a few days and I'll see what I can do, but do not get your hopes up."

"Too late!" I must have sounded like a school girl. I was so excited I gave him a kiss on the cheek. I quickly apologized. "I'm sorry. I don't know what came over me."

"That's quite all right, it's been a long time since I've been kissed by such a pretty girl. I can't wait to tell my wife."

Now red-faced, I thanked the Professor and told him how much I looked forward to hearing from him. I gave a quick wave to all in the room, thanked my lunch companions and headed for the hotel. I had always believed in the power of prayer, so that night I thanked God for the success I had experienced and asked for another door to open.

TWENTY FIVE

The General

When I awoke the next day, it was already noon. Jet lag had really taken its toll on me. I went to the front desk to see if by chance my luggage had arrived, but no luck. I asked where I might be able to buy a traveling backpack and a few clothes, preferably a secondhand store. It took the rest of the day for me to replace what I thought would be needed for the next two weeks. When I came back to the hotel, I again envisioned my luggage would be waiting for me, but still no luck. After dinner I did one last check with the clerk, who still had disappointing news for me. Then I went off to bed.

The next morning I came down around ten. As I reached the bottom of the stairs, I noticed Scott, from the day before, standing at the front desk. In my best Mae West impression I said, "Hello, stranger. Come here often?" I guess he had never watched old movies with his grandfather, because it went right over his head.

He turned and said, "I'm so glad I found you. You won't believe what happened. In all the years I've been here, I've never seen anything like it. I don't know what strings you and the Professor pulled, but it worked. After you left, the Professor immediately started to make phone calls. This morning one of his old friends returned his call. He wants you to meet with them for an early lunch today, but we need to leave right now."

I asked the man behind the counter, "Any word from the airline?" He shook his head. I took Scott's arm, turned him toward the front door, and said, "Lead the way."

As we pulled into the underground parking lot of the Consulate building, the Professor was just walking out of the elevator and said, "Your timing could not be better; I was hoping you would be able to join us. My friend is anxious to hear your story, and you tell it so much better than I ever could. He has a granddaughter about your age, and I know he would much rather hear it from a beautiful young lady than from an old man like me."

"There's nothing I'd like more. It would be my honor."

The driver took us to what must have been the most exquisite place around. It was breathtaking. I felt a little under–dressed, but I wasn't about to let it show.

The Professor introduced me to his good friend. As I shook his hand, I tried to repeat his name; I knew how important it was to pronounce someone's name correctly, especially a general's. But try as I might, I just could not get it right.

My embarrassment was obvious, so the Professor stepped in and said, "You can call him 'General.'"

The general smiled and in his heavy German accent put me at ease by reassuring me that I had come much closer than most Americans when it came to the correct pronunciation of his name. I smiled with gratitude and we sat down to order. I wasn't at all sure what the menu choices were, but I was certain about the prices. They were far more than my expense account allowed for, and I was looking for the price of a salad. I would tell them I wasn't that hungry, even though I was. I must not have hidden the expression on my face very well, because both gentlemen smiled, and the Professor turned to me and said, "This is my treat. Would it be all right if I ordered for you?"

With a sigh of relief I said, "Thank you," and the Professor placed the order with the waiter.

While we were waiting, I asked, "So how long have you known each other?" With that simple question they were off and running. I learned they had been childhood friends, what they did for fun, and the things they did as they grew up. I knew people don't care how much you know, until they know how much you care. And I really cared to know about them. Catching up with each other through the soup, salad and main courses, it wasn't until the coffee arrived when the general said, "Where are our manners? We have only been talking about ourselves."

I quickly said, "Oh, don't apologize. I've enjoyed every minute."

The general turned to his friend, the Professor. "You were right, she is very charming." Then turning back to me he added, "I understand you have quite a story; would you tell it to me?" I told the story in great detail, just as I had done the day before, ending with Commandant Schmidt and the POW who never returned. When I finished, the two men looked at each other. "You were right, my old friend. This is indeed a story worth pursuing. Perhaps we will find out which one of us as children came up with the closest ending."

Then the general asked me, "Nikki, my dear, would you accompany me to my office?"

"I would love to."

The Professor turned to us both and said, "Well, I wish I could go with you both to see what you find, but I have to get back to the Consulate." Reaching out, he clasped my hand with both of his; "I'm leaving you in good hands; and be sure to stop by to let me know what you find."

"I will. That's a promise."

Pointing his finger at me and smiling, he said, "I will hold you to it."

I thanked the Professor for lunch, and then the general and I drove to his office.

The building was beautiful, ornate, and guarded. Going through security was quite impressive, to say the least. I felt as though a red carpet was rolled out just for me. I let the general know how impressed and grateful I was. "Think nothing of it. It's not every day I get the honor to escort such a pretty young lady. This way, please." He led me to an elevator where two armed guards were posted next to the door. As we approached, the guards snapped to attention, clicking their heels together. The general had a special key to operate the elevator doors, and inside, there were only two buttons. One had a "Down" arrow and the other an "Up" arrow. He put his thumb on the down button, and a green fluorescent light scanned it.

The doors closed, and as the elevator went down I commented, "Just like in the movies."

He smiled and gave me a wink. His expression reminded me of my grandfather in earlier years. By the length of the drop, I guessed it to be about six stories down, with no stops in-between.

Before the doors opened the general said, "Nikki, do not get your hopes up, the name Schmidt is as common as . . ."

The general slowly pronounced "Smith or Jones in America. Being able to find the right Schmidt, that ran one of many hundreds of camps, is like, like . . ."

I helped him finish his sentence. "—Like looking for a needle in a haystack?"

"Ja. Danke schön. Like looking for a needle in haystack." When the doors opened, two men stood at attention, also clicking their heels to meet us. The general said something in German, and the men went into an at ease position. We both signed in and went through a door that led into a large room, where I saw more filing cabinets than I had ever seen in my life. "This is where we keep many of our records, most of which are no longer secret, but they still need to be preserved. They are scanned and put on a hard drive. They are low priority. That is why you see just a handful of people working down here. Some records, however, are still secret, and that is why you see armed guards."

As we turned the corner, we entered a small office. A gentleman sitting at his desk doing paper work sprang from his seat. I had no way of knowing what was said between the two of them, but I did hear my name. The man turned to me and nodded. I assumed it was an introduction, but for all I knew, he was being told how to dispose of my body. (I couldn't help but chuckle inside at that thought.) The general then turned to me and in English introduced me to him. "Nikki, this is Lieutenant Hans Zimmermann."

I nodded. "Pleased to meet you, Lieutenant."

The general translated for the Lieutenant, then motioned for everyone to sit. "Nikki, I am going to tell him everything you told me. If anyone can help, he's your man."

As the general related my story, I watched the attentive

lieutenant's eyes with anticipation. The story seemed to intrigue him. The general took a sheet of paper and drew a rough outline of the barracks and surrounding buildings and landscape. He asked me if his depiction was correct. I looked at it, smiled, and nodded. As Lieutenant Zimmermann and the general conversed, I recognized the name Commandant Schmidt several times, but that was about all that sounded familiar. Finally the general looked at me and said, "He thinks he can help." Lieutenant Zimmermann motioned for us to follow him. I didn't need an interpreter for that. I was right behind them.

We went deeper and deeper into a large room, turning on lights as we went. It was obvious that we were in an area that didn't get much use. The lieutenant eventually led us to a wooden filing cabinet that sat on a desk. It was about three feet high, four feet wide, and two feet deep. It had small drawers that could fit two-by-three cards. Lieutenant Zimmermann studied it for a minute and then pulled out a drawer. Moving his fingers quickly along the top of the cards, he stopped, wrote down some numbers and then put the drawer back in place.

Next, we went to another set of files, opened a drawer, and pulled out a microfiche film. I knew what it was, from some research I had done; a few libraries still used them. Going to the film reader, he placed the microfiche under the glass, turned the light on to the reader and began to talk. The general interpreted, "From the time of your grandfather's capture until the end of the war"—he held up three fingers—"there are only three possible compounds where he could have been. Two had a high turnover in commandants, which was common, and one did not."

I asked, "Why the high turnover?"

The general told me that the main job of the commandant was to make sure no one escaped. If anyone did, the punishment was quite severe. The commandant might simply be removed from his command and sent to the front line, or he might face a firing squad. Lieutenant Zimmerman continued and the general interpreted, "Hitler was very harsh with anyone that did not follow his orders. To have someone that was the same commandant for over three years, Lieutenant Zimmerman thinks that could have been only one compound."

I saw the lieutenant write something down, and we followed him back to his office. He went straight to his computer and entered what he had written on the paper. After a brief exchange with the general, he entered what must have been a pass code into the computer. Minutes later, Lieutenant Zimmerman had scribbled down the name of Schmidt and the town he was from, and handed the paper to me. In very slow and broken English, "This name of man you want—where he's from. Hope will help."

I couldn't believe my eyes, which were now filling with tears, and I could barely make out the name of the man who

That night in my room, I knelt to express my gratitude for the heavenly help I knew I had been given. Tomorrow would be another challenging day, and I knew I would need all the help I could get.

TWENTY SIX

A Ride Back in Time

The next morning, I found myself at the train station, ticket in hand, bound for a small town about three hundred miles away. Filled with nervous anticipation, I boarded the train. It was a beautiful train, nothing like the trains in the States. I soon made friends with the porter, who spoke very good English. I told him where I was going and asked about what time the train would get there. The look on his face made me wonder why what I said brought such a smile to his face.

"I'm afraid you will be waiting forever on this train," the porter said cheerfully.

I smiled back at him, "So I'm guessing I'm not staying on this train?"

"Sadly, no. This train is very prompt commuter train that goes to other big cities. You can set your watch by it. Your train, not so much. At next stop is where you transfer to another train that will take you where you need to go. It won't be as modern as mine, but it will get you there, with luck, in less than day."

I couldn't believe what I'd heard. "Less than a day? Why so long?"

"There are many halts—I mean stops—along the way. Some take longer than others. Sometimes the train will bypass stop all together, if there is no one getting on or off, or anything to drop off or pick up. That makes the trip much quicker, but is still long ride. When you get off, I would recommend you upgrade your ticket and get sleeper coach. Is not cheap, but you will find it worth every penny . . . or is it every cent?"

With a smile I told him, "Either word is correct."

He continued, "Also, when you get off, you will have time to do little shopping. There is small store very close to station where you will need to go get some things for your journey. I will draw you map."

"What kind of things would I need that I couldn't get on the train?"

"Everything! And I do mean everything, from food to anything personal." I must have had a puzzled look on my face. "You know, personal things, for the rest room."

"Really?"

He nodded and smiled. "Take my advice, and you'll do fine." The train slowed. "This is your stop." He quickly drew me a map to the store and wished me good luck.

I followed the porter's advice and went to the ticket booth to upgrade my ticket. The cost was equivalent to fifteen US dollars. When I checked my pockets, I found enough local currency to pay the fare, and hoped I had enough left to purchase the items on my shopping list. When I asked what time the train would be leaving, I couldn't get a definitive answer. The ticket agent guessed it would leave in an hour or so—at least I think that is what she said. Luckily, the little shop was close by, and it didn't take long to do the shopping, because as I was coming back to the station I heard the whistle of the train. Panic set in as I raced toward the platform. The porter was just picking up the step when he heard me call out. Reluctantly, he put it back down, and

I climbed on. I thanked him but got no reply. I had been warned that this train was more for cargo than passengers and that the next train to my destination wouldn't be leaving for another twenty-four hours.

As I looked around, I realized that the first porter hadn't been kidding when he told me this train wouldn't be as modern as his was. It was an old steam engine fueled by coal that left a big, black billowing cloud of smoke as it went down the tracks. The pathways through the cars were only wide enough for one person at a time to walk through. If another person came from the opposite direction, one of us would need to open a door to a cabin and step in, in order to make room for the others to pass. As I made my way to the cabin at the opposite end of the train, I passed by what must have been the dining car. The sight and smell of the food were not at all appetizing, and I was glad I had stopped at the store for a few supplies.

When I arrived at the sleeper car, I saw that each cabin slept four people, and that it really was meant just for sleeping. I found an empty seat next to a window and put my bags in the seat next to me. With my heart still beating rapidly, I looked out the window to see the countryside; and it was beautiful: rolling green hills one minute, and flat, spacious farmlands the next.

As the porter came down the aisle, I heard him say something I couldn't understand, but his words became obvious to me when I watched passengers hand him their tickets. He was nothing like the porter from the first train; this one wore a permanent scowl and practically ripped the tickets out of each passenger's hand. I watched him approach a young mother who held a little girl on her lap. The child looked to be about three years old and had a warm, infectious smile. Too bad the porter didn't catch it. He approached me, mumbling something in German as he extended his arm. I smiled and asked, "Ticket?" as I handed it to him, hoping for a smile in return. He grabbed it, punched it, and practically threw it back in my lap. I consoled myself by thinking, "If an adorable three-year-old couldn't get a smile out of him, I didn't stand a chance." But I had to try.

The train seemed to stop at every station and loading dock in Germany. Some delays were longer than others, but each felt like an eternity. Watching passengers get off and on, I wondered where they were going to or coming from, and what they did for a living.

The little girl I had noticed earlier wandered up and down the aisle, like a typical three-year-old looking for something to do. I didn't know that a commonly held belief in the German culture was that children should be seen and not heard. Her mother did her best to keep her occupied in their seat, but allowed her to get up from time to time. She appeared to be a conscientious mother, always keeping one eye on her daughter, and the other on the lookout for the porter. He had made it quite clear that the child was not to be walking in the aisle. I didn't speak the language, but I didn't need to. I very well understood the tone he had used earlier when he'd caught the little girl out of her seat.

In spite of the never-ending stops, I had become so enthralled with the scenery that I completely lost track of time. My growling stomach reminded me that I hadn't eaten since breakfast, nearly five hours earlier. I reached into the bag and pulled out a loaf of bread and some cheese. As I prepared the food, I looked up and saw the little girl staring at me. I caught the mother's eye and made a motion indicating that I would like to give her some food. The young mother smiled shyly and nodded her head. I placed two slices of bread and some cheese in the little girl's hand, who repaid me with an endearing smile, squealed with delight, and ran back to share the bounty with her mother. She leaned across the aisle toward me and said, "Thank you."

"You're welcome. You speak English?"

"Yes, a little."

I picked up my bags and moved closer so we could talk and share a meal together.

I introduced myself. "Hi, I'm Nikki."

"Hello, I'm June, and this is my daughter May."

I told her she was too modest; her cadence in the English language and German accent made me want to learn German.

June smiled and said, "Thank you."

"I love those names, but I have to admit you caught me off guard. Aren't those American names?"

"Yes, they are. When I was going to school, we were required to take an English class. To make it more fun we were given American names. I was given the name June, and my best friend was given May. For some reason those names stuck with us through the years of schooling. We were known as the springtime girls, May and June. May died two weeks before my daughter was born, and my husband and I decided to name our daughter after her."

"I can't get over how good your English is. I've noticed that a lot of people here speak English."

"Thank you. Mostly, it's the younger generation that speaks English, because it is taught more and more in schools. In many countries, English is the language business is conducted in. We don't want our children to be disadvantaged. My husband, Hans, speaks it very well, and he helps me. He says it also helps him learn as he teaches me. We live in the city, but I received word that my mother is ill, and I am going to see what I can do to help."

We visited and took turns entertaining little May. It was getting late, and the sun had been down for a while when I noticed that the rhythm of the train had lulled May to sleep. She slept peacefully in her mother's arms, and I couldn't help noticing that June's eyes were also heavy. "Do you have a ticket for a sleeper?"

"No, that ticket is too expensive. We should be stopping in the next few hours. We will be fine."

"I want you and May to take my bed."

"That won't be necessary."

"No, really, I insist."

"But the porter won't allow it."

I picked up their things and said, "You let me handle the porter. Follow me."

We were only a few feet away from the sleeper car when I came face to face with the porter on his rounds. June stiffened with fear and held May tightly against her chest. I gently touched her arm and said reassuringly, "It'll be all right." I smiled broadly and motioned to the porter. I used my ticket and with hand gestures explained that I was giving my bed to the young mother and her daughter. June braced herself for the argument that was sure to follow, but was met instead with an actual smile and nod from the porter. What June had not seen was the five Euros I slipped into his hand. It turned out I could speak the porter's language after all.

I turned to June and said, "Right this way." I led them to the sleeper coach. Three of the cots were already taken, leaving only a top bed available. June climbed onto it, and I lifted May up into her mother's arms.

"Thank you again, but I am worried that I might miss my stop."

"Don't worry about that. Tell me the name of your stop, and I'll be sure to let you know." June told me, and I was so happy to hear it was the same small town I was going to. Some might call it a coincidence, but I felt it was divine intervention. "Get some sleep, I'll be sure to wake you. That's my stop as well." I had a sense of peace and contentment as I watched June make her little girl comfortable in the cramped space and snuggled in next to her. A smile came across my face as I walked back to my seat and thought, "The springtime girls."

It was after two in the morning when the train came to a stop. We were the only ones to get off when I asked June, "Is someone picking you up?"

"No. You never know when the train comes in, so it's impossible to make arrangements. We'll walk; it's only a few miles. What about you? Where are you staying?"

"Now that's a good question. I have no idea. I really didn't know what to expect when I got here. Is there a hotel, or an inn of some kind where I can stay?"

"In this small town? I'm afraid not, but I do know a place where you can stay. You will stay with us."

"With no inn or hotel in town, I'm sure glad I met you. I hope it won't be any trouble for your mother."

"It's no trouble at all." June smiled and added, "This time

I'll talk to the porter, and my mother will be honored to have you. Get your things and follow me."

I graciously replied, "Thank you. Lucky for me you've got an 'in' with the porter. But wait, didn't you tell me your mother is ill? I don't want to be any trouble."

"It will be no trouble at all, not to worry."

As we walked down the dirt road, the only light in the small town was from the full moon. We took turns carrying May, and we passed the time making small talk. June's curiosity finally got the best of her, and she asked me, "What is it that brings you to my small town so far away from home?"

I willingly told her the story, and it made the long walk go by quickly. As we approached the front door, I had reached the part of the story where I had been given the name of the town where Commandant Schmidt had lived.

"The Schmidts? I know that family."

"You do?!"

"Yes, they still live here. In this small town, everyone knows everybody. I know his great-grandson. We went to school together, but I have never heard that story before. I knew that his great-grandfather was in the war, but that was about all. No one likes to talk about that time. Maybe in the morning my mother will know more." June opened the unlocked door.

"Your mother must have been expecting you, to leave her door unlocked."

June smiled and explained, "Our doors are always open. Please come in."

She lit a lamp and said, "I'll just let my mother know we're home, and then I'll show you to your room." She went to another lamp, lit it, and set it on the table so I wouldn't be left in the dark. Then June and her daughter went into an adjoining room. I could hear June's gentle attempt to wake her mother, as well as her mother's obvious joy when she realized that her girls were home. Moments later June came back into the room, a reassuring smile on her face. "Mother says 'welcome,' and she is honored to have you here. I'll show you to your room." It was a small room, but clean, and the bed felt so good after the long train ride and late night walk.

"Thank you so much. I don't know how I could ever repay you."

"You are welcome. It's the least I can do to repay your kindness. Get some rest, and we will talk in the morning."

In the morning, I woke to the smell of eggs cooking on the stove. I looked at my watch and couldn't believe how late it was. I must have been exhausted. Just then, the door opened and little May poked her head into the room. She smiled at me. I smiled back and said, "Well, good morning." May giggled and ran away. As I walked from the bedroom to the kitchen, I felt like I had walked back in time. I saw June standing over a small wood-burning stove.

"Good morning, June."

"Good morning, how did you sleep?"

"Like a rock."

With a puzzled look on June's face, she asked, "There were rocks in the bed?"

I laughed. "Sorry, that's an expression. It means that I slept very well. Thank you so much for letting me use your bed. It sure smells good in here."

"Mother raises chickens and sells the eggs and sometimes

the chickens to the market in town. Please sit down."

I sat, and together we had breakfast. While we ate, June filled me in about the locals, as well as the commandant I was looking for. The family June described was nothing like what I had pictured in my mind.

"After we clean up and my mother is settled, I'll take you to their home. It's only about four or five miles from here, and I can be your interpreter."

Everything had happened so fast I hadn't thought of needing an interpreter. "June, I can't begin to tell you how grateful I am for having met you."

June smiled, "I guess it was meant to be."

After everything was taken care of, I followed June out back, toward a large shed where the chickens were kept. Next to the shed was a fenced off area where I noticed a donkey. June led the small animal out and hooked it up to a primitive looking wagon her mother used to transport the eggs to the market. I had never seen one quite like it. We climbed up onto the wagon, and we were off.

TWENTY SEVEN

Face-to-Face

The dirt road was well worn from many comings and goings. As I was about to meet the man who had committed so many unimaginable atrocities against my grandfather and others, my mind was flooded with all kinds of emotions from the stories my grandfather and others had told me. I told myself over and over, "I'm Nikki Brown, a professional reporter. I can't let my emotions get in the way."

As we turned off the main road, I could see a home in front of us through the trees. Smoke came out of the chimney, which meant someone was home. As we walked up the steps, my heart began pounding so fast and loud I thought for sure June could hear it. June didn't knock, but called out a greeting. Before long, a woman—I guessed her to be in her late fifties, early sixties—answered the door. Warm greetings were exchanged, and I was introduced to Elsa, the daughter of the commandant.

June asked her, "How is your English?"

"Not good. Please come." She led us into the small home and asked, "Would you like tea?"

Before I could answer "No thank you," June replied, "Danke schön. Tea would be nice." She knew that accepting was the polite thing to do.

As we drank our tea, June proceeded to explain why I had made the long trip. To my surprise, a smile of excitement came to Elsa's face. She turned to me and said, "My father will be happy to see you. Finish please, tea." She excused herself to prepare her father for the visit. There was a small room off the eating area, divided by a curtain, which served as a door. Behind the curtain, I could hear the exchange of two distinct voices. I thought for sure that the father's tone would be harsh, but it wasn't. At least I assumed the male voice belonged to the commandant. The morning was mild and quite beautiful; but I was so nervous I found myself perspiring. I reached into my bag and pulled out a handkerchief to wipe my hands and forehead.

After ten or fifteen minutes, Elsa came through the curtain and said, "Father will see you now." I was about to meet the man who made my grandfather's life and so many others' a living hell. As we walked into the small room I noticed it was tidy and well lit, the day's sunlight coming through the window. The thin, elderly man sitting up in his bed looked like death had been knocking at his door for some time, but he was refusing to answer it. I knew he was a little older than my grandfather, but he looked to be ninety-five, if not a hundred.

His eyes, blinded by cataracts, were deeply sunken into their sockets. His skin was wrinkled and severely dehydrated, looking like sun-baked leather hanging from his frail arms, which rested on top of his bed covers. This was a man who looked like he had had a difficult life. Bristle-like hair protruded from his large ears, and bushy eyebrows to match.

I could see that his daughter Elsa had combed his hair and given him a fresh shave to receive his visitors. When we walked into the room, one of the floor boards creaked, and he raised his head, turning in our direction. I was surprised his hearing was still good. Most veterans I knew were hard of hearing from the damage caused by the loud explosions they had heard in the war. His countenance appeared to be dark, perhaps from a lifetime of guilt and remorse that had cankered his soul. I was also surprised to see a welcoming smile that revealed he was missing most of his teeth; he motioned excitedly with his arthritic hands for us to sit down in the chairs his daughter had brought in.

"Danke schön for coming," he greeted us in his limited English. Though I hadn't interviewed German veterans before, I knew as a rule that it took time for them to open up, normally months, sometimes years. I certainly didn't have that kind of time and neither did the old commandant. "Mr. Schmidt, my name is Nikki Brown. I'm from America and would like to hear from you your experience of the war. Are you up to it?" June interpreted. He paused, and then nodding his head said, "Ja, is time." I wanted to make sure I didn't miss a thing, so I checked my recorder to make sure it was working properly. When the commandant began to relate his story, I noticed an unexpected vitality. As the time wore on, however, his energy waned, though there remained an edge of excitement in his voice. I had come to Germany for one thing—to learn what the other choice was. I also hoped I might be able to find out why he treated his prisoners the way he did, but I knew that would be a delicate matter.

During the next few hours, with the help from my interpreters, June, and the commandant's daughter, my trip to Germany would become a success: I found out why he felt he had to do what he did and what the other choice was out in the woods. The prisoner had to go into a locked barn. I also learned what the commandant told each prisoner who tried to escape; they could give him one word that he would pass on to his family to remember them by. The commandant told me of all the single words he was given; Captain Hansen's word was one that haunted him and he tried to live by. When I asked what the one word was and what was inside the locked barn, the old commandant smiled. "You'll have to ask Captain James Hansen. He was the only man who decided to face his fears and go through those doors. I found out years later that he not only survived the barn, but became quite successful."

I couldn't believe it. Not only did I find out what the other choice was, but the name of the prisoner. I tried to get the old commandant to tell me what was inside, but he refused.

He just smiled and said, "You'll have to ask him. I'm sure he is still alive."

By this time the old man's voice was so weak and soft that June had to lean in close to hear him. The commandant took me by the hand and spoke with great effort. June continued to translate: "Please tell your grandfather and the others how sorry I am, and I beg for their forgiveness."

This old man before me was no longer evil reincarnate. With tears in my eyes, I told him, "I'll tell him and anyone else who will listen. Thank you for your time; and for sharing your story with me. I know my grandfather will be able to put his mind to rest, knowing what you have told me."

Elsa led us back to the main area of the home. She took me by the hand and told me how grateful she was that I had come, in spite of the great distance. "I knew Father had heavy heart. Now he can finish his days in peace."

"You're welcome," I told her. "And thank you for letting me come into your home. I'm sure your father's story will help heal many hearts."

The next day, June gave me a ride to the train station. She wanted to wait with me, but I knew it could be hours, so I insisted that she get back to her sick mother. I thanked her for all she had done for me, and I gave little May a kiss good-bye.

Before heading back to the States, I made one last stop at the consulate to keep my promise to the Professor and to thank those who had helped me. I let them know that with their help, I had solved the mystery, at least part one. Part two would require tracking down Captain Hansen. I assured them I would send each of them a copy of the article as soon as it was printed. And with that, I left Germany for the next plane home, without my luggage.

TWENTY EIGHT

Putting the Pieces Together

It's 3:00 a.m., and I really should be getting some sleep, but I'm wide awake. The day I returned home from Germany, it was about two o'clock in the afternoon when I walked up the steps to my grandfather's home. I took out my key and let myself in. I began walking through the house, calling his name. When I finally found him, I understood why he hadn't answered when I had called for him. He was sitting in his favorite chair, a blanket draped over his legs and his hearing aid on top of the end table. A book was open flat in his lap, and he was still wearing his reading glasses, sound asleep.

Grandpa's Favorite Chair
Photo by Bryan McClure Photography

I sat down in the chair next to him and held his hand. In a voice loud enough to wake him without startling him, I called out, "Grandpa." After a slight pause, I rubbed his hand and then repeated a little louder, "Grandpa!"

He was obviously disoriented when he awoke, but when he realized I was at his side his face lit up.

"Nikki, you're back. When did you get in?"

"Just now; I haven't even been home. I wanted you to be the first one to know."

"You found what you were looking for, didn't you?" He could tell by the look in my eyes.

"Yes, and so much more."

As his bushy eyebrows went up, he said, "Tell me all about your trip." I knew my grandfather was someone who loved to hear my stories in great detail, nothing spared. When I told him about the old train, he said he could feel the rhythm of the tracks beneath his feet. I also told him about the time I used the restroom and how grateful I was that the helpful porter had warned me to purchase my own toilet tissue. Grandpa especially enjoyed my telling the discovery of the train tracks when I lifted the lid on the commode.

He laughed. "That must have been quite an experience."

"Yes, but I think I'll leave that one out of my article. I don't think my editor will appreciate it as much as you did." I went on to tell him about the important events during the trip that culminated in unearthing the answer to the question he had wondered about for so many years. When I got to the point in the story where I had come face-to-face with his captor, I could see the anxiety on his face. "Are you all right? Can I get you anything?"

"I'm fine. Don't let me stop you. So you met the old coot,

did you?"

"I did." I took both of Grandpa's hands in mine and continued: "I found out why he was so strict and severe with his punishment." I paused while I waited for him to prepare himself. When he was ready, I continued. "He knew that if any of his prisoners escaped, it could mean his own execution. Grandpa, do you remember the movie we watched together a long time ago called The Bridge at Remagen?" He nodded his head. "Do you remember that Hitler ordered that bridge to be destroyed before the British and Americans could take control?"

"I remember."

"The man in charge of blowing up that bridge was a very good friend of Commandant Schmidt's father. They were so close while he was growing up that he thought he was an uncle. He could not destroy the bridge because he wasn't given the right amount of explosives. When Hitler found out his orders weren't carried out, the man Commandant Schmidt thought of as an uncle was executed. Commandant Schmidt was ordered to keep everyone in line and was told exactly how to do it.

"I met the commandant's daughter, Elsa. She told me the story of her father, which had been told to her by her mother. He hadn't been raised with any religion, but his mother and father had taught him to treat others with respect and kindness. This, however, was just the opposite of how he had been trained under Hitler's Army. After he was given the command of a POW camp, the power went to his head."

Grandpa Vince nodded. "Power has a way of doing that."

"After the war, Schmidt was angry with the world. He hated the British, the Americans, and anyone that was against Germany. He had been indoctrinated to believe that the Germans were the superior race, and they were meant to rule. He wanted nothing to do with his old life and took his anger to Berlin.

"The German economy was so bad after the war it was hard to find any kind of work. He met a woman a few years older than him, and they were married. The marriage didn't last long, with his anger and the nightmares that would wake him up in the middle of the night. They were more than his wife could take.

"It was about that time Schmidt received a letter from his mother telling him his father had been kicked by their horse, and it was quite serious. She told him that his father wanted to talk to him before he died. It was hard for him to go back to the place that reminded him of just how much he had changed, but he knew it was something he had to do.

"When Schmidt walked into his old home, his mother saw him and embraced him, and all his anger left him. He broke down and cried. When he saw his father, he knew there wasn't much time left. The horse had kicked him in the head, and the doctors had done all they could do to relieve the pressure building up. Through his pain, he explained to his son that it was Hitler who was to blame for what had happened to Germany, for all the promises and lies he had told the people. His father asked if he would take care of his mother and be the man he knew he could be. The son promised he would.

"Schmidt tried to let the anger go, but every now and then it would come to the surface, and he would lash out. Afterwards, he would remember the promise he made to his father and bury the anger again, hoping it would stay down. With the help of his childhood sweetheart, whom he married, the outbursts were fewer, but they never completely went away.

"Elsa told me she thought it was because he could never forgive himself. As she grew up, she could hear her father in the middle of the night calling out in terror, her mother calming him down, telling him it was only a dream."

Grandfather had tears in his eyes. I knew he could relate. When I was older, Grandma would tell me how much better Grandpa was at sleeping at night when he would share his stories with me. It was a way of getting it off his chest.

I looked at him. "Grandpa, Commandant Schmidt wanted me to ask you, and the others, if you could find it in your hearts to forgive him." I could feel Grandpa's body tighten as I held his arthritic hands.

He looked away and with some hesitancy said, "I'll have to give that one some thought." There was another long pause. "So did he tell you what was in the woods?"

"He did. When the commandant was a young boy he loved to read, mostly history. One day he came across a book about the crusades where he read about a sultan who ruled with an iron fist. The sultan would take a prisoner who was sentenced for death where he had a choice between the known and the unknown. The unknown was to choose between three doors. The fear of the unknown was too great, and all chose the known over the unknown. When Schmidt read about the choices and what was behind the doors, he couldn't believe it. When he became commandant he remembered the story about the crusades and implemented the same technique.

"The commandant would lead the prisoner into a clearing

where there was a tree with a large branch about ten feet off the ground. Behind it was to an old barn with locked doors. All the prisoners led into the woods thought the other choice was hanging. Only it wasn't. The other choice, to them, was much worse. That's why all but one chose the firing squad."

I told Grandpa what the other choice was that caused such great fear in the hearts of the prisoners: they had to go into that locked barn. Grandfather shook his head in disbelief.

"According to the commandant, a few men had decided against the firing squad to face the unknown, but at the last minute they all changed their minds. All but one, the one you saw just before the war ended."

Grandpa's eyes were wide with anticipation, and he was hanging on every word. "His name was James--- Captain James Hansen. He, too, like the others, was led up to the tree and was given the same two choices. He was given sixty seconds to decide, but he didn't need sixty seconds. He took two deep breaths and went forward to meet his fate."

"Nikki, what was inside the barn?"

"I don't know, Grandpa; the commandant was quite weak by that time, but he did say that there was definitely something inside. There was something else: the commandant would ask each prisoner at the beginning of their walk if they had just one word to give to their loved ones back home to remember them by, what it would be and he would do what he could to get it to them. Of all the prisoners, Captain Hansen's word was one he never forgot and he tried to live by."

"Nikki, what was the word?"

"I don't know, Grandpa. He wouldn't tell me. All he said

was that I'd have to ask Captain Hansen. He found out years later that he survived and was sure he would still be alive. He not only remembered the prisoner's name, but he had memorized his serial number as well. Sadly it had been too long ago and he could no longer remember it. The commandant had always hoped that one day someone would find him so he would learn more of what had happened to Captain Hansen, and I'm going to find out.

TWENTY NINE

The One Who Got Away

After I left my grandfather, I caught up on some much needed rest in my own bed, something I should be doing right now, but once I start something I have to finish it.

As I was saying, after catching up on some rest, I checked in with my editor. He wanted to run a series of the story starting the next day. He told me, "Never before have I heard of such a story; what would make it complete would be to find out what was in that barn." He asked if I thought I could track down Captain Hansen. I knew that a man with that much grit had to still be alive; if not, hopefully he had told his family what happened and I could get the story from them. I told him, "I'll need some time, but I'm sure I can do it."

"How much time do you think you'll need?" I thought for a moment. "Two weeks."

He looked at me. "I'll give you one. If you found the commandant in two weeks, you should be able to find the captain in one. This story is too good to sit on. But if you can find what was inside, it will be worth it." Then with a smile he added, "Now get out of here and get me that story."

I returned the smile and gave him a salute. "Yes, Sir!" As I turned to walk out I saw him shake his head and grin.

I used my resources at the Pentagon, and with the airman's name and serial number, I was able to access Hansen's records. The records showed that he had been shot down, and was thought to be dead. But without hard evidence, he was listed as MIA, missing in action. Just as Commandant Schmidt said, he had survived, now if only he's still alive.

The records also showed that the army found him four months after he escaped. To be more accurate, they didn't find him, he found them. One mid-afternoon, he walked onto an army base, where he discovered that the war was officially over. In his debriefing, Captain Hansen reported that he had wandered around for about four months, dodging enemy patrols, eating off the land, climbing a treacherous mountain, and making his way through the Black Forest of Germany. The file was void of details; it reported only vague generalities. I knew there was more to this story, and I was determined to find out exactly what it was. If there was more, the military files were not going to help; they were a dead-end, but I did find Captain Hansen's date of birth.

My next step was to go to the internet; and just my luck, I found over twenty with the name James Hansen. With the process of elimination and many phone calls, I was getting worried. Only two more to go. Dialing the phone, I crossed my fingers. On the third ring a woman answered the phone.

"Hello."

"Hello, is this Mrs. Hansen?"

"Yes, it is."

"Mrs. Hansen, my name is Nikki Brown. I'm doing a story on those who served in World War II; did your husband serve?"

"Yes, he did."

I became very excited; finally I was going to get the

answers to all my questions. "Mrs. Hansen, I don't know how to ask you this next question, but is he still alive and may I speak to him?"

In a soft voice she replied, "No honey, he passed away ten years ago." My heart sank. "I'm sorry to hear that. If it would be all right, could I ask you a few questions about your husband?"

"Of course my dear. I love talking about my husband, there are so many wonderful memories."

With my first question, I knew I had the wrong James Hansen. He wasn't a pilot and he wasn't a prisoner of war. I wasn't about to be rude and stop the interview, so for the next hour I got to know Mrs. Hansen as she reminisced. I thanked her for her time and for the wonderful stories.

I was down to my last James Hansen. If it wasn't him I didn't know what I was going to do. I said a little prayer and crossed my fingers. The next James Hansen was a successful man who had built a company from the ground up, doing business all around the world, but he had kept his private life very private. There were plenty of stories about what his company did and that his son was now the president of the company, but little else.

I did, however, find an old interview that had been shot in black and white film, about an hour long. It was obvious he had a great love for God, family and country. He had quite a knowledge of the Founding Fathers and the Constitution, along with the philosophers John Locke, Charles de Montesquieu, and Adam Smith, who helped shape the founders' thinking. The woman doing the interview asked how he had become so successful. He smiled, and politely said, "I've already told you. You just need to read between the lines."

Then he looked at the camera and said, "There's more, a lot more, but that's a family secret from the war. Perhaps one day I'll share that as well." I thought to myself, "Could he be talking about the barn? Did I discover a family secret? All the pieces of the puzzle fit; this is the James Hansen I've been looking for." I couldn't help but notice at that point in the interview, the woman became quite persistent, almost rude, pressing to know then, not, "one day." I could see that Mr. Hansen was not comfortable, as he graciously thanked her for the interview.

The only phone number I could find was to Mr. Hansen's corporate office. I made several calls, hoping to talk to the president of the company. He would be the vital link to more information, but I couldn't get past his secretary. I managed to get my editor to sign off on another quick research trip. Within twenty-four hours I was on a plane, headed to San Diego and the company headquarters of the private and somewhat elusive James Hansen.

THIRTY
Headquarters

The building was beautiful, all I had expected and more. I walked up to the building's directory. The company's mission statement was engraved at the heading of the directory, and below it was a list of various suites. Top billing was the Mr. James Hansen Jr. suite; of course it was on the top floor. Then something caught my eye. Some of the suites had funny names: Pulling Sticks Suite (Gym); Mommy, Daddy Suite (Day Care, Pass Code Needed); Map Room; and one suite that really had me do a double-take, Pondering Suite.

Although curious about the last suite on the list, I was on a mission to the top floor. The elevator doors opened, and I stepped out to an exquisite lobby. The wood trim lining the desks and archways had obviously been hand tooled by a skilled craftsman. Light streaming through the large windows created a shimmering design on the polished marble floors.

There she was, sitting behind her desk, an older lady with beautiful gray hair, styled in a fashion that suited her nicely. This was the woman who could determine the success or failure of my goal, namely, to speak with Mr. James Hansen Jr., the son of the man who had so bravely faced his fear of the unknown.

As I walked up to her desk, I noticed the plaque with

the woman's name and title. It looked to be Italian. Not at all sure how to pronounce her last name, I was tempted to use only her first, but then I thought she might find me presumptuous. Besides, I knew that it's human nature for people to like hearing their own names, and I wanted to get it right. If it's a hard name to pronounce and a stranger gets it right, it's like music to their ears and sure to win me some points. And I knew I needed all the points I could get with this one.

"Good morning. Are you Louise Rinomato?" I said it with a slight roll of the "R." I was worried I might have said it incorrectly, but judging from the smile on Louise's face, I was sure I had nailed it. Or she could have been laughing inside because it wasn't even close. Either way, she smiled.

"May I help you?"

"I surely hope so. I don't have an appointment, but I had to meet you, and Mr. Hansen. I'm Nikki." But before I could finish with my last name, Louise interrupted me, without a smile.

"Nikki Brown? The same Nikki Brown from the newspaper who wants to interview Mr. Hansen?"

I kept my smile and said, "Why, yes, I'm impressed that you know me by just my first name."

"Well, I should. I recognized your voice from all of your phone calls. You are the most persistent young lady I think I have ever met. I can understand why you would want to meet Mr. Hansen, but you said you also wanted to meet me as well. Why on earth would you want to meet me?" Louise asked as she leaned back in her chair, arms folded. I leaned forward, speaking softly, as if we were in a room full of people, and I wanted only her to hear. This caused Louise to do likewise. As Louise leaned forward, she unfolded her arms.

"I talk to a lot of personal assistants, secretaries, and even bodyguards, but never have I come up against one as formidable as you. I just had to meet you."

Returning to my normal speaking voice and leaning back, I continued, "I surely hope Mr. Hansen appreciates you, keeping him protected from pesky reporters like me."

With that, Louise gave a slight smile. "He does, I assure you, just as his father did before him. Not only am I his personal assistant, but one could say I'm also his bodyguard, and he pays me quite well to protect him from reporters. And that, Miss Brown, means you." Louise said, pointing her finger at me.

I knew I had just one shot with this one. "I understand. The last thing I want is for you to upset your boss in any way." I pointed to a note pad on her desk and asked, "May I?" Louise handed me the note pad. I took out a pen and wrote.

Mr. Hansen,

My name is Nikki Brown. I met your father's captor from the war, Commandant Schmidt, and I have a message from him.

I found out your father was the only one who chose to face whatever was in the locked barn. I'd like to talk to you about his escape and the family secret.

Thank you for your time.

Sincerely,
Nikki Brown

I tore off the paper from the pad, folded it in half and handed the pad and paper back to Louise. "If you would be so kind, the next time you see Mr. Hansen, could you give this to him? If he still doesn't want to see me, then I'll leave and never bother you again." With a smile I said, "So you see, it's really a win-win situation; I'll sit over there out of your way." Without waiting for a reply, I thanked her and walked over to the chair, sat down, and picked up a magazine.

I was hoping, based on the time, that Mr. Hansen was in his office preparing for the day, and sooner or later he would be calling Louise in. Twenty-two minutes later, I heard his voice over the intercom.

"Louise, could you come in here please?"

She picked up her pad and pen, along with the note I had given her, and went into his office. Louise was gone for what felt like an eternity, but it was less than five minutes when she opened the door. With a smile on her face, she said, "Your persistence has paid off, Miss Brown. Mr. Hansen would like to see you." Louise held the door open.

As I walked in I made sure to tell her "Thank you."

Louise gave a warm smile, "You're welcome."

Mr. Hansen came around his desk, my note in hand, greeted me and welcomed me in.

"Young lady, in all my years I believe you're the first reporter to ever get past my secretary. For that I must congratulate you. If what you say in your note is true, I will personally introduce you to my father. Please have a seat."

"Thank you." As I sat down I noticed war memorabilia on the walls, and a small model airplane about six inches long on the desk. It sat atop a pedestal, which allowed it to sit at a forty-five-degree banked turn. As Mr. Hansen walked around his desk to sit down, I pointed to it. "The P-51 Mustang. Is that the plane your father flew when he was shot down?"

His eyes widened a bit. "As a matter of fact it is, but then, that is no family secret. You said you met my father's captor. Tell me about him."

I quickly told him about my grandfather, the quest, and how I came to meet the commandant face-to-face, and how he told me about the locked barn. I explained why he felt he had to do what he did, and how he had longed for forgiveness from those to whom he had done so much wrong. Pausing, I thought I could see that Mr. Hansen's eyes were tearing up.

He cleared his throat and asked, "You mentioned in your note that you know about the locked barn and the family secret. Tell me what you think you know."

"I know the commandant would give the prisoner at the start of their long walk into the woods, time to think about what one word they would like for their family to remember them by. The commandant told me of all the words he had been given, your father's was one that haunted him and he tried to live by. Mr. Hansen, he wouldn't tell me what the one word was. He said I'd have to ask your father. Sir, could you please tell me what the one word was?"

Smiling, shaking his head, "Go on."

I told the story the way I imagined it might have been for his father to be locked inside that barn. "What I would like to know, Mr. Hansen, is what really happened. How did your father escape? What went through his mind as he made his way through Germany? As you can tell, I have my own ideas about what may have occurred, but sometimes my imagination can get the better of me, and I want to get it right. Can you please tell me what really happened?"

Mr. Hansen then gave me a rather strange smile, as if to say, "You really have no idea." He pressed the intercom and said, "Louise, would you please cancel all my appointments for today. Thank you." Then he picked up the phone, and while he was dialing said, "I can do one better than that." After a few seconds, Mr. Hansen spoke into the phone. "Dad, I'm coming over for lunch, and I'm bringing a guest, someone you've been waiting to meet for a long time." As he hung up the phone, he asked, "Would you care to join me for lunch?"

As we walked toward the elevator, Mr. Hansen said, "You may have found out the other choice my father was faced with, but that's not the family secret. I'll leave that to my father to tell you if he is so inclined."

As the elevator doors opened, I had to ask, "When I entered the building, I read on the directory, 'Pondering Suite.' May I ask what that is?"

Mr. Hansen chuckled. "We've had a lot of fun with that one over the years." He looked at his watch. "We have plenty of time. Let me show you around." The elevator doors closed, and he pressed the button for three floor levels down.

"What I'm going to show you today is a fraction of what my father learned as an escapee in Germany. If he feels you're the one to tell his story, he'll share in more detail later.

"The 'Pondering Suite' is where someone can go to relax and think things over, to ponder; hence the name 'Pondering Suite.' It's a technique my father was taught when he was in Germany by a very dear friend who helped him escape. Whenever my father had a crucial matter to think about, he would always say, 'I'll have to ponder about that.' So we made him the 'Pondering Suite.'"

The elevator doors opened, and we walked down the hall. On the door to the right was a plaque that read, "Pondering Suite," which included a sliding panel that could be changed to read "Occupied." Mr. Hansen invited me to check it out. I opened the door; the room was no bigger than a large broom closet. The room was dimly lit and furnished with nothing more than a small couch. I turned to see Mr. Hansen smiling, "Not what you were expecting?"

"Not really."

"It used to be a janitor's closet, but as you can see, there is just enough room for one to lie down and relax." Mr. Hansen showed me a panel with all kinds of sound effects. "My favorite is the sounds of a mountain stream. I can hear the breeze blowing through the trees, the crickets and other sounds of the night forest. Dad has a hard time picking a favorite, but he leans toward the sound effects of the ocean. Maybe it's because it reminds him of his youth when he surfed.

"We meant the 'Pondering Suite' to be a joke, but Dad got such a kick out of it, he insisted it stay and made sure the name went on the directory." Mr. Hansen smiled. "Probably just so a nosey reporter would ask about it one day."

"I could get used to a room like this."

As we walked down the hall, Mr. Hansen said, "The next room is the 'Map Room.' Other companies would call it a 'Conference Room.' Dad has a saying, 'If you want to get someplace you've never been, get a map, or find someone who has been there to show you the way. Just make sure you have the right map or guide.' Hence the name 'Map Room.'"

"I like that. Can I use it in my article?"

"It's yours. After all, my father wasn't the one who came up with it."

"Let me guess, a friend in Germany." He just smiled. The tour took about an hour; there was a lot to that building. The last place we went to was the "Pulling Sticks Suite," aka the gym. As I entered, I saw mostly treadmills with a few men and women using them and a variety of exercise equipment. Mr. Hansen said, "You should see this place during the lunch break—standing room only." I noticed a mural on the wall of two soldiers sitting down facing each other, feet together, holding onto a stick and a rifle by their side.

Pulling Sticks
Artist Rendition

"That's a beautiful mural, but I don't understand it."

Mr. Hansen looked at it and explained. "It's a test of strength. The stronger of two men will pull the other man up off the ground. It's a game called 'Pulling Sticks,' the Indians taught it to the settlers in the 1600s, and it's a game our family loves to play." I pointed to the mural; "I'm guessing the one in the flight jacket is your father and the other is another friend."

With a sly smile he said, "You catch on fast. Let's continue. We've found that a short workout helps when a person is wound too tightly or has a lot on their mind. Kind of like the pondering room. A little physical exercise gets the endorphins flowing and the creative juices going. What company couldn't benefit from that?"

"Is what you told me today part of the family secret?"

Smiling, Mr. Hansen looked at his watch. "That completes the tour. We best be going. We have a bit of a drive." He heard me; it was obvious if I was going to be told, he wasn't going to be the one to tell me.

THIRTY ONE

At Last

Going to the corporate office and meeting Mr. Hansen Jr. happened a little over a month ago. As we drove up the hillside, I remember being nervous and excited. I was going to meet Captain James Hansen. I could see that all the homes were big and beautiful. One at the top especially stood out. Not only was it the largest, but I could see that it had the best view. After we turned off the main road, we passed through a security gate and drove up a long driveway. I was not surprised to discover that we were headed to the sprawling home I had noticed at the top of the hillside. Mr. Hansen pointed to the right of the large home where there appeared to be a guest house. "When my parents first bought the land, they built that home. The Carters live there now. They are my parents' housekeepers. The large home was built in stages. As we grew, so did the house."

Looking at it, I observed, "It looks like it was built all at the same time."

"Dad had it designed with that in mind."

"Why in stages? Why not build it all at the same time?"

"Dad knows the difference between a want and a need, so the outside was built first, and as we needed the rooms inside, then and only then did that room get finished. Dad was training himself to withhold instant gratification. Growing up, whenever we saw something we wanted and asked for, Dad would say, 'I'll take care of the needs, you know what you need to do to take care of the wants.' We soon learned not to ask for wants. Christmas and birthdays were the exception, and it had to be within reason."

We walked up the steps, and Mr. Hansen rang the doorbell. "We could walk in, but there's someone I'd like you to meet."

The door opened, and we were greeted with an enthusiastic "Master Jimmy! Good to see you!" The man was elderly, but full of life.

With a hug and a couple of hardy pats on the back, he said, "Good to see you too, Alfred!" Mr. Hansen turned to me and with one arm around Alfred said, "Nikki Brown, I'd like you to meet Alfred. He and his wife Brianna live in the guest house." He then added, "Alfred isn't his real name. It's Robbie. Alfred was something I started as a kid after reading Batman comic strips. For some reason it just stuck."

"It's a pleasure to meet you, Miss Brown."

I offered my hand, "It's a pleasure to meet you, Alfred."

"She has quite a story to tell Dad. Where is he?"

"He's in the study." Then turning toward me, Alfred continued, "I must say, he is rather intrigued about you, my dear."

"Thank you, Alfred. No need to announce us. I'll show Miss Brown the way."

As we went through the entry and walked past the living room towards the study, I was breathless. The room had superb marble flooring, Victorian furniture, a grand piano that matched the time period, and an ornate ceiling. "What a beautiful piano."

"Thank you. You should hear my father play. He's really

quite proficient. He also plays an old Stradivarius violin that was given to him by a dear friend from the war."

"Your father sure has a lot of friends from the war."

"Four, to be precise. Each one taught him lessons and principles as a foundation to build on."

The room was magnificent, enhanced by a 180-degree panoramic view of the manicured backyard that looked over the ocean. I couldn't keep from commenting, "Mr. Hansen, I have to tell you, when we came up the driveway, I knew it would be beautiful inside, but I had no idea."

"Yes, it is quite a view." We stood admiring its scrutiny . . . the silence was broken when Jimmy said, "One of the lessons and principles my father was taught was how to have a good work ethic, which was passed down to us, along with giving back to the community. We don't share that with others; we keep private things private."

Confused, I asked, "Mr. Hansen, I don't understand. You know I'm a reporter, trying to get a story on your father, and yet you're telling me all this. I'm grateful, don't get me wrong." Mr. Hansen raised his hand to stop me.

"It will all make sense soon, and please call me Jimmy. Mr. Hansen is my father, whom you're about to meet."

Jimmy led me down the hall, went to two sliding doors, gave three quick knocks, then slid open the doors to the most impressive study I had ever seen. This room was on the opposite side of the living room and also had a large window, but an entirely different view of the mountainside. The other walls were filled with hand carved bookshelves from the floor to a fourteen-foot ceiling, and a rolling ladder gave access to any book.

"Jimmy, my boy, good to see you." I was expecting an

elderly looking man, but he looked more like an older brother.

"Good to see you, Dad." As they walked toward each other, I expected a handshake, but instead a warm embrace with two slaps on the back. I couldn't help but think, "This is like my family, who love to hug." I had a preconceived notion that all wealthy people were a little stuffy and cold.

"Where's Mom? I'd like her to meet Miss Brown as well."

"Her sister Joyce called last night, and she needs her help. She shouldn't be gone for more than a month. She left just before you called."

Then Jimmy turned toward me and said, "Dad, I'd like to introduce you to Nikki Brown. She has come a long way to ask you a question. Nikki, this is my father, James Hansen."

I extended my hand to shake his. Taking my hand, with a warm smile he said, "Well, Miss Brown, what is it you would like to ask me?"

"Mr. Hansen, I'd like to know what the one word was you gave Commandant Schmidt and what was going through your mind when he left you alone in that barn to die?" He looked at his son, and they both smiled. Jimmy nodded. Catching me completely off guard, Mr. Hansen gave me a big hug, and then held me at arm's length by my shoulders as if to get a better look at me.

"Nikki, my dear, I have been praying for this day for a long time. I was beginning to wonder if it would ever come. Please have a seat." He led me to two leather chairs in front of the desk and invited me to sit. As he walked around his desk, he asked, "Can I offer you anything to drink?"

"I'm fine, thank you."

"So Nikki, tell me, how on earth you came to know about

Commandant Schmidt and the choice? And don't leave anything out. Lunch won't be ready for a while, and I want to hear everything."

"I'm not sure where to begin."

"How about at the beginning."

I told him about my grandfather and how as a little girl I loved his stories. I told of his days as a prisoner of war and how he had seen a prisoner leave the camp with the commandant under guard, but the prisoner never returned. I told him about my experiences in Germany and how I had come to meet his captor, Commandant Schmidt. I was somewhat hesitant to tell him that the commandant hoped to be forgiven, because of my grandfather's reaction, but I ultimately told him.

Mr. Hansen sat back in his chair. "I let go of that anger a long time ago. I found that anger and hatred can eat at you like a cancer; it can grow until it consumes our whole being. Anger is among the list of the seven deadly sins, along with greed, laziness, pride, lust, envy and gluttony. I'm not perfect by any means; I still have to be just as careful as the next guy not to allow them to find a place in my heart. But some traits I've come close to mastering, and some I still have to work on. In my many years of experience, those deadly sins all lead to tragedy and destroy lives, yet anger especially creates walls that trap us in and others out. I choose love instead.

"From the way you described the commandant, it sounds like he's tortured himself most of his life. That's too bad; I would like to tell him myself that I have forgiven him, but perhaps it will be in the next life."

I told Mr. Hansen, "Not only did he remember your

name, but your serial number as well. He memorized it, hoping that one day he could put it to good use. With his information, you weren't hard to find. The hardest part was getting past Louise Rinomato." Both Mr. Hansen and Jimmy laughed at that remark.

"Did you know you were the only POW who didn't pick the firing squad? The commandant was so frightened that he would be put to death for giving you a chance to escape, he never told anyone, except his family, and he swore them to secrecy. Mr. Hansen, I can understand why he didn't dare say anything, but why didn't you?"

He leaned back in his chair and clasped his fingers. Putting them under his chin, he thought for a moment, then said, "For the last ten months, I've been more nervous than a long-tailed cat in a room full of rocking chairs."

I put my hand up to my face to cover my smile.

"A very good friend of mine told that one to me. I'm guessing you've never heard that expression before?"

"I haven't, but for a moment I thought I was sitting in front of my grandfather."

"Sounds like the kind of man I'd like to meet."

"You two would definitely get along, or should I say, you're like two peas in a pod."

Mr. Hansen chuckled. "As I was saying, I've been going through my journals trying to compile them and write my life story." He reached into his pocket and pulled out a notebook. "See this? I carry this with me during the day. When I think of or hear something that I feel is important, I make a quick note. Then before I go to bed, I write the thought or idea in more detail in my journal." He reached into the drawer, then placed a journal on the desk. He looked at

Jimmy, who then pulled out a notebook from his pocket. "Nikki, you can bet that your name will be written in two journals tonight."

Mr. Hansen held the book so I could see the binding. "When one journal is filled, I store it on the bookshelf behind me and start a fresh one." My eyes went to the bookcase above his head. One of the shelves was lined with books like the one he was holding. It looked as if there was room for about five more books before he would have to start a new shelf.

"As you can imagine, going through all those journals will be quite a task. I'll need someone to help me. My journals are random thoughts mixed with what I think are pearls of wisdom; at least I'd like to think so.

"Nikki, I have a proposition for you. If you will come and work for me and help me with the task of compiling these journals for my biography, I'll tell you what really happened in that barn so you can finish your article, and complete your obligation to your editor. I'll have my legal team contact your editor to make the necessary arrangements for the time I'll need. Now don't worry. They'll be more than compensated for your absence. But I'll only tell you what happened when you get back. Your newspaper earned and deserves the story. But the story after the story is mine, and I'll decide who deserves that.

"These first four journals contain the details of everything that happened to me after the commandant slammed shut the barn door. Those experiences in Germany gave me the groundwork of what I needed to know to be successful in life. They are why I have led the life I have. I would like you to tell those stories, to help others get through the trials they may be going through. I will tell you this: I believe there are two kinds of fear. One is good, it keeps us safe, and the other keeps us from being great. I learned that fear can be an opportunity for growth. The E, in F.E.A.R. can have several meanings. For example, False Evidence Appearing Real. With no, or false evidence, we can work ourselves into a frenzy. I'll bet that happened to you on your first phone call for an interview"

"I'll never forget it. It took me hours to get up the courage to make that phone call, and I did work myself up for nothing."

James smiled. "Sometimes the E in F.E.A,R, stands for environment. You think everyone around you is judging your every move. I'll tell you a little secret—for the most part, everyone is wondering what everyone is thinking about them. Nikki, I can tell you this, you'll have friends and family tell you, you can't do that, it'll never work, you're just wasting your time. Yes, and as you become more and more successful, some of those friends and even family will want you to fail; recognize it when it happens and get new friends. Too bad you can't get new family." He smiled. "Nikki, my dear, sometimes fear is real and you need to take action. I believe God gave us the ability to know when it's real and when it's not.

"So why have I waited so long to tell my story? I explain that on the last page of the fourth journal, and I would like for you, young lady, to tell that story. I'm willing to triple whatever it is you're making now. You won't have to worry about relocation details. I'll take care of everything. There are plenty of rooms to choose from here, and I think you'll find the accommodations quite comfortable. A car will be provided and an expense account set up—whatever you need to complete this task in less than six months, all you have to do is ask. You may question why the time limit? For me the clock is ticking. The doctors say I have anywhere from six months to a year left."

I was shocked. "But you look so healthy."

He smiled. "Thank you. I have more good days than bad, but I don't know how much longer that is going to last. We all meet our Maker sooner or later. I just hope I can return home with honor. After I'm gone, you can publish the book, and for your devotion I will arrange for you to receive the royalties. I know this is a lot to think about, but I need to know your answer. I'll give you a minute to think it over."

I learned Mr. Hansen knew from experience that a self-motivated leader could make difficult decisions quickly. As the three of us sat in silence, he watched my eyes rapidly moving back and forth over the books. He said it was like watching a ticker tape machine processing everything in my brain. I knew it meant leaving my family and friends, and stepping out of my comfort zone. In spite of the many factors I had to consider, I felt an overwhelming peace and calm come over me, and I knew it was the right thing to do.

I looked him in the eye and said, "Mr. Hansen, I'd be honored to take on this task with you."

He looked at his watch and smiled. "Less than thirty seconds, not bad. If you're going to work for me, you can call me James. Mr. Hansen was my father. I don't know about you, but I'm hungry. Let's eat."

After lunch we returned to the study. I asked, "Mr. Hansen—" but I stopped suddenly at his changed expression—a cocked eyebrow and stern smile. I knew immediately what I had done wrong and quickly corrected myself, "I'm sorry—James."

James smiled. "That's better."

"Forgive me for asking, James, but I don't' understand why you haven't shared your story with the rest of the world? Your story of how you faced your fears could have helped so many others. Why didn't you publish it long ago?"

"There are plenty of books already written about how to face your fears and improve yourself." He leaned in toward me and whispered, "The secret is, when you find wisdom in a book that resonates with you, read it over and over again, not just once. Study it! Make it part of your life! Apply it! Whether it's the scriptures or some other book like Og Mandino's Greatest Salesman in the World. If it's a book you really enjoy, it'll be like getting re-acquainted with an old friend. Each time you read the book, you'll find something new that applies to your life at that time. It'll be like a whole new book each time you read it, not to mention that most books are now on audio, so you can turn your car into a rolling university. I've learned leaders are readers."

"Forgive me, James, but that really doesn't answer my question."

James chuckled, "You're right. My apologies; sometimes when I say something I think of something else and wander off into the bushes."

James tried again. "There are two reasons why I have waited so long to tell my story. One I'll share with you now and the other when you come back. One of the reasons comes from a lesson I learned from George Washington." James went to his bookshelf, took down a book, and sat back down. It was quite a thick book. When he opened it, I could read the cover: The Real George Washington. It had obviously been read many times, because when he opened it, some of the pages fell out. James turned to a page toward the back and spoke. "When George Washington was alive, a good doctor friend of his wanted to write his biography, but Washington made it quite clear about his feelings on the matter in a letter:

> "'I will frankly declare to you, my dear Doctor, that any memoirs of my life, distinct and unconnected with general history of the war, would rather hurt my feelings than tickle my pride whilst I live. I had rather glide gently down the stream of life, leaving it to posterity to think and say what they please of me, than by any act of mine to have vanity or ostentation imputed to me. I do not think vanity is a trait of my character.'"★

James closed the book. "Nikki, I knew if I allowed someone to write a book about what I went through in Germany, people would have focused more on me and not on what I learned from the experience. There are two kinds of fame. One that comes from doing good, and the other is of course the opposite. I've seen what both kinds of fame can do to most people, and I've tried very hard to show my family, by example, to do good and not to let it be known.

"My wife, Karen, and I have set up a number of charities anonymously. They were set up so that others, who feel so inclined, can donate and receive the blessings that come from giving. You see, I truly feel that when we contribute with a giving heart, and without any fanfare, we receive blessings."

★ The Real George Washington, p.451. Andre M. Allison, Jay A. Parry, and W. Cleon Skousen.

I said, "Sounds like the Sermon on the Mount, not letting your left hand know what the right hand is doing."

James smiled, "It is. I am, however, human and must admit I would like my name to carry on forever, to be part of a legacy. There's a good chance the last name of Hansen will fall off the genealogical tree. So after I'm gone, then, and only then, will my name go on the charities that Karen and I have set up. My youngest son Ryan has his own law firm. Ryan has been named the executor of my estate, and his siblings are trustees. They will see to it that all of the charities are well funded.

"I'm grateful for the family I have been blessed with. I have two sons and two daughters. Among them, they have blessed my wife and me with fourteen grandchildren, and eight great-grandchildren, all of whom are girls with the exception of two boys, Sean and Raymond, who will carry on the Hansen name. Sean is Ryan and Jennifer's son. Sean and his wife have three girls, and they tell us that their family is complete." James chuckled. "That's what Jimmy here said, but he and his wife Reese had a surprise in later years and had Raymond, our youngest grandson, and he isn't married; evidently the right one hasn't come along yet. So you see the odds are not in my favor for a continuation of the Hansen family name."

I said, "I think I understand your first reason for 'flying under the radar,' so to speak. You're a private person and for noble reasons wanted to stay out of the limelight. But what was the second reason?"

James smiled, pointing his finger at me. "You're not going to trick me into telling you the second reason. You'll have to wait until you get back."

"You can't blame a girl for trying," I told him.

One corner of his mouth went up. "If you didn't try, you wouldn't be the girl I'm looking for. Tell you what, I'll tell you the first part of what happened to me when I tried to escape." He sat back in his chair. "When I made my break for it, I tried to talk two others into coming with me, but they wanted no part of it. They did say that they would do all they could to cover for me at roll call. They were able to give me a two-day head start.

"I traveled mostly at night following the sounds of the big guns. I knew that's where the front line was. If I could get close enough I would hide myself, letting the Germans fall back as the allies drove them past me. Then when the allies came towards me, all I had to do is come out of hiding and be rescued. At least that was the plan. I would rest by the day, getting what little sleep I could. When I wasn't resting I would look for anything to eat. I could see plenty of small wild game, but no luck in catching any of it. With what little food I was fed in the prison camp and nothing while on the run, I was running out of energy and I was afraid of getting caught before I could put my plan into action.

"I thought with my going through water, backtracking, and doing everything I could think of to disguise my scent I would throw off the dogs. Those dogs were so well trained I don't think I slowed them down for more than a minute. When the dogs caught up to me, they bit me so hard in the leg and arm it was a miracle I was able to climb a tree to get out of their reach. The guards finally caught up and called off the dogs. They were so angry for all the work I put them through, when I climbed down one took the butt of his rifle and landed it right to my head. I hit the ground like a sack of potatoes. After a few swift kicks to the ribs, they finally stopped and marched me back to camp."

James smiled. "When you return, I'll tell you what happened next and it will all be made clear. I do know that the time has come for my story to be told. Perhaps it will help others, and inspire them to face whatever it is that's holding them back and keeping them from reaching their full potential. So report back to your editor, let your family know about your next adventure, and hurry back. When does your flight leave?"

"I don't have one. I had no idea how long it would take me to get past Louise, to get to you!"

James laughed, then turned to Jimmy and gave him a nod. Jimmy knew what his father wanted him to do, and he immediately got on the phone. I overheard him say, "Have the jet fueled and ready to go." As he was making the arrangements, James asked me, "Today is Wednesday; can you be back here in two weeks, ready to go?"

Reviewing in mind everything I would have to do, I didn't want to disappoint him. I started to say, "I'm sure—"

Jimmy cut in, "Dad, I'm sure Nikki will need at least a month to put things in order."

"You're right; please forgive me, in my excitement I forgot my manners. How much time do you think you'll need?"

"I'm sure a month will be plenty."

"Great!" He looked at his calendar. I'll have my grandson Ray pick you up from the airport on the first Wednesday of next month at nine o'clock. By the way, Ray is also going to be your pilot. I think you'll like him. He's about your same age, and he loves to travel."

On the way to the airport, Jimmy told me, "I was afraid

you were going to tell my father you could be ready in two weeks. I have something in mind, and I'll need at least a month to pull it off, but I'll need your help."

I was intrigued. "What do you have in mind?"

"There's something you should know about my father. He loves to surprise people. I think I have a way to top all the surprises he's ever pulled off."

"Count me in." As we drove to the airport Jimmy laid out his plan. The drive was just long enough for the two of us to work out all the details in his plot. I couldn't believe the length Jimmy would go to, to pull off a surprise on his father. I couldn't wait to see James's face.

When we arrived at the airport, we went to a private hanger. The doors were closed, but on the tarmac was a Gulf Stream 150 fueled and ready to go. I had seen a few at a distance, but I never dreamed that one day I would be able to fly in one. I was introduced to Ray, who was dressed in regular street clothes, not like the commercial pilot's uniform I was used to seeing. He had a smudge of grease on his forearm and another on his ear; I couldn't help wondering if he had been working under the hood of his car when he got the call to get the plane ready. Ray took my bag and helped me onto the jet. I asked if I could sit up front where I could see the panels. Ray said he didn't mind as long as I didn't touch anything. I never let on that I had my pilot's license.

THIRTY TWO

Back Home

Because of the time zones, it was late evening when Ray and I landed. I thanked him and disembarked the plane. I headed off to catch a cab, but before I had gone twenty feet from the jet, a limousine pulled up. The driver exited and went around the front to open the back door. "Good evening, Ms. Brown. Mr. Hansen wanted to make sure you arrived home safely. May I take your bag?" Pleasantly surprised, I handed him my bag and climbed inside the limo. He closed the door, placed my bag in the trunk, and drove me home. I have to be honest— that was the first time I'd ever been in a limo, and I must say it was nice. When we pulled into the driveway, I offered the driver a tip, but he tipped his hat and said, "Thank you, Ms. Brown, but that won't be necessary. Everything has been taken care of."

As the driver began escorting me up the front walk, I told him, "Thank you, but you don't need to see me to the door." He tipped his hat again and said, "Mr. Hansen's orders. I'll pick you up next month at eight o'clock sharp and drive you to the airport. Have a good evening, Ms. Brown.

The next morning I went directly to see my grandfather, eager to tell him about all that had happened. I went into detail about how I had gotten past Mr. Hansen's bodyguard. I love Grandpa's laugh and knew how much I was going to miss our long talks. I knew that with me so far away and a project that could take quite awhile, there was a chance I might never see him again, at least in this life.

I spent the rest of the day and the weekend rewriting the first article and making it even better than before.

It was Monday morning when I put the finishing touches on the story titled "Fear vs. Freedom." I was nervous, anxious and excited when I finally walked into Mr. Baker's office. Everything I had rehearsed in my mind went right out the window when I came out with "Mr. Baker, I need an extended leave of absence." I handed him the article, and without giving him time to respond I started to tell the entire story.

He picked up the papers and waved the pages in front of me. "Would it be okay if I take a few minutes to read this?"

I was embarrassed for having blurted it all out like that and said, "I'm sorry . . . of course." What I didn't know was that Mr. Baker already knew what I was going to say. He had already been in contact with the owners of the paper. I sat down and nervously watched his reactions as he went through the pages, turning each page face down as he finished it. As he turned the last page and placed it neatly face down on top of the others, he leaned back in his chair. "This is by far the best piece you have written since you came to work for us. There's just one problem. Your assignment was to find out exactly what happened in that locked barn. You don't have an ending to the story."

"I know, that's what I was trying to tell you."

Mr. Baker raised his hand to stop me. Smiling, he opened a drawer and took out some papers. "Mr. Hansen has already approved of these; they'll need your approval and signature. He assures us that once you start work next month, within one week you'll have the ending of the story on my desk. We'll start the series in three weeks, which should time it just right for the climax. We're sure going to miss you around here, but I couldn't be happier for you. If you ever need anything, do let me know, and we look forward to your coming back."

Saying goodbye to my fellow workers was harder than I thought it was going to be. I had never realized how much I loved them, and how they had become like family. There are three people I'll miss the most. Rachelle, with her infectious laugh and Andrea's and Andi's competitive spirit.

It was a lot of work, but after getting my affairs in order I was ready for my new adventure. It was a Wednesday morning, and all of my family and friends came to the house to see me off. At eight o'clock sharp, the limo pulled into the driveway. The driver got out and began putting my luggage into the trunk. There was a lot more this time than last, that's for sure. While the luggage was being loaded, I said my goodbyes. Mom dished out the same advice she had been generously sharing with me all week, but this time she did it through tears. Dad did a good job of holding his tears back when he gave me a kiss and a hug. Then it was Grandpa's turn. He took me aside in his gentle manner that made me feel like a little girl again. He told me, "I had a nice, long talk with that new boss of yours a few weeks ago; he seems like a really nice guy."

"He is, Grandpa. You are two of a kind. What did the two of you talk about?"

"Lots of things, but mostly about you." Pointing and shaking his finger in my direction, he said in a stern voice, "I told him he'd better take care of you, or else!"

I smiled and gave him a big hug. Grandpa looked at me. "I remember being able to hold you in these two hands." Giving me one last kiss on my forehead, he said, "Have I ever told you I think you have the prettiest blond hair and blue eyes?"

"Yes, Grandpa, but I never get tired of hearing it from you, and I love you too." As I climbed into the limo, I waved, gave one last good-bye, and I was off to start my next adventure.

THIRTY THREE

A New Adventure Begins

This next part happened last week, and I'm still excited about it. The limo pulled up to the jet, this time a Gulf Stream 650. At the same time the limo driver opened the door, Ray opened the door to the jet. The steps unfolded and he stepped out, but this time he was wearing what appeared to be a new, freshly pressed uniform, from his shiny black shoes to his captain's cap. As he walked down the steps, he gave me a playful salute and a friendly smile. With the morning sunlight shining down on him, it was as though I was seeing him for the first time.

When he tipped his cap and said, "Good morning," I wasn't sure if I saw a wink with his smile.

I wasn't looking for a relationship, but I do like to flirt. I walked right up to him. "My, don't we clean up nice? I like a man in a uniform," I said as I brushed the four bars on his shoulders. Ray's face flushed, so I thought I'd go the extra mile, and I winked. "Shall we go?"

Ray took off his cap, and, pointing up the stairs, said, "After you." The luggage was stowed, the door closed, and minutes later we were taxiing toward the runway. The wheels were up at nine o'clock sharp.

Ray was making a gradual ascent to 30,000 feet. Once we reached 10,000 he asked me, "Would you like to take over the controls?"

"Really?" I must admit I was quite surprised.

"Why not? You're a pilot, after all."

Grinning, I said, "Been checking up on me, have you?" Ray smiled and I took the controls, informing traffic control of the tail number and requesting clearance for flight level 4. 0. 0. Request was granted, and I pushed the throttle forward and pulled back on the yoke. I found myself leveling off at 40,000 feet so fast I couldn't believe it. Pulling back on the throttle, I tried so hard to play it cool; but there was no way I could wipe the smile off my face.

Ray looked surprised but couldn't help but smile along with me. I think he was impressed. He locked his fingers behind his head and leaned back. "I wish I had known on our last trip that you could fly. I could have gotten some rest."

I couldn't help myself—I had to have some fun with him. "Let's see if this baby can do a barrel roll." I leaned toward Ray as if I were going to do it.

He sat upright in a flash. "Let's not!"

I started to laugh, and Ray knew he'd been had. During the flight we got to know each other better and discovered we had many things in common. Thirty minutes out from our destination I began a descent to 5,000 feet in preparation for our approach into San Diego Montgomery Field. I contacted approach control, requesting clearance to land on runway two eight right.

Ray turned to me, his eyebrows up. "You've flown into Montgomery Field before?"

I didn't say anything, only smiled. "Take over the controls, Captain."

Ray gave a salute and took the controls. I couldn't help but notice the butter-smooth landing, the softest landing I'd ever experienced. "He's showing off," I thought to myself. Ray taxied around to the front of the hanger. The doors to the hanger were open, and I could see the other planes as Ray pointed the nose of the jet toward them.

"Are these all yours?"

Ray smiled, and in a jovial tone to let me know he was kidding. "Sure are, every one of them." I knew he was flirting with me. "These are just a few of my fleet." Ray opened the hatch and walked down first.

Turning, he extended his hand to assist me. I was perfectly capable of walking down the steps myself, but he was being such a gentlemen I couldn't refuse. A limo pulled up, and the ground crew started to remove the luggage. It was then I saw it—fully restored and ready to go. Now it was my turn to show off. I wanted to run, but I played it cool. As I casually walked over to it, I couldn't believe my eyes. I ran my hand along the smooth surface of one of the props, and said, "The P-51-D Mustang! Did you know this little baby was considered to be one of the greatest single-seat fighter planes used in World War II? Of course that was after they replaced the 1,100 horsepower Allison engine with the Merlin."

I could have stopped there. Ray was obviously impressed, but I wanted an excuse to check out the plane up close and personal. As I walked around the outline of the plane, Ray stood back to watch me. I walked down and around the wing, my hand along its edge. I continued, "Wing span, thirty-seven feet. Length, just over thirty-two feet. Height, just under fourteen feet. Six fifty-caliber machine guns. This baby could fly over forty thousand feet, with a cruising speed just under three hundred." I turned my head to look at Ray: "Max speed, over four hundred. Distance, you're looking at a thousand miles, at the cruising speed, of course."

Ray replied back with a smile on his face. "Of course." He was definitely flirting with me, and I knew it, but then again, so was I; and I can flirt with the best of them. I could have gone on, but I restrained myself. No one likes a showoff. "This is like the one your grandfather flew."

"No, it is the one he flew and was shot down in. I know he's looking forward to telling you all about it."

I couldn't believe it. What were the odds of finding the same plane he flew? Ray smiled. "Let's get you to your new home."

As we pulled up to the house, the driver gave a few taps on the horn, and Alfred, Jimmy and James came out to greet us. They each grabbed a bag, and James led me to my room. Outside the door, Ray stood behind me, his hands over my eyes as they led me in. "Ready?" Ray asked.

I nodded my head and said, "Ready." Ray removed his hands. I couldn't believe my eyes. It was perfect, from the bedspread to the fresh paint on the walls; it had all been done in my favorite colors. I turned to James, pointing my finger, and said, "Someone has been talking to my grandfather."

James asked, "Did we get it right?"

"It's perfect. I love the color, and the smell of fresh paint. The three of you did a great job!"

"What makes you think we painted your room?" Ray asked.

"Well, unless your nail polish is the same color as my new

room, then I'd say you had a hand in it, along with your dad, who, like his father, missed a spot when cleaning up. You both have paint on your left ears." Ray checked his hands while James and Jimmy pointed at each other's ears and laughed. "I guess we can't pull one over on an investigative reporter."

Alfred came in carrying a box beautifully wrapped with a bow on top. "Is now a good time, Sir?"

"Your timing couldn't be better, thank you." James took the box and handed it to me.

"This is for you."

"What is it?"

"You'll have to open it to find out."

"Whatever it is, there is no way it could top what the three of you have already done." But I was wrong. Inside were two brass model airplanes mounted at a forty-five-degree banked turn—the P-47 Thunderbolt, and the P-51 Mustang. As I picked them up, my tears fell on the wings.

"The T Bolt is from your Grandfather Vince, and the Mustang is from me." I was speechless. All I could do was give him a big hug.

After taking some time to get settled, I reported to James in the study, where he asked me, "So how was your flight?"

"Very nice, thank you. I've never been in a Gulf Stream G-650. I must say, it was very impressive."

"So he picked that one for you, did he? I'm not surprised. When Ray got back from dropping you off, he spent a lot of time at the house asking all kinds of questions about you."

I could feel my face blush. I wanted to hear more, but thought it best to play it cool, so I said, "Shall we get started?"

"That's what I like, down to business."

As I sat down, I reached into my purse, took out my recorder, and placed it on the desk. Next I took out a notepad on which I had written all kinds of questions I had been compiling for the last month. Looking at James across the desk: "Mr. Hansen. . ." there was that look again. "Sorry, it'll take a little time to get used to calling you James. So James, when we last met, you said you would tell me what happened in the barn the commandant locked you inside of; and the second reason, why you haven't told your story."

James sat back in his chair. "There are two parts to the family secret. One, I'm ready to tell you now; and part two, after you send off your story to your editor, Mr. Baker. Part two is going to take quite a while."

I stopped him before he could continue. "James, before you start your story, which I really want to know, would it be all right with you if I could ask you a few questions first?"

"What would you like to know?"

"I know so little about your personal life that I would like to get to know you. I feel if I know you better I'll be able to bring your story to life."

"I like that. Ask away."

"What I'd like to know are things like who your parents were; what they did for a living. Do you have any brothers or sisters? What were you like as a kid? Things of that nature."

"Sounds like a great place to start. My father's name was Raymond, and my mother's name was Jideen. She was one of a kind, and so was the spelling of her name. Her father's name was James, but everyone called him Jimmy. Her mother's name was Maudeen. So they put the two names together to come up with Jideen, spelled J-i-d-e-e-n.

"Different spelling continued with their firstborn, but not on purpose. My sister was born in a hospital that would not let my parents take a newborn home without putting a name on the birth certificate. In fact, if my memory serves me right, the story my mother told is the hospital needed the name after the delivery, in the delivery room. They were expecting a boy, so when my sister popped out it was quite a surprise. When asked what the name was going to be, dad said he liked the name Renée and Mom agreed. Just one problem, when they were asked how to spell it, they weren't sure. There are several ways, but the one my dad remembered was R-e-n-é-e with the accent over the e. Only dad remembered the accent to be an I, so on the birth certificate it was spelled R-e-n-i-e."

I smiled, "So you were named after your grandfather, and your grandson Ray was named after your father. Tell me about him."

"So you'd like to know more about my grandson, would you?"

James smiled as I stumbled over my words. "No— I mean yes. I mean, about your father, tell me about your father."

He knew what I meant; he was just having a little fun with me. "My mother and father were the hardest working people I ever knew." I could see him reflecting back in his mind. He smiled. "Dad called me 'pepper,' one day, and it stuck. He knew he should give my younger brother Mack a nickname and tried to call him Salt, but it didn't last. After my father served in the army, he had many different jobs. You name it, he probably did it. He was never too proud to work. If it was honest work, he had no problem doing it. 'No job should be beneath any man when it comes to providing for his family,' he would tell me. I learned a lot about work from him, and I'll always love him for that. He would say, 'If you do a good job, they might tell one, but if you do a lousy job, they'll tell twenty. I'll give you twenty to one odds on what you should do.' I've never forgotten that, and I apply it to all of my business dealings.

"My mother was a school teacher, and like all loving mothers, she did whatever it took to see that our needs were met. When she wasn't teaching, she did odd jobs for people. I remember her taking in laundry. She would scrub shirts on a washboard and then iron and fold them late into the night. During the fall, we helped her harvest apples from the orchard and tomatoes from the garden. The apples became delicious applesauce, and when our cellar shelves were full, the surplus was sold at the mercantile. We helped her bottle stewed tomatoes, and the 'merc' was happy to sell them as well.

"Mother was a very generous person. She must have been dog tired most of the time, but she never turned her back on a person in need. She cared for an elderly neighbor for years, and I remember many occasions when there was an extra plate on the table for a child she looked after while the mother worked as a sole provider. Mom nursed critically ill friends back to health during the flu epidemic, took them meals, and ran errands for people in need. She didn't do those things for pay or with the expectation of getting anything in return. She did it because it was the Christian thing to do. That was my mother, a true Saint."

I learned a lot about James. He described a happy, normal childhood with his brother and two sisters, and he shared some funny stories from his youth. His sense of humor reminded me a lot of my Grandfather Vince's. I can't remember the last time I had laughed so hard. James is a great storyteller.

One particular story was about his only friend in the neighborhood, a boy named Joe who was three years older than he was. Joe loved getting into trouble, but he didn't like doing it alone.

He must have told me a dozen or so stories, but there are three I just have to write down. He started off by smiling and said, "I remember a time when Joe wanted to smoke, so he talked me into sneaking a pack from my Dad's night-stand. We found the perfect place to light up. Unfortunately, amidst a stack of baled hay. We pulled out a few of the bales to make a hole where we could hide, and by the time we were on our second cigarette, we could hear the sirens from the volunteer fire department. 'I wonder where the fire is?' Joe said, as he kicked back and puffed on the cigarette. One minute we were thinking how cool we were, and the next we were looking down the nozzle of a fireman's hose.

"I'll never forget the look on my father's face. One fire-man took us both by the back of our shirts and raised us up to show my Dad what he had found. Dad told him to put us back in the hole and turn on the hose."

"Did they do it?"

"We were dropped back in the hole, scared to death. They were ready to give us a drenching we'd never forget. Dad stopped them at the last possible moment, not wanting to ruin the hay by getting it wet. He may not have drenched us, but he did the next best thing. He sent Joe home and told him to tell his folks before he did. You see, back then if you did something wrong you got punished twice, once by the neighbor that caught you, and once by your folks.

"After he sent Joe home, he took me to his favorite tavern, sat me on the bar stool, and had his friend behind the bar bring him two cigars. 'If you're going to smoke, smoke like a real man,' and he lit both cigars. He really didn't want me to pick up his habit. Let's just say— I never smoked again. Come to think of it, I believe I was the only one in the service that I knew who didn't smoke. That was really hard on the ones in the POW camps, because cigarettes were hard to come by. In the camps the prisoners would barter with what they had. Anyone who had cigarettes could get top barter, even with the guards."

The next story he called "The night the lights went out."

He started this one with a sly grin. "I don't know what it is about boys and caves, but every boy I've ever known has built at least one cave in his lifetime. Joe and I worked on this one for weeks; and let me tell you, she was a beauty. I don't know how deep it was, but it was deeper than the power pole that we dug underneath of, because one night, the entire south end of our little town was without power. It just so happened that the power pole had a transformer on it. It wasn't hard to figure out who the culprits were, because the tunnel started in Joe's back yard behind the garage. I can still see Joe standing between his mom and dad, when he said, 'I told you we had big gophers!' His folks didn't buy it, and since I was always his partner in crime, neither did my parents."

I was laughing when James looked at his watch and commented, "Would you look at the time; how did it get so late?"

I knew that was his cue to stop, but I begged him for one

more.

He smiled. "All right, one more. I suppose since I told you about the time we caused all the lights to go out, it's only fitting to tell you about the time we caused all the lights to go on. Nikki, my dear, I don't think I've ever told anyone this story; I didn't want to give anyone any ideas. I don't know how he did it, but somehow Joe got his hands on a stick of dynamite. I snuck out of the house after my folks went to bed. Joe had begun to drive by this time, and we drove about five miles out of town. He didn't have a fuse, but Joe was convinced he could set that stick of dynamite off with a flashlight. He stuck the wires in both ends of the stick, laid it in the dirt, and then we ran about fifty feet away and crouched behind a rock. He wrapped the ends of the wires around the batteries, and we counted down from ten. I covered my ears and braced myself when we got to one, but nothing happened. Joe tried all kinds of combinations with the wires; let me tell you that after about thirty minutes we were no longer counting down. I was bored and was about to stand up when KA-BOOM! That thing was so loud I had a ringing in my ears for a week or more. We were laughing so hard we almost wet our pants. We could see down the canyon that all the lights in town were coming on, and it didn't take long before we could see every police car and fire engine coming up the only road that led straight to us. I'm not sure, but I think Joe did pee his pants."

James had me laughing until tears rolled down my checks. After I composed myself, I asked, "Tomorrow, if it's all right with you, I'd like to know more about the rest of the family."

"Your timing couldn't be better. Karen will be back in the

morning, and Saturday I have a surprise for you." As James and I were walking down the hall, James told me a little secret about Ray. "In high school, Ray was on the swim team, and they called him Sting Ray."

"Thank you. I'll put that to good use."

THIRTY FOUR

Nikki Meets Karen

It was just last Thursday when I walked down the hall. I could smell breakfast cooking, and it smelled so good. When I came into the kitchen, I was surprised to see Ray standing over the eight-burner stove with an apron on and a spatula in his hand. Good thing I had put my makeup on. I tried to sneak up on him, but I had to go around the kitchen island, and he saw me out of the corner of his eye. He turned and smiled.

"Good morning. Trying to sneak up on me?"

I smiled back. "Good morning. Whatever gave you that idea? So a pilot and a chef. I could smell breakfast all the way down the hall. What are you making? . . . Sting Ray."

Ray looked surprised, as I knew he would. "Been checking up on me, have you?"

Smiling, I said, "I'll never give up my source."

Ray smiled back. "Hope you like eggs Benedict."

"I do. I can't remember the last time I had them." I asked if I could help.

"I can always use an extra hand." He pointed. "There's an apron in that drawer."

I selected an apron, put the strap over my head, and started to tie the other straps around my waist. Ray came up behind me. "Here, let me help you with that." I didn't need any help, of course, but I knew what he was up to.

"Thank you. What would you like me to do?"

"The sauce needs stirring while I check the ham and start the eggs." Just then, James walked in.

"Smells good. What are you two cooking?"

Together we said, "Eggs Benedict." We looked at each other and pointed, and together we said, "Jinks!" We started to laugh like a couple of school kids. James just smiled and started to set the table.

I noticed a plaque on the door that led to the garage: "Return With Honor." Curious, I asked James what it meant. He looked at Ray and said, "I think it would be appropriate for you to tell her."

"Be happy to, Grandpa." Turning to their inquisitive guest, Ray explained, "Every member of our family has a plaque like that in their home, usually by the door that gets used the most. It's placed there to remind us who we are, and that we should have the utmost integrity when dealings with others."

James walked by carrying the flatware. "Tell her the rest."

Kiddingly, Ray said, "I'm getting to it. Just hold your horses." I smiled at the thought that Ray had picked up his grandfather's clichés. Ray continued, "When we start to date, it reminds us to treat, and be treated, with respect. But the true meaning behind it is something Grandpa James learned as an escapee, it means . . ."

Just then, Karen walked in from the garage with her sister and brother-in-law Joyce and Jack. "It sure smells good. I hope there's enough for three more." With hugs and kisses all around, Ray introduced me.

"Grandma, I'd like you to meet Nikki Brown."

I tried to give her a hand shake, but Karen gave me a big

hug instead. "Nikki, my dear, I've heard so much about you. It's good to finally meet you."

During breakfast, James announced, "I've been going over some of the family photos I thought you'd like to see."

Ray jumped in: "If they're the ones I'm thinking of, it's a good thing I came by."

I looked at James and whispered loud enough for Ray to hear. "And if they're not, you'll have to show those to me later."

James smiled and gave me a wink. We spent the day going over the many photo albums. That evening, before James retired for bed, he told me, "Don't stay up too late; tomorrow I have a surprise for you." I tried to get it out of him, but it was no use.

Ray and I talked about what things were like growing up. How his family made sure he didn't get whatever he wanted and how he had to work just like his dad. We really do have a lot in common. I found out about all his girlfriends in high school and college. He said he would have liked to find someone to have a serious relationship with, but nothing really developed. When he tried to find out about my boyfriends, that's when I looked at my watch and said, "Would you look at the time?" He tried, but there was no way. When I was in my second year of college, I fell head over heels in love with a guy who broke my heart, and I promised myself I would never let that happen again. That story could definitely fill up another journal.

It was after two o'clock in the morning when Ray and I finally said good night.

THIRTY FIVE

The Reunions

That brings me up to last Friday. We had just finished breakfast when the door bell rang. Because Alfred had the day off, James asked me if I could please see who it was while he finished the dishes.

When I opened the door I found Jimmy and my Grandfather Vince standing there, grinning from ear to ear. "Hi, Pun'kin, surprised to see me?"

I wrapped my arms around him. "Why didn't you tell me you were coming?"

"And miss the look on your face? Never!"

I turned around and saw James with a big grin on his face. I pointed at him and gave a look that said, "You got me."

That day was spent listening to the two of them banter back and forth as though they had known each other their whole lives. From whose squad had more adventures to who had the better plane. Grandpa Vince tried to get me to take his side, but I put up both hands: "Don't drag me into this."

As the day went on, more of the family arrived. I recognized many of them from their photos the day before. I took James aside. "What's going on?"

"They're part of another surprise. Didn't I tell you?"

"No, you didn't."

There was that half-smile again. "The rest of the family

will be here tomorrow for a little reunion. They're all eager to meet the person I've been waiting for, for such a long time."

Not knowing what to say, I asked, "The family is coming to meet me? Why?"

"It's part of the family secret they know about, and one day you'll know too. But for now you'll just have to be patient."

I still didn't know what to say, so I told him, "I look forward to meeting everyone."

It was Saturday afternoon, and the house, as well as the back yard, was filled with family. The grandkids and great-grandkids were busy setting up the tables and chairs, while Ray introduced me to everyone. Jimmy came up to me and whispered in my ear, "They're here," and walked over to James. Suddenly I realized I hadn't prepared my grandfather for the surprise Jimmy had planned for his father. Looking around, I spotted him next to James, and I followed behind Jimmy.

I heard Jimmy say, "Dad, there is someone here who would like to meet you in the study. Vince, you're welcome to come along as well." As Jimmy led his father away, I took Grandpa Vince by the arm, letting Jimmy and James get about ten feet ahead. "Grandpa, in all the excitement I forgot about the surprise that was planned for James that you need to know about."

Grandpa Vince gave my hand a pat of assurance. "I'll be fine. Jimmy gave me a call a few weeks ago and told me all about it. I'll be honest with you, when he told me, I had many emotions run through me, two of which were fear and anger. I didn't know what to do. Then I remembered I was the one who taught you to face your fears head-on, like we had to when we flew our airplanes into danger. What kind of an example would I be if I chickened out? I can't believe it, but I'm looking forward to meeting the old coot."

Jimmy tapped on the doors and slid them open. There he was, Commandant Schmidt, sitting in his wheelchair, his daughter Elsa standing behind him. James recognized him right off from the way I had described him when I told my story. He smiled and said, "Commandant Schmidt, is that you?"

He still looked like he was refusing to answer death's door. But there was something else—his countenance was much brighter. It was as though a dark cloud had lifted off him. Elsa leaned over and whispered in his ear. With all his strength he stood and held out his hand. I could see how nervous he was.

With his hand stretched out, in broken English, holding back tears, he spoke. "Could you ever forgive me?"

James walked up to the commandant, and like the true Christian he is, embraced him and told him he had forgiven him long ago. No interpreter was needed. Helping him back into his chair, James looked at me. "There's someone else who would like to say hello."

A familiar voice from behind and to the side started to interpret. "June?" I turned. There she was, with little May hiding behind her and peering between someone I assumed was her father. May smiled and gave me a wave. I walked over and gave June and May a hug. "And you must be Hans, June's husband."

Hans shook my hand and in clear English spoke. "June has told me so much about you. It's nice to finally meet."

I turned, pointing my finger at Jimmy. "I see your dad isn't the only one who likes to surprise people." I quickly introduced everyone and then turned to the commandant.

I touched his hand and in a soft voice said, "Hello, Mr. Schmidt."

He smiled that toothless smile and in his thick, limited English German accent replied, "Hallo, Nikki, is good to hear your voice again."

"I'd like to introduce you to my grandfather. Do you remember what I told you about him?"June interpreted.

Commandant Schmidt nodded, "Ja." He struggled to stand and held out his hand as he spoke. June interpreted. "I'm so sorry about your leg. I know the doctors were anything but kind. They saw so much carnage done to the German people I'm afraid they took it out on the prisoners. I hope you can forgive me."

Grandpa Vince took his hand. "That's all I needed to hear. I may not be as forgiving as Captain Hansen here, but I too forgive you." Grandpa Vince helped him sit back down.

We visited for a while when Alfred entered. "Lunch is ready when you are."

James leaned over and picked up the box of tissues that sat on his desk. There wasn't a dry eye in that room.

Outside, the tables were arranged to have a table of honor. There was a place setting for each of those who had been in the study. James introduced the family to the new guests.

I sat next to Karen, with Ray on my left. As the lunch was coming to an end, I asked Karen, "I can't help but notice how much in love you and James are in after all these years. What's your secret?"

Karen smiled warmly and touched my hand. "We've had

our ups and downs, just like everyone else. It helps to understand the diverse personalities that everyone has, and the differences between men and women. Men are simple creatures, they really are. For most men, the top three priorities are bed, food, and sleep. You may have thought I repeated myself with bed and sleep—I assure you I did not." Karen gave me a wink. "Men rank "bed" and breathing about the same. Women, on the other hand, for the most part are just the opposite. We're not called the opposite sex for nothing. For us, it's sleep, and I do mean sleep. Then food, and yes, "bed" every now and then is nice. We also like breathing, it's just that we can hold our breath a lot longer than men. We're wired differently, and that's where many of the challenges begin in relationships between men and women." The women who were listening smiled, nodding in agreement. James stood up, tapping his wine glass with a knife, and everyone gave him their attention. Karen lovingly patted my hand, and whispered, "James and I are looking forward to telling you more, and yes, it is part of the family secret."

"Thank you all for coming," James said. "I hope everyone had enough to eat. If not, it's your own fault, because I see there is still plenty of food." The family laughed and raised their wine glasses in approval. Martinellis for the kids, of course. "For all who would like to hear Nikki's story, we'll meet in the theater room. After that, we'll have dessert."

I stood up along with everyone else. "I wasn't expecting that. Why didn't you warn me?"

James looked at me, threw out his arms and said, "Surprise!"

I shook my head. "I don't think I can take any more

surprises." James put his right arm around my shoulders, and with his left arm stretched out he said, "Shall we?" He led me to the theater room. Everyone followed behind us.

In a low voice, I told James, "I don't think I can do this. I've never talked in front of so many people before."

"Nonsense. If there's one thing I know about you, my dear, it is this: You can, and you'll have fun doing it. Just remember . . ."

I said, "I know, I know. F. E. A. R."

James smiled and touched my nose. "That's my girl. Besides, they're not people, they're family."

The smell of the popcorn wafted down the hallway as we made our way to the theater room. I could see Alfred behind the counter working the popcorn machine, the kind you'd see at any movie house; his wife, Brianna, was ready to hand out the bags of popcorn to any who wanted them. I took center stage, the big white screen behind me and numerous rows of luxurious theater seats in front of me. I watched everyone come in, and I appreciated their supportive smiles and words of encouragement. James was right. I loved it.

I faced my fears and found myself wondering why I had worked myself up into such a nervous state. I told my story, starting from the time I flew imaginary airplanes with my grandfather—everyone laughed at that one. Grandfather Vince, being the ham he is, stood up and took a bow. When I told of my experience in Germany, I could see Commandant Schmidt smiling his toothless smile as Hans interpreted. I was surprised when I looked at my watch and realized I had held a captive audience for almost an hour. Ray, sitting on the front row, was the first to give me a standing ovation.

When it was time for the Schmidts and company to leave, I asked June where they were staying. Jimmy had arranged for them to stay at The Grand Del Mar, a five-star hotel. Grandpa Vince said, "You should see this place, Nikki. It's incredible."

Turning to June, I asked, "What are your plans?"

"Didn't Mr. Hansen tell you? The State Department, along with the Veterans of Foreign Wars, is sponsoring a tour for Commandant Schmidt to speak to them, and Hans is going to be his interpreter. Your grandfather was also asked to join him."

"Is that true, Grandpa?"

"I'm thinking about it."

I gave him a hug. "I think you should do it."

We gave our customary good-bye, as he cupped my face in the palms of his hands, kissing my forehead, and my telling him, "I love you too." As the driver of the limo opened the door, Grandpa turned, smiled and said, "I could get used to a taxi like this."

It was Sunday morning when I walked into the kitchen. Five little children were eating cereal and chit-chatting as little kids are prone to do. Their aunt Kathy was putting away the milk when I heard one of them rhythmically say, "Good morning, Nikki. We're not fasting, because we're little."

I replied, "Good morning. What do you mean?"

As Kathy closed the refrigerator door she said, "Once a month the family goes without two meals. It's called fasting. It's something in the Bible that a good friend of Grandpa James taught him while he was in Germany."

"Sounds like more of the family secret."

Kathy smiled. "I know he's looking forward to telling you all about it. When the kids get older, and they want to, they can fast with us. Can I get you anything? I can put on a pot of coffee and scramble some eggs for you if you like."

"No thank you. I think with everything I ate yesterday, I could go without a few meals myself."

James walked in and greeted everyone. He was wearing a perfectly tailored suit and coordinating tie. Ray, right behind him, was looking just as dapper.

"Church starts in less than an hour. You kids better hurry or we'll be late." James turned to me. "You're welcome to join us, or you can stay here and make yourself at home. I invited your grandfather and the Schmidt party over for dinner; they should be here around four."

I looked at Ray. "I can be ready in fifteen minutes." As I passed by Ray, I heard him say, "Fifteen minutes? Can't be done!" Ray has sisters, and he knew how long it always took them, but in fifteen minutes I was ready. I think Ray was impressed and surprised. He complimented me on how I looked and that my dress matched his tie. I smiled and said, "What a coincidence." I let him wonder if it was.

After church, I asked James if we could get started with his story, since the guests wouldn't be there for a few hours.

"Not today," James explained. Today is a day of rest." His answer came in a soft tone, not one that made me feel embarrassed or uncomfortable. His ability to put people at ease was one of the traits I found so appealing and that endeared him to me.

After dinner everyone retired to the family room, where we all got to know each other better. That night as I lay in bed, I reflected on the day. It was one of the most enjoyable

Sundays I could remember.

As my thoughts turned to Ray, I found myself smiling. Catching myself, I said, "Not so fast. I've got a job to do and I'm not going to fall for just any flyboy." I have been preparing a list of qualities I'm looking for in a husband, ever since my grandfather taught me about setting goals. And let me tell you, it's a long list. I just wished I'd remembered to use it when I was in college.

I had a hard time falling asleep that night as well. I remember thinking before I drifted off . . . "Tomorrow I find out what happened to James after Commandant Schmidt left him in that barn to die and what made him who he is. What could he possibly have learned wandering through Germany? Who are these four friends I keep hearing about? What kind of fears did he have to face? Why did it take so long to get to safety? And how long is it going to take to go through those first four journals and then the others?" With those thoughts running through my head, I drifted off to sleep.

THIRTY SIX

The Choice

It was Monday morning after breakfast when James and I retired to the study. James sat down in his chair and began, "So you would like to know what the one word I gave Commandant Schmidt and what happened to me after he locked me in the barn." I smiled, took out my recorder and turned it on.

He began, "I'll start when I was shot down. We were flying cover for the bombers when we noticed all the top turrets turned to six o'clock and pointing up. It almost looked like they were aiming at us. We turned to look at what they were aiming at, but the sun was in our eyes. The German pilots were known for this maneuver. They were hard to see, but coming in fast were Messerschmitt 262s, six of them, the first time I'd ever seen a jet. We were told they could go over a hundred miles an hour faster than the top speed of P-51s. The bombers aren't built for speed and we were carrying reserve tanks, which I ordered to drop, and then for us to climb.

"Pushing the throttle wide open, we climbed. As we dove down, picking up speed, one 262 came right into my sights. I let him have it, but I undershot. My wing man, however, took him out. The 262s might be faster, but because of their speed I knew the Mustang could outmaneuver them. We fought tooth and nail, a dogfight that would go down in history. The 262s took out three of the bombers, and there was no way I was going to lose any more. We took out three more of theirs, leaving them with two.

Me 262
Artist Rendition

"One of the Messerschmitts came in on the right waist gunners of the bombers and took out one more. He flew right in front of me, and I fired. Again I couldn't adjust for the speed. I was so angry I did what no pilot should do—I took off after him without my wingman. All I could see through my anger was to get revenge.

"As I dove down after him he knew I was on his tail and he pulled away. I didn't give up but stayed on his tail. He had to pull up sooner or later. What I didn't see was the last jet right behind me. He did, however, get my attention when I saw the tracers whizzing by my canopy. My wing man followed him down, but he was out of range to do any good.

"There was one more short burst and I was hit. The jet in front of me was long gone and the one on my tail broke off. He must have been out of ammo, or else he would have finished me off for sure. I leveled off and tried to climb, but it was no use. I was losing oil pressure too fast.

"My plane was too low for me to bail out and I could see no safe place to land. I was in a real predicament, to say the least. Desperately scanning the landscape, I saw a small opening in a group of tall trees just ahead. I quickly calculated the distance, altitude, and air speed. I didn't see how I was going to make it, but somehow I did. There must have been a headwind just right to keep me airborne. I kept the wheels up as long as possible to avoid any drag on my aircraft.

"As I came over the top of the last tall tree I could hear the branches scrape against my P-51. Quickly bringing down the landing gear, I could feel the small saplings break against the wings as I touched the ground. I held my breath as the plane's wheels hit every mound of dirt that had been pushed up by whatever was making their home in that clearing. I hoped that one of those mounds of dirt wasn't a big rock. Just when I thought I was going to make it, the trees at the end of my little makeshift landing strip were getting closer and closer, and I wondered if I should have landed with the gear up. Then snap! The left wing hit a tree that wasn't going to give way. I spun around like a top. When my Mustang came to rest, I quickly took inventory of myself and couldn't believe it—nothing was broken but the wing. I knew the Germans had seen where I went down, giving me only seconds to hightail it out of there. I eluded them for a while, but they eventually caught up to me.

"I was taken to be interrogated, but all they got out of me

was name, rank, and serial number. I was beaten to a pulp and deprived of any real food. I was fed hard black bread and water for many days. How many days? I had no idea. My cell had no windows, and they left the light on the whole time I was there. When they could see I wasn't going to cooperate, I was to be dumped at a prison camp. Hundreds of other POWs, and I were crammed into boxcars packed so tight there was no room to move. We had to sleep standing up. It took days before we were let out. When the doors opened, the ones standing up against the door fell out from the weight of the others pushing against them. I remember when I could finally move my legs, how hard it was, stepping over some of the dead who had fallen. We were given water and the same hard black bread. This time I was so hungry it tasted pretty good.

"From there we were divided up. Transport trucks showed up and loaded in as many of us as they could. I was the last one on. As the tailgate closed, I could see the rest of the POWs being loaded back on to the box cars. I thought to myself, 'At least there will be enough room for them to lie down.' We were under heavy guard, no chance to escape. It was a bit of a drive, and we had no way of knowing where we were when we pulled into the prison camp. When we stopped, the guards ordered us down. I couldn't move as fast as they wanted, which won me a prize — a hit to the gut with the butt of a gun.

"While being marched into camp, I caught my breath and went in standing as tall as I could. I wasn't about to let them think they had gotten the better of me. We were placed in an area inside the fence and I could see the other prisoners, but none came up to us. I learned later it was against one of the many rules. No one speaks to a prisoner. The commandant alone lays down the law. We must have stood there for at least an hour. Come to find out, the commandant was waiting for another truckload of prisoners to arrive; there was no way someone of his great importance would make an appearance twice in one day, to lay down the law.

"As I stood there and looked around, it was evident the other prisoners were anxious to greet us and learn of any news about the war. As a prisoner, there's a love-hate feeling toward new arrivals— they love to get an updated report as to how the war is going, and hate because there is no more room in the inn. But this didn't matter to the Germans, they just crammed us in. I couldn't believe my eyes. Some of the men looked like specters. Many of their clothes were rags, and I could see the ribs on most of them. Those who still had some fat on them must have been the newer arrivals.

"No way was I going to end up looking like that. I had a wife and a newborn baby back home that I hadn't even held yet. I was enraged to think the prisoners were being treated as badly as they were.

"Finally, two large trucks pulled up to the gate, and the camp came alive. More guards came out of their living quarters and retrieved their dogs to greet their new house guests. As the men climbed out of the back, some were so bad off they buckled under their own weight as they hit the ground; it was then that the dogs would attack, bringing them quickly to their feet. One prisoner, out of reflex, hit the dog, and that's when we learned one of the rules the hard way: Never, and I mean never, touch one of the dogs. He was so weak it only took one blow of the rifle butt to the head. It made such a sickening sound, and we knew he was dead; there was nothing anyone could do. As the men lined up with the rest of us, I watched two guards drag his body behind one of the buildings; it was the last time anyone saw him.

"Finally it was time for Commandant Schmidt to make his grand entrance.

Commandant Schmitt
Artist Rendition

He came out of his office dressed to impress. Shiny, black leather boots that went just below his knee. A black trench coat and matching gloves, with a crop under his arm. He stood there letting us bask in his presence. I remember thinking he was quite a young punk for a commandant and wondered what strings he had pulled to get his job. But still you knew you didn't want to cross him.

"There he was with his high-arched hat and a stiff neck, looking us over. He slowly walked down the three steps to inform us of his rules. His first one we had already learned—never touch the dogs. With each rule he would slap the riding crop in his glove, and when it was one that needed extra attention he slapped it against his boot, making such a crack that most of us flinched. I could see he especially enjoyed that. As he walked around delivering his rules, he stopped in front of me and looked me right in the eye. 'Never, and I do mean never, try to escape. You will be caught, and your punishment will be death.' With each 'never' came a crack of the crop. We were all assigned a barrack, and that's when the other prisoners could greet us and help us to our quarters. Some of this I've already told you, so I'll make it short.

"I could feel myself getting weaker and weaker by the day and knew if I didn't make a break for it soon I wouldn't have the strength. It was a night when the moon was just a sliver, and with the cloud cover it was pitch black. I tried to talk two guys that I had gotten to know a little to come with me, but they wanted nothing to do with it. They said they would try and cover for me at roll call. I timed the search lights just right and made my way through the fence, past the guards, and disappeared into the woods. It took a while, but the dogs found me and ripped into my leg and arm. When the guards brought me back, Commandant Schmidt came out and greeted me with a smirk on his face. 'Welcome back, Captain. Care to take a walk?' He took only a few guards and a dog. With my hands tied behind my back, I was no threat.

"I knew I was going to die. The commandant informed

me on our walk that if I had made my way to safety, the punishment for him would have been the firing squad, or if he was lucky, the Eastern front. At the beginning of our walk he told me to be thinking of a word I would like for my family to remember me by and he would do what he could to pass it on. But it could be only one word. I kept thinking to myself, what is the one word I could give my son to live by, a son who I never even had the chance to hold; I needed a word that would guide him for the rest of his life. Nikki my dear, you've had quite some time now knowing this part of the story, what one word would you have chosen?"

"James, I have to admit I've given it a lot of thought. I think the one word for me would have been Love."

"Good word, that was on the top of my list as well. Many thoughts ran through my head as we walked into a small clearing. There was a barn with an old dead tree in front of it.

A large branch about ten feet off the ground would be perfect for a rope to be tossed over for a hanging. When we walked under it, I stopped, but they kept going. The commandant turned and looked at me. 'What, you think you are to be hanged? You should be so lucky. No, your fate is what is in that barn.'

The Choice
Photo from the private collection of Gary J. Sumner

Commandant Schmidt looked at his watch. 'You have sixty seconds to decide.'"

"James wait a minute. Is that where you got the idea when you gave me a minute to think it over, whether or not to take this job?"

James smiled and gave me a wink, "It was a huge barn with a heavy board across the two doors, locking in whatever was inside. What could possibly be in there? Perhaps wild, starving animals, ready to eat me alive. No, not wild animals, but the dogs that seemed to love to rip the prisoners to shreds. Perhaps it was full of booby traps that would spring some kind of a tortuous, slow, agonizing death. All of the worst kinds of death ran through my head. Perhaps, once I was locked inside, they would set the barn on fire, burning me to death. It felt like ten seconds when I heard the commandant tell me my time was up. I was about to pick the firing squad, as had all the others before me.

"Then all of a sudden I had a feeling I couldn't explain. Something in my gut told me to pick the barn. I took a deep breath and told the commandant my choice: 'I choose the barn.' I was led up to the door, and the heavy board was removed. The commandant took out his knife and cut my hands free. The guards opened the door, but I had to walk in on my own accord.

"So captain, what is the one word you have chosen?"

"I looked at him right in the eye . . . Integrity, and then I added, without it, you have nothing.

"Once I had cleared the door, I heard it slam shut behind me. The big, heavy board slid down in place, locking me and whatever else inside. The slamming of the door caused what seemed to be hundreds of birds to fly around. My heart was pounding in my ears so loud I could barely hear the flapping of the bird's wings. What sort of death was I going to face? My imagination went wild. Dust was everywhere, and with the shadows from the birds and the dust reflecting off the beams of light through the cracks of the barn, I thought my heart was going to come right out of my chest. I stood there choking from the dust, waiting for the worst. Once the birds and the dust settled down, my eyes became adjusted to the light, and I saw the back door to the barn was ajar. It was a trick: if I made a beeline to what appeared to be freedom, I knew for sure I'd spring some kind of trap.

"I stood trying to figure out what I should do. Should I go straight to the door? No, that would be too obvious. Maybe if I stayed against the wall of the barn, that would be safer, but which way? I didn't know what to do; I froze dead in my tracks. Tired and hungry, I couldn't think straight, but knew I had to do something. I closed my eyes and took in a deep breath. As I slowly exhaled, I opened my eyes. The right side, yes, the right side is the way I'll go. With the wall of the barn against my back I knew at least no one could come up from behind me. Inch by inch I carefully moved the loose hay, looking for any trip wires. I was half way when I heard some movement from the loft above. I stopped. I looked around for anything I could defend myself with. A stick, rock anything; but there was nothing. I stood there straining to listen, but there was no sound, only the pounding of my heart.

"Once again I started to move. Out of the corner of my eye I saw a shadow, and I quickly put up my fists to fight. Whatever I saw was gone. My nose started to bleed, and I could taste it in the back of my throat. My blood pressure must have been going through the roof to give me a bloody nose. I put my head back to get the bleeding under control. When it finally stopped, I remember telling myself, 'If I don't pull it together I'm going to be the one that kills me.'

"Again something out of the corner my eye went into the hay about ten feet in front of me. Was it real or my imagination running wild? Do I go back and start over and go down the other side? I'm almost there; I kept staring at the hay where I saw whatever it was go in. Again it moved, and again I could feel the blood start to run over my lip and in the back of my throat. Just then it leaped out and ran away from me. It was a cat with a mouse in its teeth, and it disappeared through a hole in the wall.

"Blood was now streaming down my face. Trying to stop the bleeding, I started to move again. Inch by inch I went looking all around, waiting for the worst. I thought for sure

I was going to step on a landmine, or a trip wire that would spring a trap that would kill me slowly. I don't know how long it took, because I was frozen with a fear that filled my mind.

"When I finally reached the door, I leaned against the wall and looked out the door, keeping my head inside. I was certain that the second I stepped out into the clearing, I would be cut down, so I decided to wait until the sun went down. I figured I would have a much better chance in the dark than I would in broad daylight.

"As I waited, I started to calm down. My breathing and heart rate slowed to a more normal rate, and my nose finally stopped bleeding. It was then that I noticed a small backpack by the door. Do I open it? What if it's a bomb? I decided to leave it alone. As I kept looking through the cracks, watching to see if I could spot anyone, I kept looking at the backpack. I couldn't take it any longer; I had to see what was inside. I opened it carefully and saw that it was filled with jerky, black bread, and a canteen of water. I remember chuckling to myself, thinking the commandant was giving me my last meal before the execution. I picked it up and went up into the loft to hide and wait until it was dark enough to make my move.

"As I lay there, staring at the food, I wondered whether or not I should eat it; after all, it could be poisoned. I decided that if they were out there waiting for me, I was going to have to make a run for it. The adrenalin that had coursed through my body earlier had subsided and left me feeling weak and shaky. I knew I was going to need energy to make a run for it, and my only source for renewed strength was in that backpack. So I took a couple of bites of the jerky and bread and washed it down with a big gulp of water. I have to say, it sure tasted like a Thanksgiving feast.

"With what little we were fed in camp and while I was on the run, I wasn't able to find any kind of food to live on. It was the first bite of food I had had in many days. I wanted to devour it all, but my stomach had shrunk so much that the few bites I took filled me up. It only took a moment, and my stomach started to cramp. Fear of having eaten poisoned food overtook my reality, and I started convulsing. I wasn't positive what was and wasn't real. Fear eats at you like a cancer, and unless you take control of it, it will eat you alive. Was it poisoned, or was it my fear getting the best of me? I told myself over and over, 'The food is fine, and I'll be fine.' Thoughts are powerful, as is faith; my stomach calmed down and I was able to eat the rest of the bread.

"I waited there for what seemed like an hour. In that time I was able to finish off one of the pieces of jerky, and half of the water in the canteen. Having regained some strength, my spirits lifted. I climbed down from the loft and made my way toward the door. It was dusk, and I remember looking through some of the slats, trying to figure out which way would be the best to make my break.

"The light was perfect. It was time to make my move; dark enough to make me a harder target to hit, and light enough so I could see my way without running into a tree. I found a rock by the door and picked it up. I threw it as hard as I could to create a distraction. As I heard it hit some trees, I made a run for it, carrying the backpack of food and water with me. When I didn't hear any gunshots in the direction of the rock, I thought, 'Great, they didn't fall for it, and I am about to be cut down.' I ran as hard and as fast as my aching legs could carry me, zigzagging as I went. When I made it to the thicket of trees, I kept on going. To my surprise, I never heard a shot, or anyone following me. I don't know how far I ran, but it felt like miles before I fell to the ground exhausted. I hid myself the best I could and waited for the worst, but it never came.

"As I began to calm down, I could smell the aroma of the woods and hear the sounds of the night. It was then that I realized I was free. The only thing that had been holding me back was fear of the unknown. It was at that moment that I decided I would never let that happen again. I don't like talking about what I went through in the war; it was very personal and emotional. Men died before my very eyes after everything I could do to save them. And yes, men died by my hand. I've only told family members the barn story, and that was only when I thought it would hold a special meaning for them. Those whom I shared the story with were to tell no one else. I'm a very private person, and I don't like the attention. And now Nikki, my dear, you know that part of the family secret. It's time to share it with the rest of the world. I've tried to teach my family not to be afraid of the unknowns in life, but to push forward to achieve all that life has to offer. Don't be afraid to fail. It's from our failures that we learn.

"Sometimes we have to learn the same lessons over and over, but that's life. So why are we so afraid? It's that fear of the unknown. If we don't face our fears, how can we ever expect to overcome them and grow? I've always said, 'If you're going to fall down, fall on your face. At least that way it'll be easier to pick yourself up, and you'll still be facing forward.'"

James smiled. "What you've learned so far is only part one of the family secret. You could call it 'facing your fears head on.' Or 'fear will only hold you back.' For me, I call it 'from fear to freedom.'"

I could tell he was going to stop there. "Can't you tell me just a little of part two?"

He hesitated. "I'll tell you this much. After I went through the barn into freedom, I was lost. I didn't have a clue as to where I was or where to go. That's when I met four very good friends who helped me. They not only got me to safety, they gave me a foundation on which to build my life."

"Are those the four Jimmy told me about?"

"They are. I was taught that the world doesn't revolve around me, that I needed a purpose in life. For me it started with a spiritual need, a reason for living. I always had in the back of my mind three questions: Where did I come from? Why am I here? And where am I going after this life? I think everyone has those questions in one form or another. They helped me so I could find the answers to those and many other questions. That's why I'm not afraid of dying. I learned that we need to understand one another, given the different personalities we all come with and what makes us so different. They taught me to respect one another's religion and beliefs. I learned what makes America so different and what the founders sacrificed to give us our freedoms. And I learned how to control money—not to let money control me. I call part two of the family secret 'Lessons Learned Escaping Nazi Germany.'

"There's more, a lot more. Finish your article and I'll tell you, as Paul Harvey would say, 'The rest of the story.'"

James stood up to stretch. "Nikki, my dear, that should satisfy your editor, Mr. Baker, to fulfill your obligation. I told him it would be on his desk in one week's time. When you've completed your article, come find me and we'll get started. It's going to take quite a while to go through those first four journals."

And with that he gave me a strange smile, as if to say, "I can hardly wait to tell you what happened next," and he left the study. As I sat pondering, I now understood why Commandant Schmidt couldn't tell me what was in the barn. For each prisoner it was his own hell that he had to face and go through.

As I come to a close to this chapter in my life, I can smell breakfast cooking, and I'm looking forward to "part two," of the Hansen family secret.

EPILOGUE

Grandfather Vince decided to go with Commandant Schmidt on the speaking tour. Somewhere along the way the name "The Captive Captor Tour" was given, and it stuck. To have both of them on the same stage did indeed heal many hearts.

James had his doctors look at Mr. Schmidt, and they put him on a special diet to help him gain weight and strength. The cataracts were removed, and tears rolled down his cheeks as he looked upon his daughter's face. It had been years since he could see, and she was as beautiful as he remembered.

Over the next several months as the two former enemies talked to other veterans, the crowds grew bigger and bigger. As their fame grew they were asked to talk to congregations from all different churches, telling their story of forgiveness.

Nikki stayed in touch with her grandfather as the two of them toured. One time as he was saying his good-byes, he said, "I'll wave to you tomorrow." The next day before she and Mr. Hansen got started, James turned on the television. There they were, the captive and captor. Once again James pulled off one of his surprises. Nikki got such a kick out of seeing the two of them on *The Good Morning America Show* that when her grandfather waved, she waved back.

Whenever Nikki talked to her grandfather, she would tell him all about Ray. He was the one who pointed out to Nikki that she was falling in love. It took months for James to cover the first four journals that contained what he had gone through as an escapee in Germany. On the last day when James told Nikki the final family secret, Ray proposed.

As The Captive Captor Tour came to an end, the old commandant finally answered the door that he had been refusing to answer for so long. He passed away peacefully in his sleep.

Though Grandpa Vince swore he would never set foot in Germany after the war, he accompanied the commandant's body back to Germany with the family. He promised Nikki he would be back in plenty of time for her wedding. Germany was nothing like he had remembered or imagined. He was shown around, and fell in love with the good people of Germany.

Vince extended his stay and met with several German veterans and told them all about The Captive Captor Tour. It was two days before he was to fly home when Nikki got the call. Grandpa Vince was in the hospital with a heart attack and couldn't be moved. James had the plane fueled and cleared for Germany within the hour. The doctors met with Nikki and Ray before they went in and gave them the same bad news they told Vince. It was doubtful he would make it through the night. When Nikki walked in, she saw that same smile as when she had first come running into the living room smothered in her grandfather's old flight jacket.

"Hey Pun'kin, don't look so sad. It won't be long now before I get to see your grandmother. I'm sorry I won't be able to keep my promise." Then he added. "But I'll be there in spirit."

Over the next few hours Nikki and Ray stayed at his bedside. Vince had a good man-to-man talk with Ray, telling him to take good care of his little Pun'kin. Too weak to lift his hands, he said softly, "Have I ever told you I think you have the prettiest blond hair and blue eyes?"

"Yes, Grandpa, but I never get tired of hearing it from you, and I love you too." Nikki bent down so he could kiss her forehead. He smiled, closed his eyes, and took his last breath.

Nikki knew her grandmother was there to greet him and take him home to a loving Heavenly Father. As she sat there holding his hand for what she knew would be the last time, she reflected back to a warm memory pulling him forward into the bedroom where a treasure chest awaited. His hands firm but always loving were like worn leather from the hard, back-breaking work he had done throughout his life to provide for his family.

Hands now arthritic that went to war in hopes to once again hold his loving wife and young son again. Giving a soft kiss to his hand, Nikki whispered, "You're in the hands of God now." She took her hand and straightens his hair, "Until we meet again Grandpa."

AFTERWORD

I hope you enjoyed the book and found it worthwhile. If you received any good thoughts from it, please share them with others by going to www.amazon.com and enter *From Fear to Freedom* by Gary James Sumner and leave a customer review. Thank you.

I wrote *From Fear to Freedom* to give readers pieces of a puzzle. When putting together a puzzle, you start with the corners and edges. Then you put the pieces in groups that are of the same color and pattern. Next, you start to look at the shapes of each piece and study them. Soon your mind is trained to see how the pieces fit together, and before long the puzzle will start to come together.

With the corner and edge pieces as the stories from history, you will build your own puzzle. The centerpieces are the pages of history, not only from the past, but the present as well. As you start to put together the pieces of the puzzle, you will be able to see the historical patterns that always seem to repeat themselves. As George Santayana once said, "Those who do not remember the past are condemned to repeat it."

As with any research, you can always find facts that contra-dict other facts. Yes, it can be confusing. Think of each fact as a puzzle piece and you're putting together a masterpiece. Some pieces will appear to fit at the time, and then you come across new pieces that will throw a monkey wrench into your masterpiece. Don't give up. Keep digging. The trick is to keep an open mind. Don't force the pieces together just to make them fit with what you think the puzzle should look like.

The Next Book

I hope you enjoyed *From Fear to Freedom*. In the next book you will learn more of the family secret, what Mr. Hansen discovered after he went through the back door of the barn. In that book I cover a few areas I have gathered in my readings and life experiences that have helped me and I hope will help others. The title is *Lessons Learned Escaping Nazi Germany. Sub title, Captain Hansen's Secret to Success.*

What are the Odds?

About six months after the first printing, I was in the home of a lady who had a photo on her wall. I'd seen the photo many times, but never on anyone's wall, so I had to ask why? She pointed to the man on the far left side of the photo and said, "That was my husband, Commandor James Ricect." I looked at her and said, "Are you telling me your husband was at the Yalta Conference?" To which she replied with a smile on her face, "He was. You know about the Yalta Conference?" I went to my vehicle and returned with a copy of my book. I showed her the chapter that covers the conference. "What are the odds I would meet the widow of someone who was there?" In chapter five, I tell the Hank Tussy story. With his wife by his side, he told me of his experience. When he finished, I was invited into his office. Among the many photos on his walls, one caught my eye. It was one that I had seen in many books and documentaries. I said to Hank, "I know that photo." He looked at me and smiled. "That's me in the center, number seventy-two." You'll find the photo on page 44. About two years later I was talking to a lady about the book and told her the Hank Tussy's story, when I showed her the photo I asked if she had ever seen it before? Many time's I hear yes, so when she said she had, it wasn't all that surprising. But when she pointed to the man in front of Hank and told me he was her uncle Philip Tellez, I couldn't believe it. What are the odds? Hank passed away May 2018. I'm so grateful for having known him.

How much is true

I've been asked how much of the book is true. I wrote *From Fear to Freedom* as a historical novel based on true events. The story line of Nikki, her grandfather, and Mr. Hansen's family were created to tell true historical events the way I like to learn: in story form.

A story you may think is made up but is true would be the *Hogan's Heroes* story. Robert Clary, who played Lebeau, was a victim in a real Nazi concentration camp during the war; and he has the serial number tattooed on his arm to prove it. There were other actors on that show who had lived in Germany at the time of Hitler and had to deal with the Nazis as well. The autobiography of Robert Clary, From the Holocaust to Hogan's Heroes, tells his story in a very moving way. His story, like so many others needs to be told and remembered.

The story I call, "The Choice" comes from a sermon I heard as a kid in the sixties. WWII was still fresh on everyone's minds so when I heard it, I believed it to be true and it made such an impression on my mind I never forgot it. In all my research I have not come across the story so it made me wonder if it were true or just a story that was made up to make a point in a sermon. When the book was published with the first one thousand copies being a limited edition, I gave one to a bookstore manager at a major university who was retiring in a few months. I didn't know it then, but he is a renowned historian. When I told him the barn story, he looked at me and said. "You do know that the roots of that story comes from the crusades, don't you?" I had to admit, the crusades were not in my wheelhouse. He gave me the name of the sultan and I wrote it down. When I returned home I placed the note in a safe place to later research, knowing I would be doing a reprint and I wanting my readers to know where the story originated from. Fast forward two years and I'm now looking for that note and as you can imagine I can't find it for the life of me. I was able to track down his home phone and talk to his wife. Unfortunately he had been in and out of the hospital and wasn't doing well at the time; she gave me his number and thought if he were awake he would love to visit. I called and he answered. After telling him who I was he remembered my book quite well but couldn't remember the name of the sultan.

In August of 2017, I had the honor of interviewing a man who can't go anywhere without being recognized. He is best known as, "The Beard of Knowledge." His name is Mark Patton; Mark is the director of Clark County Museum, Las Vegas Nevada, and is related to General George S. Patton Jr. When I told Mark about the chapter I call, "The Choice", he was familiar with the story and agreed it's a lesson that should be taught. When Mark told me the amount of books he owns, I was honored he accepted one of mine.

The Charlie story in chapter seven is based on a true story. It was given to me by knowing a member of his family, whom I'm grateful to for allowing me to share a part of his life with you. The man in the rowboat from the island was an American, not German. I had to use literary license to have Charlie captured again and sent to Commandant Schmidt's concentration camp so the story could be told to Grandpa Vince, so he could pass it on to Granddaughter Nikki.

Charlie is no longer with us, and I thank him for his service. He also had many other experiences that could fill a book, and I'm told a family member is working on it. Keep an eye on www.gjsumnerbooks.com for when it comes out. Just as this book was going to print, my official military sources got back to me about the prisoners whom the Russians sent off to the salt mines; to this day their fate and their names are unknown.

In my research I found common traits among the POWs: there were those who would entertain the others to help keep their minds off what they were going through. So I created Pat O'Kelly to honor them. The stories of Mr. Hansen's mom and dad are about the author's parents, and they are true stories. Yes, even Joe the troublemaker.

The stories of Grandpa Vince's brothers, Evan, Ellis, and Joe, are true. They are my wife's uncles. I've seen the letter that is mentioned in the first chapter. The brother George is a compilation of all who never came home to loved ones.

You might also like to know, that Caroline (Grandpa Vince's mother in the story) was my wife's grandmother, and she really did have five boys and five girls. I want to thank my mother-in-law, Carol, and her brother Evan for sharing their stories with me, to share with you. Read through the book again, and when you come across a story and you wonder if it is true or not, simply enter a few key words into a search engine and go exploring. That's how I found the section on economics where Nikki teaches the teacher in chapter four. After entering hyperinflation around the globe, I found many sites to choose from. I liked www.lewrockwell.com and added that information in the story. There are many sites to go to for World War II aircraft. I like Dave's War birds at, http://www.daveswarbirds.com

RECOMMENDED READING

Here are some of the other resources used for my storyline. I highly recommend them in no particular order.

List of books mentioned in *From Fear to Freedom:*

A Distant Prayer, by Joseph Banks and Jerry Borrowman.

The Bible.

The Berlin Candy Bomber, by Gail S. Halvorsen

Democracy in America, by Alexis de Tocqueville,

The Wealth of Nations, by Adam Smith.

The Five Thousand Year Leap, by W. Cleon Skousen.

Victory, Tales of a Tuskegee Airman, by Les Williams and Penny Williams

The Tuskegee aviation experiment and the Tuskegee airmen, by Le Roy F. Gillead

The Real George Washington, by Parry, Allison, & Skousen.

Not mentioned by name but alluded to and highly recommended:

The movie *Red Tails*, by Lucas Film Ltd. I had the opportunity to meet three of the original Tuskegee airmen who worked on the movie. George Lucas invited them and others as consultants, so as to get everything right. I asked, "With the way Hollywood embellishes things, how accurate was it?" I was told, "He got it between ninety-five to a hundred percent right." In talking with Dr. Daniel L Haulman PhD that number is high. On the DVD, go to extras and watch *Double Victory.* I can't recommend it enough. In chapter three, I already knew some of what is covered in *Double Victory* and a lot that was new. The man who treated them fairly, Noel Parrish, I found in *Double Victory.*

Three against Hitler, by Jerry Borrowman, is the story about Helmuth Hübener and his two friends as they did their part in fighting Hitler. There is also a DVD called *Truth & Conviction: the Helmuth Hübener Story.*

Unbroken, by Laura Hillenbrand. As I would tell people about my book, so many of them told me I had to read Unbroken. Laura covers the Pacific Theater extremely well and tells the story of Louie Zamperini in a breathtaking manner. I knew the Jesse Owens story but never knew the story of Louie Zamperini. I remember in the 1960s, my father talking about a man who ran in the 1936 Olympics so fast that he would have been the first man to break the four-minute mile if it weren't for the war. Dad had to have been talking about Louie. After reading *Unbroken*, I just had to find a place to put that story in mine. Thank you, Laura and Louie. The story of the Japanese amputating Fred Garrett's leg also came from her book. I did know about the "Rape of Nanking" from my friend Graig. Laura covers it in greater detail than I do in mine, and she still left out a lot of what happened. I'm sure she, like me, couldn't put down on paper what happened to the women and children for others to read. If you want to learn more about Nanking, you'll have to look it up for yourself.

Just as this book was going to print, I found *A Higher Call*, by Adam Makos, with Larry Alexander. Adam is a real journalist, historian, and editor on the military magazine *Valor*. He's the real "Nikki Brown," and I highly recommend his book. (I'm looking forward to reading his other books.)

I've been asked where I get my information from. Primary sources, along with autobiography, are the best. Secondary sources are also reliable, along with documentaries. My favorite place is Costco. I can almost always find a new documentary, and for a few bucks, it goes into the cart. Many great authors cover history in a way that it comes to life, and you'll find chivalry on both sides. It's my hope that after your reading *From Fear to Freedom*, it has sparked an interest in wanting to learn more.

THANK YOU

Since the early eighties I've wanted to tell the barn story. When I questioned my childhood friend Kerry if he could recall the sermon about the POW who faced his fears by going into a locked barn, he couldn't remember. I told him that throughout my life the story always gave me the courage to face my fears and step out of my comfort zone. I told him I was going to write the story in a pamphlet form in hopes to help others as well. He thought it would make a great booklet and encouraged me to write it. Thank you, Kerry.

When telling a good friend of mine, Graig, about the pamphlet idea, he told me I had the makings of a novel. I told him I don't know of any novels ten, maybe fifteen, pages long. Graig knew my love for history and convinced me to build the barn story around true events. After giving it much thought and prayer, I created Nikki and her grandfather Vince. Graig has what is commonly known as a photographic memory, and I think he has read about every book there is that deals in history. There are those who like to take a book into the bathroom to read, and as a young teenager his favorite book was the encyclopedia (true story). Whenever I talked with Graig and told him some of the stories that were going into the book, he would remember at least twenty stories to my one along the same subject. Some I knew and had forgotten, but for the most part, his stories were ones I had never heard, and he would go into great detail. With all the stories he shared with me, if I included them in this book, it would have made *War and*

Peace look like a short story. Thank you, Graig, for all your help and resources. Your friendship means more to me than you'll ever know.

I want to thank my wife, Karen and dear children, Ryan, Rachelle, Andrea, and Brianna, thank you for your willingness in offering your helpful suggestions, edits and proofreading.

Thank you to Renie Williams, Diane Davidson, Jeanette Carter, and Mike Wade, who also put in hours of proofreading and editing in the early stages of the book.

A special thanks to my two final editors

Thank you is a word that can't begin to describe what the two of you did for me. I consider both of you good friends. My first editor is a member of the English faculty at a major university for many, many years (now retired). He taught classes in literature and Dutch, and also edited the journal of a national humanities academic organization. He is focusing on a very busy schedule during his "retirement" years, and therefore is officially anonymous. I very much appreciate the time he gave me. With your mentorship I learned so much. Thank you.

Professor Don Norton: Proofreader, editor, teacher of English usage (grammar), teacher of multiple writing classes at two major universities. He ran the Faculty Editing Service for twenty-five years at another major university, in which he edited some seven to ten thousand pages of faculty writing annually (with the help of student editors); articles, books, theses and dissertations came from a wide variety of departments. Though now retired for nearly thirteen years, he continues to do oral histories of veterans (over 1,000 so far), which he and his student employees and interns transcribe and edit. Professor Norton, thank you is insufficient for all you did for me and for what I learned. I am so blessed to have also known you. Thank you.

GRANDPA JIMMY

My Grandfather James—Jimmy to his family and friends—had a great love for the founding fathers and the sacrifices they made to give us our freedoms. He studied the Constitution, and though he only had an eighth-grade education he had a remarkable understanding of that great document. While his father was away serving a calling from his church, James was put in charge to be the man around the house helping his mother. Grandpa Jimmy learned to raise chickens and soon developed a love for them. He became quite well known for his knowledge in breeding. He was also known for riding the rough stock. If it was said that a horse couldn't be ridden, the call "Go get Jimmy" went out. I was given his name and developed a great love for both America and the Constitution. I know nothing about horses, and everything I know about chickens I learned from Colonel Sanders, founder of Kentucky Fried Chicken.

My grandfather was a great student of history. In 1977, I remember him telling me how concerned he was for America. He saw that the freedoms for which so much blood and treasure had been spent were eroding away. As my wife and I studied history and the Constitution back in the late 70s early 80s, we, like my grandfather, saw a pattern. It's my hope that *From Fear to Freedom* will give you a desire to want to learn more about history and the Constitution and how they affect our lives. In the beginning of this book, Nikki wonders about how many civilizations lost their freedoms before their very eyes and for how many the warning bell sounded. This is my way of sounding the warning bell in hopes more will hear. In my next book, Lessons Learned Escaping Nazi Germany, I give you a foundation and more pieces of the puzzle, to remind readers how our Founding Fathers gave us ways to keep our freedoms intact. Thank you again for your time.

— GARY JAMES SUMNER

ENDORSEMENTS

Command Sergeant Major (Retired) James E. Slade, "N" Co 75th Inf Rangers

This book is dedicated to any soldier who has been to war, and also to his family. All of us who served as combat soldiers in Viet Nam feared being taken as a POW. Those few who lived through the degradation and terror of all wars are held in great respect. *From Fear to Freedom* has history and mystery. Through the eyes of Nikki's Grandfather Vince, a POW from Commandant Schmidt's camp in WWII, we learn of the ugliness of man's inhumanity to man and the determination of the human spirit to survive.

Soldiers, no matter their experiences, often return from war and store their mementoes in an old attic or closet. Maybe someday someone will ask about these memories, and maybe enough time has passed and the horrors faded enough that the soldier can finally talk about them.

This book records many of those facets of war and human emotions. We feel the tenderness and devotion between a grandfather and his granddaughter, even if it isn't with spoken words. Nikki, a young journalist, is driven to travel to Germany to discover a secret buried for sixty years which her grandfather tells her about. One secret leads to another, and Nikki goes on the hunt for another POW from Commandant Schmidt's camp. I couldn't put this book down, not only because of the intrigue of the story itself, but because I knew it was based on actual soldiers' experiences.

— Command Sergeant Major James E. Slade

Jared Verbeek with his mother Rosalia and father Travis

The date was June 21, 2011, when our home was rocked by the true pains of freedom. I had just stepped outside to work on my car's air conditioning system, before leaving for work. As I was leaning over the passenger-side fender, I observed three military service members approaching me. It was a Marine Corps staff sergeant (SSGT), a Marine Corps captain (CAPT), and a Navy chaplain. It didn't sink in why they were walking down the sidewalk, and then I heard the SSGT ask in a loud, clear voice, "Are you Travis Verbeek?"I stood up and answered yes.

SSGT Cardinal walked directly toward me, and upon arriving where I stood, he softly asked if we could go inside. I leaned on the car fender again, supporting myself with both hands, pausing for a moment, as their purpose registered in my mind, then sank into the recesses of my soul. I realized they had come to notify my family and me of our son and my daughter's brother's death. I knew at this moment that Jared had been killed in Afghanistan. I stood up and told the SSGT standing before me, "Come in."

We walked up the sidewalk to our home, and as we entered I could hear my oldest daughter sobbing, calling out to her mother, "Mom, Mom!" She had seen the three men in uniform, walking on the sidewalk, past the front of the house to the place where I was standing, looking at my car. Her fears overwhelming her emotions, she had begun to cry, calling out to her mother, who was in the bedroom.

I proceeded to our bedroom and asked my wife to come out to the living room. "Why?" she asked with urgency. "What is going on?" She had heard our daughter's sobbing and calling out for her. Upon entering the living room, she observed for the first time the three servicemen I had just met moments ago, and she began to cry loudly, exclaiming, "No, no!"

SSGT Cardinal informed us that Jared had died from his wounds while on patrol in the Helman Province in Afghanistan. When I asked what had happened, SSGT Cardinal informed me that Jared had stepped on an improvised explosive device (IED) while on patrol and had succumbed to his wounds. I asked if his wife had been informed of his death. I was told that a team was conducting the death notification at the very moment at the wife's home on Camp Pendleton. I told the Marines that Vanessa, Jared's wife, had driven up from Camp Pendleton last night and was at her parents' home.

When SSGT Cardinal asked if I knew the address, I informed him I did not know it but could drive to the home if he wished to follow. "Yes, I need to make contact with her before the news is released by any other means," he replied. I turned to my wife and daughter, still both crying and holding on to one another, "Ladies, do not call anyone until Vanessa has been notified."

My wife, daughter and I got inside our car, and with the casualty notification service members following behind us, we drove to Vanessa's parents' home. My wife and daughter continued to cry, and I remember my wife saying several times as we were driving to their home, "Oh my God, Vanessa, how will she take this? . . . Oh my God, she's all alone."

Upon arriving to their home, just a short drive from ours, the SSGT asked us to remain outside until they made the notification. Then they would let us know it was okay to come inside.

I remember hearing a loud scream, and I knew Vanessa had received the death notification of her husband. The navy chaplain stepped outside the front door and motioned for us to come inside. Upon entering the home I saw Vanessa on her knees, screaming, "No, no, no!" My wife and daughter attempted to console Vanessa, yet no words or embraces could soften this devastating and painful news. The three women continued with their mournful cries.

I knew I had to maintain my sanity, fight back the tears that were welling up inside of me, and ask details of the SSGT what next steps would take place. He informed me we would be picked up from our home later that evening and flown to Dover Delaware Air Force Base, where a dignified body transfer would take place the following day. Later that evening I remember two vehicles arriving at our home to take us to LAX, to fly into Baltimore Metro International, where we'd rent vehicles and drive the rest of the distance to Dover.

While en route to LAX we were delayed for three hours on top of the grapevine on I-5, due to construction on the roads. Upon arriving in Los Angeles, we rented a hotel room for only a couple hours, just to try and get some rest. We fell asleep for the few hours we could get, which felt like seconds. We checked out of the hotel exactly two hours later and checked in at LAX, to continue on our travel to meet our son's body returning to the United States.

As we traveled across the United States via several airports, USO workers assisted us, expediting the process of getting us to where we needed to be, and providing us with food and drink, knowing we had no time to stop for nourishment. I believe all of us were in a state of shock; a feeling of numbness is how I would describe my own personal state, unable to really think, a headache that seemed to reach deep into my mind, the likes which I had never felt before.

June 22, 2011, we arrived at Dover Delaware Air Force Base and were put up in the Fischer House, a facility where families are billeted, awaiting the bodies of service members who have died during deployment and are flown back to the States. I don't recall just when we arrived, but I do remember the tiredness, the headache that wouldn't stop, and the sadness on every family member's face, knowing well that the price of freedom's pain was cutting deep into the very souls of their beings.

As night fell, a military cargo jet flew in, and we were informed that our son was now on US soil. We were taken by bus out to the airstrip where the aircraft that carried our sons' body was parked. We exited the bus and stood at a distance as the dignified body transfer was conducted. I remember my wife crying loudly, and her sister telling her to stand proud, "With your head held high. Look upon your son, he is a man. He did what he wanted to do, and he did not waiver, even though he knew this could happen."

His flag-draped casket was slowly escorted from the aircraft and transferred to an escort team that took it to the morgue on base.

Those who do not know the sacrifices our service members make, whether it be the comforts of everyday life, or the ultimate sacrifice one could give serving their country, it is a shame not to give these unselfish individuals who have fought for this country all the honor our nation can give, because they are the true heroes of the freedom most of us take for granted. For were it not for them and those who have served this country before, we would not be the nation of freedom we are today. Yet the freedom bestowed upon us by these individuals is truly felt by those who knew and loved them; they especially feel the true pain of freedom, and realize the saying that "freedom isn't free" is true in the truest sense.

Since that time, in Visalia, California where Jared was raised, we have held an annual golf tournament in his name, whose proceeds benefit the Wounded Warrior Project. We have also held an annual Memorial Motorcycle Ride in Jared's name in San Diego California, just as a memorial. Recently our city's minor league baseball team, the Visalia Rawhides, honored him at the last game of the season. Also in Jared's hometown, the Giddings overpass has been named the Cpl. Jared Verbeek Overpass, by Assembly woman Connie Conway. Further, I have put up a facebook page honoring Jared, where friends and family can post: Facebook Jared C. Verbeek.

We realize that these honors are being performed to keep

his memory alive, because the worst injustice would be to forget those who have paid the ultimate sacrifice.

This book is an excellent and easy read, and I recommend it to everyone. It looks at the cost of freedom from a different perspective than others I have read. Excellent book!

— Travis Verbeek, Gold Star Dad

Mark Terry with his father Roger

As the son of one of the Tuskegee Airmen whose story is touchingly told by Gary Sumner, I heartily recommend this unique and heartfelt book.

— Roger Terry

ABOUT THE AUTHOR

Gary J. Sumner comes from a long line of patriots. John Colton Sumner, known as Captain Jack, was the guide for Major Powell when he made his first trip down the Colorado River. Captain Jack also served in the Civil War.

Jack's grandfather was Robert Lucas, twice governor of Ohio and the first territorial governor of Iowa. Robert also distinguished himself by keeping a journal of his experiences in the War of 1812. Robert's father, William, was a captain in the Revolutionary War. Jack's wife's grandfather, John Brown, also served in the Revolutionary War.

Going back seven generations was Senator Charles Sumner, who was nearly beaten to death on May 22, 1856. Days earlier, Rep. Preston S. Brooks had heard Senator Sumner's speech against slavery and was angered by what was said. Waiting in the Senate chambers until Senator Sumner was alone and sitting at his desk (in those days desks were bolted down), he walked up to the Massachusetts Senator and with his heavy walking cane struck him several times until it splintered. Two House members ended the attack but not until Sumner ripped his desk loose in the effort to defend himself. The damage was done—he was rendered unconscious. It took him three years before he was able to resume his duties.

As an additional note, Senator Sumner and Abraham Lincoln were good friends. When Lincoln was assassinated, Senator Sumner was by his side throughout the night.

Gary had a grandfather by the name of James Gardner. But his family and friends called him Jimmy. He passed onto his grandson Gary his love for America. After more than thirty years of research on the lives and events of Americans who gave so much for their country, Gary shares a few of their experiences in such a unique way as to intrigue the reader into wanting to learn more.

Gary and his wife Karen married in the mid-seventies. They raised their four children in the San Francisco Bay area in California, where they live yet today. Gary has always been a successful entrepreneur, operating several different businesses over the years.

It is Gary's hope that through his and other's books, one's love and appreciation for America will deepen.